BLACK CRACKER

BY JOSH ALAN FRIEDMAN

BOOKS

TELL THE TRUTH UNTIL THEY BLEED

I, GOLDSTEIN: MY SCREWED LIFE (with Al Goldstein)

WHEN SEX WAS DIRTY

WARTS AND ALL (with Drew Friedman)

TALES OF TIMES SQUARE

ANY SIMILARITY TO PERSONS LIVING OR DEAD IS PURELY COINCIDENTAL (with Drew Friedman)

NOW DIG THIS: THE UNSPEAKABLE WRITINGS OF TERRY SOUTHERN (co-editor, with Nile Southern)

ALBUMS

SIXTY, GODDAMMIT

FAMOUS & POOR

THE WORST!

BLACKS 'N' JEWS

JOSH ALAN BAND

BLACK CRACKER

Josh Alan Friedman

an autobiographical novel

WYATT DOYLE BOOKS

new texture

Wyatt Doyle Books
from New Texture

Cover by Wyatt Doyle with Andy Biscontini

Wyatt Doyle, Editor
Editorial Consultant: Sandee Curry / SandeeCurry.com
Book design by Wyatt Doyle

Special Thanks:

Peggy Bennett, without whom . . .

Chloe Mae, Wyatt Doyle, Pete Brown, J.D. King,
the Glen Cove Police Department

The *Glen Cove Record-Pilot*, which reported on local NAACP
meetings of the '50s and '60s

Black Cracker.fm

NewTexture.com

Booksellers: *Black Cracker* and other New Texture books
are available through Ingram Book Company

ISBN 978-0-615-35417-0

First Wyatt Doyle Books Edition: February 2010

Printed in the United States of America

10 9 8 7 6 5 4 3 2 1

FOR KIPP FRIEDMAN,
my youngest brother

*And to all my
long-lost friends and teachers
at South School
from another time, another century*

Contents

NOTE: The archaic terms "colored" and "Negro" appear throughout, being accepted usage in the time this book takes place. Usage of the word "nigger," however, is timeless.

Prologue: Back Road Hill

I RETURNED TO GLEN COVE AFTER thirty-five years. My family moved away when I was ten in 1966. From first through fourth grade, I attended South, the last segregated colored school on Long Island. I was the only white kid. Four years—an eternity to a kid—of readin', 'ritin' and 'rithmetic. Then we moved to be closer to New York City and get away from South School. It closed anyway after the 1966 school year.

My elementary school, the last remnant of Negro education, was still standing at the bottom of Glen Cove Avenue when I returned. It was now used as an administration building. I was thirsty and longed to wet my lips once more from what was, *de facto*, the last "colored-only" water fountain on Long Island. But it was late afternoon and the doors were locked.

So I strolled up the Back Road Hill to the old "colored section." The humble Lincoln House—an old settlement alone in a field, not unlike something Lincoln himself might have lived in—was now a modern community center. Lincoln House was built by Long Island Negroes still heartbroken over The Great Emancipator, *Marse Lincum's* (Master Lincoln's) assassination. Young Abe was once beaten up by a gang of runaway slaves in the woods, and to this I could relate. (Man, did they get the wrong guy.) Somewhere out in our woods, before developments encroached, was a forgotten Revolutionary War graveyard. I discovered the toppled gravestones as a boy, covered by underbrush of briers, vines and trees. You might catch "dead man's fever" if you intruded—so the Catholic families warned, and I believed them.

The projects on Glen Cove Avenue, a short hike up from South School, were built after President Johnson's War on Poverty and the Civil Rights Act of 1964. Until then, a Negro shantytown existed that could have been transplanted from the Carolinas, from where the South School elders had migrated. My friends stayed there. When construction on the projects began, people were forced to evacuate their clapboard homes in the woods. They carted their meager possessions through the snow in a long march across Glen Cove Avenue.

So now I went searching for my old Black self, the inner nigger of my youth. It's obnoxious when affected white crackers lay claim to Blackness. As if the Wizard of Oz bestowed upon their necks an Honorary Negro medallion. Only a few born-whites qualify—militant abolitionist John Brown, R&B maestro Johnny Otis and New Orleans pianist Dr. John. Not me. But I was privy to both the show-biz world of my parents and the shadowy slums of Glen Cove— sometimes referred to by locals as the Back Road Hill. Of course, slums are in the eye of the beholder, and not all Blacks in Glen Cove lived in squalor. Outside might be slums, but behind someone's door was a home. Sometimes.

At the reception area of the projects, two teenage Black girls worked the front desk. Both seemed puzzled.

"You went to *South School*? Back when it was *segregated*?"

"Yeah. I was the only white kid."

"That is *so* cool," chimed the young ladies, perking up in unison.

I asked if they knew the whereabouts of Melvin Bullock.

The girls named three friends their own age, whose

father they figured was Melvin.

Father? That seemed impossible. Melvin was a ten-year-old boy, the smallest kid in class. I wrote a sketch play we both performed in fourth grade. We were a salt 'n' pepper smash.

A wino loitered around the sidewalk where Bobo's shack once stood. I might have been a bounty hunter or private eye for all he knew. He grew less suspicious when I told him I went to South School back in the day.

"Bobo Monk?" I asked.

"Dead."

"How?"

"Narcotics," said the wino. More than ten years ago.

"Jeffrey Lincoln?"

"He dead, too. Narcotics. Same time as Bobo."

"Torrence?"

"He in prison down in Florida, for life."

Torrence was never tough, he couldn't fight. He just sang and pranced.

The gray-headed wino wore a coat, even though it was spring. Suddenly he didn't look so old, maybe my own age. He eyed me carefully. "Yo' face look familiar," he said, squinting through the decades. Slowly and surely, he said: "I remember you."

"James?" I asked.

"Yes."

Glen Cove Avenue intersected Robinson Avenue, an uphill trek that was my personal freedom run. My very own Mason-Dixon Line, from colored to white world. I'd been chased downhill by nigger-hatin' white ladies, and chased back uphill by cracker-hatin' Black ones. I'd been up and down that hill thousands of times. Finally, as a grown man, I was ready to pit myself against the haunted memory of this hill and eat it for breakfast.

I checked the second hand on my watch. Then began my adulthood sprint. But there were hellhounds on my trail. The boy ghosts of Bobo and Jeffrey and Mumsy called my name, *Jock! Jock!*, the way I hadn't heard it mispronounced in 35 years. Their families—janitors and scrubwomen— came up behind, ladies whose natural scent, I thought, was that of ammonia and Comet and Mr. Clean. A permanent smell acquired, as Iceberg Slim would later put it, from a lifetime of "cleaning the stink out of white people's homes." They carried mops, pails and brooms—*the tools of ignorance.* Then came their daughters—the little girls of my class, about whom a white girl once exclaimed, "Look, Mommy! Baby maids!"

And then all hell broke loose. Once-innocuous images of Black folklore, from the days when Southern aristocrats believed in the marked superiority of colored cooks: Here come Rastus up the middle, aka Mr. Cream of Wheat, having clawed out of the slave burial ground, with his red bow tie and puffy white chef's hat; kindly old Uncle Ben, escaped from the rice plantation, marching like a zombie; and everybody's favorite, *Hecha Momma* (Aunt Jemima), waddling behind, from pancake box to corporate fox, batting her spatula at my head.

Most grown-ups have few memories of first grade—just a glimmer or two, usually the name of their teacher. Mine came flooding back. In my four years at South I was baffled by the Negro's hatred of whites. Now I needed to fill in all the blanks. I learned the history of what was going on in the adult world at that time. The NAACP had been working hard to shut down our school.

The run took a minute. As a poor little rich boy, it had taken ten times longer. After a snowstorm, it took what seemed like an hour. Back when I was a little Black cracker.

1. Colored School

September 1962

I HAD ALWAYS WANTED TO BE AN adult, and the magic day had finally come. It was the first day of first grade. The mothers had just abandoned their children and I sat there, alone and frightened, but anxious to start being an adult. I was actually sitting at my own desk, which made me feel like a real businessman. The classroom was my office, and the school was like the bustling editorial enterprise where I'd seen my dad at work.

There were twenty-five other people who shared my office. With one exception, each one was a colored kid, although I hardly knew the difference. What seemed stranger was one other sparkling-clean white kid sitting there, with red hair and a dense army of orange freckles covering his face. He sat pert and proud in a Buster Brown suit and black oxford shoes.

The teacher, a gruff white matron, handed out fat yellow pencils; she explained that we wouldn't be using pens until third grade. Then she handed out thick yellow paper and told us to write down the numbers one to ten. Those who hadn't been to kindergarten were unable to do it, but me and the other white kid, with kindergarten diplomas under our belts, had no difficulty completing the task. A few other kids sat in deep concentration, trying to recall the numbers, while others didn't even pick their pencils up. Nobody made a peep.

Then the door slammed open as an exasperated teacher ushered two colored boys pushing desks into the room. They were both being *lef' back*. First came a gawky, oversized boy, his lip hanging low. He sluggishly pushed a desk into the room. Being *lef' back* was a long, futile march backward. His undersized pants, tied at the waist with rope, rode high above the ankles.

The kid who followed behind pushed his desk with gusto. He was extremely well-dressed, in something akin to a sharkskin suit. After every few steps with the desk, he performed a few slick dance moves, emitting short bursts of laughter, shaking his head, lost in some private joke. He also sang aloud fragments of a James Brown tune, too sophisticated for any of the new kids to fathom, much less the teachers. The entire class' attention focused on the two in silent awe. No one dared interrupt. Our teacher looked as though she were about to get a year-long headache, but sat patiently waiting for the second kid to get settled. But he continued to drag his desk toward the back, shifting the exact destination, searching for the perfect spot. He serenaded the teacher escorting him back to first grade:

> *Got to, got to, got to*
> *Get some learnin'*
> *Without an education*
> *You might as well be dead, now.*

It was the chorus of "Don't Be a Drop-Out," James Brown's public service announcement.

That was the first time I ever saw Bobo. His utter disrespect and rudeness toward authority struck me as the funniest thing I'd ever seen. A whole new style of behavior for me to mimic. Under his influence I became wild, but remained a mere sidekick to Bobo, who set new standards of mayhem. He was incorrigible and acted beyond his years. He spat at cops. He urinated on other kids and their books in the lunchroom. During intense Dick-Jane-and-Sally reading sessions he would stand up and blurt out, "YOU WASTIN' MAH FUCKIN' TIME," then barge out of the class while yanking up some girl's skirt and leaving our elderly teacher in a state of fury—and me in a state of hysterics.

The superintendent of schools, Dr. O'Kane, came to deliver an address at Glen Cove's most humble school. He was the boss of all principals. That made him more intimidating than the police. All classes and faculty assembled in South School's auditorium. Right in the middle of his speech, Bobo leapt up on stage and imitated a saxophone, scat-singing some Charlie Parker-type bebop riff. When the superintendent froze in disbelief, Bobo tiptoed back to his seat, shushing everyone.

Bobo Monk had a sidekick, Jeffrey Lincoln. Jeffrey was a handsome fellow, always serious, and sure enough troubled about his height.

"Just cause ahm short don't mean ah can't kick a big kid's ass, that right, Bobo?"

"That's right, Jeffy. You can kick anybody's ass 'cept mine." Jeffrey Lincoln looked up to Bobo like an elder brother. When their playful sparring accelerated into full-fledged fights, Jeffrey got slaughtered. But Jeffrey would come back and apologize.

Actually, all the kids respected Bobo and listened to whatever he said. After all, he was a year or two older, having been *lef' back*, maybe more than once. The colored girls liked him. Even a teacher or two, much against their better judgment, laughed when he danced. But teachers were his natural enemies. They were unable to discipline him. I admired Bobo from afar, began to copy a few of his stunts, and started getting into trouble at school. That's how we became a team.

It was an honor to serve an afternoon's detention with him. That's where we first met. And escaped. We beat up older kids together, played hooky, hitched rides on the backs of trucks, and walked along the third rail of train tracks. We ordered 25-cent hamburgers and Cokes at the diner across from school, then ran out on the check. Acting on impulse, Bobo did almost anything he wanted to do. And as far as I was concerned, Bobo was even funnier than Jerry Lewis.

South School was less than a mile from my home. Each morning I took my own route—I could traverse a wooded hill or just walk down Robinson Avenue. At the bottom, across Glen Cove Avenue, stood a three-story red-brick school building, circa 1920s. The other side of life.

The inside smelled of industrial cleansers; our custodian, Mr. Gaines, scrubbed the halls nightly. All the teachers and faculty were white. Once, a Negro administrative aide came to work in the principal's office. It was said she'd taken a special course at college designed to root out Negro inflections in the voice. But she still said "y'all," and she didn't last long.

Our principal, Miss Margaret Tiger, had an obsession with oral hygiene. The school ran ongoing dental education programs stressing the importance of daily brushing. A retired white tooth doctor came every year to display diagrams of cavity-ridden molars. The colored kids sat uninterested and restless. The school handed out little dental-care kits equipped with Tommy Toothbrush and Red Cross toothpaste. But there was no way most of those kids were going to brush their teeth. Maybe some of the girls, but not the boys.

For that matter, some kids were so poor, their families used the Yellow Pages for toilet paper. The school allocated tax dollars in its campaign against tooth decay, but overlooked subsidizing toilet training. However, there were frequent head-lice exams by the nurse, and a yearly rectal check for worms. A feared problem discussed at P.T.A. meetings was the possible epidemic of either malady. The school managed to pull another old decayed white doctor out of retirement to do the worm checks, along with your basic head-lice search. We hated to line up single file at the nurse's office every fall. One at a time, the next in line had to march in and shut the door.

Sabrina, an indignant little spitfire, stood silent in line every year—until her turn came. Then teachers had to drag her in as she kicked and screamed, "Ah ain't lettin' no doctor go diggin' up mah butt for no worms! He just interested in mah natural born ass!"

Bobo, Jeffrey and I were friends with a guy named Mumsy Leech. Mumsy stunk. In fact, he smelled like something dead, and this drove away other kids like James, who was himself a pariah for being disgusting. Luckily, Mumsy didn't show up in school too often. But when he did, the girls in class—wearing charm bracelets and wool sweaters, altogether tidier than the ragamuffin boys—kept their noses turned up and away, and fanned themselves in annoyance.

Mumsy's desk, often unoccupied, was stationed in back, isolated from everyone. Once he shat in the boys' room urinal. I don't think he did this out of spite, he just wasn't hip to exactly what a urinal was for. Nobody ever showed him. His papa got kilt and left him. His mama left him. He lived with an Aunt Nellie. Mumsy was a drooling specimen, easily frightened, and only spoke in monotone. His most prominent physical feature was the size of his nostrils. They were the largest I'd ever seen. He could slide both thumbs into one nasal passage, and would proudly demonstrate with a smile.

Rumor had it that Mumsy lost his father under puzzling circumstances. The story, whispered on the playground with cryptic overtones, went down like this: Mumsy daddy, a menial laborer, was walking home from work one night. A fancy Cadillac pulled up to the curb. There were well-dressed colored men inside. One of them leaned out the window and asked, "Do you want to come for a ride in our car?" Mumsy daddy say yes, having never rode in a car, much less a shiny new Cadillac. He jumped in with the strangers. No one heard from Mumsy daddy until he was found dead in an alley the next week.

2. Dead Man's Fever

"**W**OW, YO' DADDY MUST HAVE A thousand dollars!" cried Jeffrey, the first time he saw my house. He was just as amazed seeing my home as I would be seeing his. Bringing kids from South School into the neighborhood often stirred up trouble. They were awed by the "rich people houses," with front lawns and gardens.

"Jock, ah cain't believe you actually live here!" said Mumsy, in a rare display of emotion. "Wow!"

I was embarrassed by my home at 53 Robinson Avenue, and the whole neighborhood. It seemed like proof that I was really white. Someday, I assured them, I'd be moving in with them down on Glen Cove Avenue, where I belonged. But we wrestled in my yard and threw crab apples, and swung on the tire my dad had rigged up from the tallest tree.

Bobo, however, was never impressed with anything. He always wanted to break something. I was stronger than Jeffrey and Mumsy and could always pin them in wrestling. Bobo was stronger than all three of us, and showed no mercy in play fights. He would knee kids in the balls from out of nowhere for no reason. He fought dirty. If he had Mumsy in a headlock, he'd keep it there till it hurt.

"Lemme be, lemme be," begged Mumsy. "What ah done to you?"

We ran into my house, whizzing past my nanny, Mrs. O'Leary, up the stairs to my bedroom. I plopped my school books on the bed. Carrying school books could be a real hindrance when being chased, but I always held on. Bobo never worried about that. You never saw him with school books. He was dead set against learning how to read or write, and would lose his books soon after they were issued.

"Is that a rat?" asked Jeffrey. No, I explained, that's Sitting Bull, my guinea pig, whose cage was stationed by my bedside. Occasionally, he slept with me under the covers, but mostly slept in his shoebox within the cage—a rodential castle. The crisp rhythm of Sitting Bull's front teeth began rat-tat-tatting on the cardboard. He could have had a job serrating paper in a factory. He chewed up several shoeboxes a month.

"What foods do he eat?"

Lettuce, carrots and celery were the big three favorites—aside from his guinea pig pellets. Sitting Bull then backed up three steps, his face taking on what I imagined to be a solemn expression. As he performed the guinea pig's most prolific activity, I too would back up three steps and salute patriotically.

"Shitting Bull, Shitting Bull!" yelled Jeffrey.

Bobo took no interest in animals. I didn't appreciate the slight sneer of contempt that registered whenever he saw mine. Mumsy and Jeffrey had an unusual fear of dogs.

We ran downstairs and out the screen door, which sprang shut behind us. On a brisk autumn day, Mumsy wore only a stained white undershirt. He declared nothing kept you warmer than an undershirt, it was all you ever needed, even in winter. But undershirts were all he had. Mrs. O'Leary referred to Mumsy as "that poor, poor child," being the most pitiful of my friends. Bobo, Jeffrey and I wore jackets.

"There go a nigger!" cried Jeffrey, pointing to a front yard. Bobo mimicked the wide-eyed stable jockey holding a lantern. Sold at gardening stores, the jockeys came from a coonsmith foundry. They were so common on front lawns, I never noticed.

"Look like yo' daddy."

"Look like yo' face."

"*Is* yo' daddy!"

"Look like yo' butt!"

Mumsy lagged behind because he smelled. A car slowed down as it passed. The man inside shook his head and waved an accusing finger at me. I threw an apple as the car trailed off. Nobody else was outdoors, and we walked unhindered down the road.

We skidded down dirt hills and climbed the edges of cliffs. From there we saw vistas of unsettled Glen Cove. The train tracks came into view. Bobo and Jeffrey didn't even know where the train went.

"It goin' to New York, where you get yo' sef a shoe shine," said Mumsy.

"New York?" said Jeffrey. "Ain't that where King Kong run loose?"

Only Mumsy and I rode the Long Island Rail Road into New York City. If you followed these tracks all the way, you'd wind up in New York.

"See way out there where the sky turn red?' said Jeffrey. "That's China."

"Shut up. You fulla shit," said Bobo, climbing upon a lightning-scarred tree stump by a creek. "Wow! There go a big ol' momma rat!" he yelled, staring into the running water.

"Where? Where, Bobo, where that rat at?"

"Momma rat, momma rat, where you at?"

The creek was inhabited by water rats. At least that's what everybody called them. Bobo spotted one. They were larger than regular rats, long and slinky. They glided gracefully underwater down the creek. They knew where they were going. Their size, we figured, indicated their place in the family; as they got larger, they gained in family rank.

By the time the rest of us reached the creek, the strange creature disappeared.

"Damn, where is he, where is he?" asked Mumsy. "Ah wanna see that rat!" Everyone's eyes scanned the creek, whale watching for another. This was better than any zoo. The water rats lived in dark fissures along the bank. Odd varieties of vegetation grew in the babbling creek. Like at the dumps, things didn't seem natural.

There was a splash in the middle of the creek and a huge water rat slithered through the current. Everyone gasped and stepped back.

"Wow! That must be a granddaddy!"

"Hecha Momma rat! Hecha Momma!" It zigzagged into oblivion.

"Musta seen yo' face!"

"Musta smelt Mumsy!"

Mumsy sat upon a fallen tree branch in a world of his own. He stripped the excess fiber from a cat-tail reed. He took it in stride to keep his stinking self at bay. There were cat-tail reeds all about. Dipped in kerosene, they made excellent torches, or so said Bobby Mortimer.

The faint echo of a horn came from afar. Everyone ran toward the tracks. "Here come the train! Here come the train!" Time to separate the men from the chickens.

Telephone poles followed the track far as the eye could see, with strange-looking transformers and secret lockboxes affixed to them. They smelled like wet tar syrup, which seeped out from crevices in the brown wooden poles. The stuff adhered to your finger like glue, especially on a hot day in the sun, when it dripped down the pole. I wondered what it would taste like on pancakes. I tried to climb a telephone pole a few times, but gave up halfway. The oddest thing was when you saw a lineman perched at the top of one, talking into his portable phone. The linemen had these fat rotary-dial contraptions on their belts, and could plug in to the telephone lines. It seemed cool to make phone calls from the top of a pole. But you had to work for the phone company.

We dashed over and lined up on the tracks. Bobo spit in his hands and rubbed them together. A smoky train smell rose up from the gravel and wooden railroad ties. Blotches of black syrup bubbled up over the beams. It was a nice smell, like bus fumes. Jeffrey had an ecstatic grin on his face as he stood between the tracks rubbing his own hands together. "Oh, boy, here it come."

Mumsy was reluctant. "We could get in trouble. Big *white* trouble."

The face of the giant machine appeared instantly from around the bend. I felt my blood jump. This was the Long Island Rail Road. Rickety old train cars, built long before the 1960s. They were often off schedule, and the conductors who collected tickets were burly, short-tempered goons.

Still, when one of those trains rounded the bend at top speed while you were standing broadside of the track, it was terrifying.

"Rich white crackas inside," Jeffrey surmised. "Ah ain't goin' no where."

"Squish yo' butt like a cockroach," said Bobo.

As the train got closer our hearts beat faster. I had that roller coaster feeling in the pit of my stomach. I put down a penny on the track, which would squish out thin and shiny. Wouldn't be as neat if one of us got hit.

Mumsy jumped off the track first and ran. "Ah don't play this shit." His voice was drowned out by the next warning blast of the locomotive horn. But I was determined to stick it out another few seconds. This was insane.

Jeffrey dashed off. It was between me and Bobo. My muscles were tense and ready to spring to safety. The giant metal creature was almost upon us, blasting an angry warning from a hundred yards. The engineer up front was probably livid. Bobo lurched over and jumped me, holding tight. I couldn't move. He was holding us both there, like a suicidal maniac. And then we tumbled down the embankment.

The train blasted through where we had stood only seconds before. It brought a huge gust of wind, which blew my mop-top Beatle hair straight up. I never wanted to play this game again. Heads of white businessmen zoomed by in the windows like eggs on a conveyor belt. Jeffrey waved at them, watching the parade. The caboose whirled by, leaving a gust of wind.

"The winner!" proclaimed Bobo, hoisting up his hands. "Y'all chicken shit."

"Ah ain't no chicken shit," retorted Mumsy. His huge nostrils flared indignantly.

"You a chicken butt," said Bobo.
Mumsy's head hung low as he rubbed his shoe over the grass. "Ah ain't," he muttered.

I went up to the track and fetched my copper Lincoln penny. It was shiny and flat, the size of a quarter. The edges were sharp.

"Wow!"

We followed a recently plowed dirt path off into the woods. An alligator-like imprint of tractor tires was caked into the reddish dirt. The trees got taller and older as the delicate, wild odor of the woods grew more intense. We came across a toppled fence. Behind it were chipped, weather-beaten, lopsided tombstones sunk halfway into the earth, covered with moss. There in the underbrush in a thick growth of vines, briers and trees were the fallen gravestones of Revolutionary War dead, barely discernible.

HERE LIETH THE BODY OF OSGOOD BARNES, AGED 33, WHO DEPARTED THIS LIFE IN BATTLE FOR HIS COUNTRY ON APRIL 5, 1777.

I wondered if he had been from Mrs. O'Leary's stony

Long Island stock. Nobody dared touch a tombstone.

"Ol' dead crackers down there?"

"Yeah, man, *real* daid."

"Scary, man."

"What if they ghosts get angry? Then what we gonna do?"

"What you wanna do, Jock?"

"You crazy."

"Shhh! Just walk slow! Don't be stompin' cn no grave."

"Hey, Bobo."

"Shut up!"

Every leaf that crunched made us jump. Yet there was something idyllic and peaceful about the weave of the vines and trees. Maybe it was somehow okay to be here. But my Catholic neighbors, the Applebys, had warned if you got too close to a grave, you could catch *dead man's fever.*

About fifty yards away was a clearing. A few plots were covered with tarps, a pile of freshly interred earth alongside each one. Americans who founded the country. Had somebody been here to dig them up? And then, from a hole came a spray of dirt. A man was in there, waist deep, digging away. Tire treads led up to the hole, but he was all alone. A burly Negro in lumberjack clothes. He waved.

"Hey!" he said, forking the shovel into the dirt. We began to backpedal. He waved again. "Hiya, boys!"

"Hey!" we yelled back. We stopped. He smiled and mopped his heavily sweating brow with a handkerchief.

All four of us approached.

"What you boys all doin' out here?"

"Nothin'. What are *you* doin'?"

"Well," said the burly man, figuring how to explain. "This here my job. Diggin' ditches."

There was a toppled tombstone where he stood and a canvas wrap on the ground.

"What kinda ditches you dig?"

"Well . . . Ah digs nigger graves, mostly. But this here a re-interment."

"What dat?"

"These fellas done passed a long time ago. A *long* time ago. They in heaven since before yo' great granddaddy born. Houses comin' up around here soon. It's time to make way and move 'em on to another pasture. 'Course, hardly much lef' of they mortal remains, bless the Lord. What's yo' names, boys?"

"I'm Bobo. This here Jock and Jeffy and Mumsy."

"Well, pleased to meet you fellas. They call me Nigger Digger. The only Black man in Local 365, Cemetery Workers and Greens Attendants. Dig, for short."

He seemed awfully friendly for a guy with such a ghastly profession. I wondered if he'd laugh at doo-doo jokes. Revolutionary War soldiers—real Long Islanders, like Mrs. O'Leary—lovingly dug up for re-interment by Mr. Digger. The dust of the American Revolution was down in that hole, and nobody was left in the modern world to pay respects.

"Skeleton bones down in there?"

"Well, sometimes. Might be a few at that, by and by."

Where would they take these skeletons? The dumps at Garvies Point? The Museum of Natural History, where our school took a field trip each year? We didn't dare ask.

"Mah daddy daid and buried," volunteered Mumsy.

"Oh, yeah?" said Digger. "Well, ahm sure sorry to hear that, son. Maybe ahm the one what buried 'em. Where he buried at?"

"Ah don' know," said Mumsy.

"He in the kingdom of the Lord God Almighty. Yes he is."

Another train horn blared. Trains always passed by unpleasant nooks and crannies. Out-of-the-way places that nobody knew were there.

"Whadda we have here, boys?" said Dig, waist deep in the hole. "Wanna take a look?" He poked his shovel upon something then reached down and pulled it out. Then he tossed it at us. "Somebody bone!"

The four of us screamed and scattered. We ran out of the woods, as the laughter of the strange man with the even stranger name diminished in the thick of trees and brush.

"Yahhhh!"

3. Nigger Chasers

On MY SIDE OF THE TRACKS lived the poorest white family in all of Glen Cove. A former Appalachian clan of ten Caucasians, who ate mostly saltine crackers and threw firecrackers. Big Willie Wilshire got drunk on firecrackers. He smelled like gunpowder. He licked the silver residue from his fingers. The more he lit and threw, the more intoxicated he became, cackling like a hyena.

One day, I spied Big Willie, who was about eleven, with a group of real teenagers smoking cigarettes on the street. I watched from a distance. This must have betrayed my early desire for inclusion in the brotherhood of juvenile delinquency. All of a sudden, they waved me over.

"Wanna hang out with us?" said the greaser in charge, who had a pompadour. They all laughed.

"Okay," I mumbled.

"If you wanna hang out with us, then you gotta go home and step into your old man's boots," he instructed, with mock sincerity.

"What old man?" I asked.

"Your old man. You know, your daddy, your father. You gotta put on your daddy's boots."

This was my big moment. I walked back home to my dad's closet, where a hundred ties hung from a rack. I couldn't find any boots. I tried on a random pair of shoes.

Then I trudged back down the street like an idiot, falling in and out of the giant shoes.

"Naw, not those," said the greaser. "They ain't right. You wanna hang out with us, you gotta fill some bigger boots than that. Go back and get your daddy's boots." So I marched back to the house and put on another pair.

These guys had never bothered with me before. I was just a squirt, invisible. They were teenagers. Teenagers were really big, they did important things, they had girlfriends, switchblades, three-speed bicycles and did homework for hours.

"Are teenagers bad?" I once asked my dad, after seeing *West Side Story*.

"No, just a few," he said.

I worried about the homework situation looming in the future. Someone told me teenagers had to do four or five hours of it each night. I questioned my mom about this, and she assured me that when you become a teenager, you're ready to handle it. But these guys down the street didn't seem to have any homework. They just hung around, lounging against telephone poles, smoking cigarettes, part of some mysterious ritual I couldn't begin to understand. They must have been a few of the bad ones.

When I came back wearing the second pair of shoes, the leader sized me up. "Well, I guess they'll do. . . . But where's your hat?"

"What hat?" I asked, crestfallen.

"Your daddy's hat. You can't hang out here without your daddy's hat. Right?" The other greasers nodded.

So I went home, found a hat and trudged back again. They had a good laugh. I sensed I was their idiot, but hadn't reached my threshold. These were real teenagers, sort of like the ones in *West Side Story*, and I had a chance to hang out with them, whatever that entailed.

An unpainted, gray jalopy pulled up to the curb. Behind the wheel sat the very oldest, first-born Wilshire brother,

who rolled down the window. He had recently joined the
Army and was rarely seen in the neighborhood. Now he was
on leave, or AWOL. Or maybe he got kicked out. The dubious
soldier spoke quietly to the gang, comporting himself on a
higher plane than the rest of them. A pack of cigarettes was
rolled up in the sleeve of his undershirt, and when he got out
of the car, I saw he had a slight gut.

"Hey, Whitey, you really got 'em?" asked one of the
greasers.

"Yeah, I got 'em," said Whitey Wilshire, opening the
trunk of his jalopy. The greasers were more excited than he
was. He reached into a green duffel bag and brought out a
cache of fireworks called Nigger Chasers. Each package had
a caricature of a bug-eyed darkie on the run, hair a-frazzle,
a puff of smoke bursting after his airborne ass. A cartoon
balloon said the usual *Feets do yo' stuff.*

It seemed odd that somebody would manufacture a
product specifically designed to chase off colored people.
Maybe it was a package from long ago. Everyone knew
fireworks came in on slow boats from China, stocked "under
the counter" at Chinese laundries. They were illegal in
New York. But in China, they'd never set eyes on Negroes,
only heard of their legend, like dragons. Nigger Chasers
were like that exotic Asian toothpaste called Darkie, with
the grinning minstrel on the box.

"You can hang out with us now," decided the head
greaser. "Wanna come for a ride?"

Pvt. Whitey Wilshire was the oldest person I'd ever met
in the kid world. But he didn't say a word to me. I got in
the back seat between two greasers, while Big Willie sat up
front. I felt a creeping unease in the back and remembered
what had happened to Mumsy's father.

We drove down Continental Avenue, past the new
Grant's department store. I felt an odd sensation, being
driven in someone else's car other than my father's Buick.
The shock absorbers were shot and the upholstery was torn

and riddled with charred burn marks. Whitey paid no mind to traffic lights or stop signs, driving to his own drummer. Maybe you could do that if you were in the Army. There was no such thing as seat belts yet, and we bounced with every bump.

The car puttered along past Vic's candy store, where my father got his newspapers and cigars, and I got my monthly copy of *Famous Monsters of Filmland*. The arrival of each new issue, hot off the press, was one of the great thrills in life. When it snowed or rained, old Vic threw sawdust on the floorboards, so the whole place smelled like a heady mix of candy, sawdust and fresh newsprint. Now I saw it from the odd perspective of Whitey's car.

The greasers watched out their windows attentively. They were on a mission. The streets in town were virtually Negro-free, you would rarely see colored kids. Once when I was little, a group of angry young colored women confronted my mother on the sidewalk. They shouted a barrage of anti-white epithets as my mother hurriedly led me away by the hand, spilling groceries. It was the first time I'd seen such militant Black anger—something I'd be seeing more of in the future, and plenty of it.

But the colored folks mostly kept to their small neighborhoods. Big Willie and the gang aimed to keep it that way. When we reached the bottom of Robinson Avenue, Whitey took a left at my school.

"He goes t'da nigger school," said Big Willie.

"That right, Bagel, that where you go?" asked the head greaser. "You go to school with the niggers?"

I was at a loss for an answer.

"No wonder you so stupid. You King of the Jews, that right? King of the Jews?" said the greaser. I had almost no idea who the Jews were, or why I was king of them.

"We got the King of the Jews wit' us here."

They spotted their first quarry near the Carvel Ice Cream drive-in. An effeminate baby-headed Negro teen, with a checkered scarf around his conk, licked a chocolate cone as he bounced down the sidewalk. He held it with pride, as if this were a gift from the gods. Big Willie Wilshire, the young commissioner of fireworks, readied his ordnance. His older brother and defender of the free homed in on the scarf-headed teenager. The front window rolled down. And the games began.

"Hey, Mr. Chocolate, roll over!" Willie tossed out a Chaser, the fuse sputtering. Then the tube took off after its target like Chinese New Year, frantically hissing hither and thither. Mr. Chocolate dropped his ice cream cone and dove for cover. He screamed like a girl and held his head rag. The firework did as advertised, like some heat-seeking device for Negroes. It hissed around like a snake, until the final charge made it leap out one last time before exploding. Mr. Chocolate stood mournfully over his splattered ice-cream cone. He probably couldn't afford another.

"Next time, try vanilla!" Whitey hit the gas pedal, and the greasers fell back, laughing.

"Hey, Chocolate, roll over!" they repeated, bobbling their ice creams. "Man, you see duh nigger's face!?" They traded expressions, mimicking the scare they put into the guy, then fell back laughing hysterically. Coon hunting was a good ol' boy tradition. They usually threw garbage out the window at Negroes, or smacked 'em with baseball bats. Colored people, especially in do-rags, were slapstick funny when scared, screaming and dodging for cover. The greasers were self-assured in their actions, like this was the way you gotta treat 'em, this was how you dealt with the Negro Problem.

"That one of your friends, Bagel? He in your class?" said the head greaser as they tailed a raggedy kid. The kid was Mumsy! I sat frozen in the middle, like an intimidated poodle.

"Burnt toast!" yelled Big Willie, tossing out a whole pack of firecrackers, which exploded in rapid bursts. Each bang was satisfying, like the crack of a baseball bat. Mumsy could only run slowly, but threw a rock as Whitey drove off.

"Goddammit you!" yelled Big Willie. There was murder in his eyes. He reached for a baseball bat on the floor, breathing heavily, but his older brother said, "Naw, never mind that."

The car drove down to Continental Place, where a cul-de-sac of working-class Negro homes appeared. The houses were small and shabby, with dirt yards, clotheslines and fences. A man in overalls pushed a wheelbarrow while an old mama stood in the doorway of her shack, looking poor. Whitey beeped his horn full throttle. Willie let loose with a handful of Nigger Chasers, lighting and throwing them into as many yards as he could while Whitey u-turned through the cul-de-sac.

"Happy New Year!"

There was celebration in the car. An outpouring of juvenile delinquent glee. On the way back, Whitey drove up on front lawns, veered onto the left side of the road and went the wrong way down one-way streets. Just like Mr. Magoo. He actually stopped before an old colored lady crossing the street. The lady nodded her appreciation, as if thankful that this crazy cracker didn't run her down. Even Big Willie showed mercy, and didn't light anything.

The colored kids had no resources for such amenities as fireworks. They didn't know about Chinatown in New York, where white teenagers copped their contraband at laundries. Firecrackers were a white kid's artillery. Anytime I passed a Chinese laundry, I imagined boxes of firecrackers under the counter, and wondered what might be the code word. Swordfish? Who did you have to be to buy them?

Firecrackers, cherry bombs, ashcans and M-80s—power and loudness increasing in that order—were banned throughout New York and all surrounding states. An M-80 was alleged to be a quarter stick of dynamite. A pack of firecrackers, wrapped in exotic Chinese paper adorned with leaping tigers, was like heroin for kids. Forbidden as opium, intoxicating as nudist-colony magazines.

Whitey drove back to the Wilshires' slum house in my own neighborhood, which stuck out like a Depression-era Hooverville. The coon hunters pulled up behind the house, littered with junkyard debris and weeds. It was really cool. As a token of farewell, the greaser who invited me to hang out put his face up to mine:

"A Jew ain't nothin' but a nigger turned inside out."

4. The Back Road

THE COLORED SECTION SPREAD OUT upon a hill beyond the school, up Glen Cove Avenue. Although it was a suburban ghetto, reeking of garbage and poverty, it felt to me like entering a beautiful nightmare, inside a dark oil painting. Lincoln House was a dilapidated recreational barn, its lumber blackened and rotted over time. Built in 1917, it was named after the 16th president, who some considered the Negro race's greatest hero.

"It's a club," said my friend Mumsy Leech. "It's a boys' club." Lincoln House seemed far off the road to progress, but held local meetings for the humble Glen Cove chapter of the National Association for the Advancement of Colored People. It had a boxing ring. You had to be a colored boy to be a member. I was not admitted.

During the Kennedy years, when I first ventured up Back Road Hill, the air itself was spicy and wild. Unfamiliar smells drifted from doorways and alleys. My adrenaline spiked, wits sharpened. Along Glen Cove Avenue stood a broken-down apartment building, a sparse grocery store called Foods, and a shabby collision-repair shop. The names were scrawled upon signs. The weeds seemed better fed than the people, growing several feet high in empty lots. But weeping willows and oaks obscured the conditions from afar.

Behind the broken road, however, was where things got weirder. Hidden out of view was a shantytown of unpainted, tarpaper shacks, the wood rotted and gray, nailed together by untrained Negro hands. People who had migrated North for a better life, mostly from the Carolinas. Homes stood for years without plumbing, electricity or telephone lines. Windows had odd geometric shapes, their spaces sawed without measure, cubist in perspective. Broken windows stayed broken; others were boarded up. Crooked steps led up to unleveled front doors. Dirty clothes were boiled in an iron kettle outside. Clotheslines ran between trees. Yellowed pairs of long johns swung in the breeze, and jumbo lady pantaloons hung out to dry. It looked like a place for livestock.

Indian trails wound through the wooded area. Elderly gray-skinned Black women with mammoth breasts roamed barefoot through the woods with shotguns to kill squirrels or Long Island possum for supper. Though squirrels were hardly edible, they used them in stew. These mothers of my classmates were spiritually and physically stronger than their menfolk, some of whom had up and gone, died or resided in jail.

White crackers were not welcome in this grim little village. I didn't actually know any other white folks who'd ever been there. The colored people just lived over in those woods somewhere. If a white cracker came, he risked life and limb.

The freckled white kid with the Buster Brown suit in first grade had been transferred to St. Patrick's. Built at the turn of the century, its foreboding Irish Gothic steeple loomed from a hill over the opposite side of town from South School. A Catholic stronghold, I was never welcome there either. It was Glen Cove's highest structure, after the water tower.

Young Freckles ventured all by himself up Glen Cove Avenue in search of an after-school soda pop. He was spotted by some big colored boys. They were on their way to the train station, headed for Penn Station in New York with shoeshine kits. Backed up against a wall, the white kid could do nothing but take a shivering gulp and offer them a nickel to shine up his oxfords.

"We'll shoeshine yo' *face*," came the reply. A can of Kiwi boot black was rubbed and buffed into his kisser. He arrived home with a high-luster finish. His parents immediately removed their pride and joy from South School. Thus, I became the only white kid amongst several hundred colored ones. But somehow, it never really struck me that I was different until years later.

By the end of my first year at school, I naturally developed the same speech as my friends. It disappeared before white people. My parents never seemed to detect it. Most of the time, maybe as a survival tactic, I believed I *was* a colored kid.

"He a white nigger," Bobo and Jeffrey would explain upon introducing me to wary relatives.

"He don't look like no nigger to me. You sure?"

"Yeah, ah'm sure. He just got light skin."

"Well ah don' know. . . . I'll take your word for it, but he still don't look like no nigger."

I stood spellbound as strangers eyed me suspiciously. I was utterly perplexed as to why the grown-ups here hated white people. I made some narrow escapes. But I always came back.

5. Bobo's Place

By THE TIME I REACHED SECOND grade, home base in the Back Road became Bobo's house. If I ever got into a tough scrape, I could rely on Bobo to hide me in his shack. Then when it was dark, I would sneak out of the colored section and run up the hill to my home. Alongside Bobo's shack was the collision repair shop where his Pops had worked with his Uncle Limpy before going to jail. The back wall of the building was where the colored philosophers of Glen Cove Avenue wrote. There was one particular phrase that always caught my curiosity. It was written bigger than the other scribblings, and everyone was careful to write around it in respect: "Pussy Is Good." I wasn't exactly sure what this meant, but it must have been good—all those bathroom walls couldn't be wrong. White kids in America didn't know what the word *pussy* meant yet. They said *cunt*.

In second grade I gave a pretty Puerto Rican girl named Iris a ring from the A&P bubble gum machine, which she treasured. Of course it meant we were going to get married later on, and when the news spread, Bobo and a few older guys came up to me.

"Hey, how big is her pussy?"

"I don't know how big her pussy is. How big is yo' pussy?"

"Shit man, you don't know nothin'."

They walked away shaking their heads. Bobo was the only kid in my grade who claimed to know about pussy. He said he could show me some from a girl named Babes. That's what he called her. Jeffrey said Babes was so tall, you'd need to stand on a ladder to fuck her. Babes lived in an old white brick building, one of two apartment houses by Cecil Avenue in the colored section. I was looking forward to Friday afternoon when Bobo said he'd take me to meet Babes. But first he wanted to stop by his place, then visit his Uncle Limpy.

Bobo's shack was first on the hill of Glen Cove Avenue. We climbed a flight of gray splintery steps to reach the porch, which was always littered with eggshells. Inside was a stale unfurnished room with a couch in the center—and on that couch was Bobo's mother tucked under blankets. Every time I ever visited Bobo, his mother was lying on that couch looking half dead. Bobo had four younger brothers and sisters crawling around on the floor. I guess he had to take care of them all since his mother seemed so lifeless. Whenever Mrs. Monk addressed me directly, she tried hard to sound like a white by pronouncing the words slowly and carefully. Or maybe she just spoke that way because of some illness. She was the most peaceful mother I'd ever met on Glen Cove Avenue—yet she had the most volatile son. Bobo always sobered up before his mom, moving at a slower pace. She said softly to Bobo, "Come here, chile. Tell yo' white fren that he welcome in our home." Mrs. Monk was polite and always greeted me this way. Then she extended a swollen arm from under the blanket and motioned me to come over.

"You been kind to my Bobo, takin' him out to lunch an' all, so ah want you to have this gif'." She dropped two nickels into my hand as though it were a small fortune. I thanked her, realizing that she valued every nickel. Then she asked Bobo to get a razor and some pads so he could cut off some of her corns, and I could help if I wanted to. I backpedaled to the door, and was relieved when Bobo said he'd do it later.

Next stop was Uncle Limpy's place. He was laid up in bed from yet another car crash. He'd lost his license again. The means by which Limpy scraped by were mysterious, for the Monk Bros. collision shop was closed more often than not. I'd never seen it open. But Limpy had a quality that charmed the pants off the ladies. Especially fat, ugly ones, judging by the ladies who insulted the very mention of his name. Bobo said his uncle sweet-talked quite a few into marriage, and would marry another without even getting divorced from the previous one.

Bobo led me to a big white house that we entered without knocking. The premises were swarming with toddlers. For a moment I figured we walked into some nursery school by mistake. All of them were left unattended, smashing dishes and toppling over furniture, just about wrecking everything in sight. We walked up to the second floor, which was no different from the first—there were more little kids. One, who was covered with vomit, started to gag and out came what seemed like quarts more. I asked Bobo who these babies were.

"They all bastards," said Bobo. "They mah cousins and shit." Apparently, Uncle Limpy had felt an obligation to populate the world with dozens of little Limpys, all in his image.

The third floor was a bit more private. Uncle Limpy lay on a bed by the window with a broad beaming smile. The top of Limpy's head was wrapped in a handkerchief, tied in a bow around his proud pompadour. His hair dressing of choice was called Lucky Brown, a can of which sat on the dresser. (Avoid krimpy bad hair and you could be a Lucky Brown!) The "process" was invented to straighten Negroes' hair and make them look white, the accepted standard of beauty. But it somehow made them look ten times Blacker.

"Hey, Bobo," said Uncle Limpy, pointing to his Philco, tuned in on a baseball game. "You see dat guy? He hit dat ball."

"Yeah, ah see it," said Bobo.

"He hit dat ball . . . outta dat place," said Limpy, drowsy and slurring his words. "You know, ahm really messed up dis time, Bobo. A cracker smacked up Miz Washington ol' Packard. Ah was testin' it at the shop. Didn't go but 'round the block."

His eyes closed and he drifted off a few moments. There was a bandage on his forehead where he'd received stitches. Uncle Limpy was oblivious to the racket from the infants downstairs. He opened his eyes and just stared up at the ceiling, delirious. Bobo became angelically serious, as with his mother. Bobo came to the bedside, and they started whispering to each other in falsetto. Then Uncle Limpy pulled him down to his chest and wept. I stood over in the corner and turned my head because this seemed like a personal family matter that I had no business attending.

A stout old woman came from another room carrying a bowl of mashed-up food.

"Ah can't stand any more yo' slop!" Limpy barked at the woman. "Hey Bobo, fetch me a gallon dat Borden chocolate ice cream." He fished out some change from the dresser at his side. "So ah can have my se'f a party. So I can sit top the terlit and eat and shit all night! The best party in town. Heh, heh, heh!" he suddenly roared. And then he looked most decidedly my way, with a nod and a wink. "Diarrhea is the *po' man's pleasure*."

"You shut up and res'!" said the woman. "And you eat what you get."

A naked infant, who'd boldly attempted to crawl downstairs, lay crying at the bottom, defeated. He left a trail of evidence behind.

"Arthur done doo-dooed down the stair," Bobo alerted them.

"Fetch him *hyeah*," ordered the woman, pointing at the couch.

Bobo set the infant down. He whispered some final words to his uncle. The old woman started to mop Uncle Limpy's brow. As we headed for the door, Uncle Limpy dug his fingers into the old woman's massive rear end and winked at her seductively.

"Ahm a loser, baby," he said with a husky chuckle. "Ahm just a fuckin' loser."

We stopped off at the grocery store to steal two sodas and some candy. Since Bobo never had money, he just took what he wanted and tore ass. The sodas were for us, and the candy was for Babes. Bobo knew exactly how to handle women. How could he not, being the protégé of Uncle Limpy? The stolen candy was sure to guarantee us some pussy if things didn't go smoothly.

Babes lived on the seventh floor. We rode a small, clunky elevator. It was the only elevator I'd ever ridden in Glen Cove. Bobo knocked on the door and the mother answered.

"What ch'all want?"

"Is Babes home?"

"Yeah, come on in."

Bobo entered and she reached out her hand to stop me from going in. "You stay out here." I was accustomed to *Crow Jim*—reverse discrimination—treatment by now. They were just adults anyway. Through the door I faintly heard something that made me wish I hadn't come at all. I was nervous enough to begin with.

"Ah got a fren outside. He wants to know if you can show him yo' pussy." The door opened, and there was Babes.

"This the fren ah was talkin' 'bout."

I started to tremble and said, "I don't want no one to show me nothin'!"

"Well you ain't *gonna* see nothin' 'cause ah ain't showin' mah pussy to a whitey." She was a few years older than us and had her hair in braided pigtails. She was taller than Bobo and me, just like Jeffrey said, and wore a training bra beneath her undershirt. Bobo took a debonair bow and held out two candy bars.

"Well, can you show *me* yo' pussy?"

"Well. . . ." Babes went for the candy. "All right." So the both of them walked into Babes' room and left me standing in the hallway with the front door open. Hell, I didn't want to see no one's pussy anyway, I thought to myself, but secretly I did. *I'll just wait out here and Bobo can tell me what it was like.* About a minute went by and I heard a commotion. It got louder and out of the room came Bobo carrying Babes with her dress held all the way up.

"Look, here go some *fine* pussy!" shouted Bobo. She was kicking and screaming for him to put her down but seemed to be smiling.

"Yep, sure is fine," I said and just stared at the thing. In the midst of puberty, she had kinky hairs around that mysterious *line* that girls had. But I still didn't get why they wrote "Pussy Is Good" on walls. It didn't look so good to me, at least I wasn't sure. A strange feeling came over me, and I wanted to leave. All of a sudden Babes' mother shot over and grabbed Bobo.

"Leave her be! What 'chu doin' to mah daughter, messin' with her bidness?" Bobo broke loose and we started to run for the stairs. "When Isaiah come home he gonna *kick* yo' butt, Bobo!"

Bobo was snorting devilishly through his nose as we ran, and I heard the mother yelling at Babes, calling her a tramp and Miss Goody Sweet Ass. It was dark now, and we ran right across Glen Cove Avenue through the traffic, past the grocery store and stopped at Uncle Limpy's collision shop wall. Bobo was still cackling and I was a little shaken from seeing my first real live pussy.

"How come you didn't get yo' sef some pussy? Ah was holdin' right up there for you to get some," he said.

"How you s'poze to get *some* pussy? She only has *one*. How do you get it?"

"Shit, man," said Bobo. "You don't know nothin."

6. Principal Tiger

BOBO AND I WERE CALLED SEPARATELY to the principal's office for bothering Babes. The principal of South—otherwise known as "the nigger school" to outsiders—was a powerful-looking, no-nonsense white woman with a short-cropped hairdo. She referred to us as her "pyu-pils." Each of the photos on her office wall showed her at different stages in life, posing with a group of colored children in the snow. She pointed to snowmen in the photos, while the colored kids looked off in other directions. She suffered some odd speech impediment, her voice trailing off in tics, like an exotic bird.

Miss Tiger's office was a sanctum of dread. She sat me down politely, then walked over to her desk, opened a bottom drawer and produced two pairs of Everlast boxing gloves. They were red.

"So you like ta bother girls, eh?" She tossed one pair onto my lap and slipped her hands into the other. To laugh or run—that was the question. After her gloves were tied (the final slipknot accomplished with her teeth), she jumped up and started shadowboxing. Miss Tiger wasn't kidding around. Her head squatted between her shoulders as she shuffled toward me, moving skillfully on her feet.

"You wouldn't hit an old lady, would ya?" she asked while dancing around me, slapping her jab. "Stick and move, stick and move," she repeated, in a circular demonstration. Unlike our first grade teacher, no Jell-O jiggled beneath the principal's arms when she raised them. She was built out of something hard. Some of her jabs tapped me. I started to cry. The blows kept stinging. Tears started rolling down my cheeks as she jabbed and dove. Though she encouraged me to counterpunch, I didn't dare fight back. She finished off with a few body shots that sent me tumbling into a bookshelf stocked with volumes of *The Journal of Negro Education*.

Out of breath and instantly friendly, she said, "You see, lad, bothering girls doesn't get you anywhere, right, eh? Right? I can handle myself pretty well for an old lady. And I can whip any kid in this school, you betcha. But the point I'm trying to make is that bothering girls doesn't get you anywhere, does it?" And then she walked back to her desk with a twinkle in her eye as though her wisdom had profoundly changed my life. Dismissed.

I had more than my share of fights. Some of the colored boys fantasized about becoming boxing champions. Everyone knew the names of Floyd Patterson and Sonny Liston, and especially the emerging Cassius Clay. Local boxer Hubert Hilton, who fought out of Lincoln House, was currently undefeated as a heavyweight. "A man should fight with his gloves, not with his mouth," Hilton said in the papers, publicly challenging Clay. Hilton was the pride of the local community on the Back Road Hill. Although a sanitation man by day, he was considered a gentleman. He trained behind the garbage truck, trotting along, sparring, while dumping cans.

But Bobo didn't learn from the likes of Hubert Hilton, or from the boxing program at Lincoln House. Bobo was a street fighter before he could count and would knee someone in the balls whilst looking over yonder. He only fought dirty. The term "Black" was a racial insult, and if muttered by a white cracker, them was fightin' words. Any colored kid that wanted to learn had *someone*—older brother, paroled uncle or mother—to teach him to fight.

"Man, mah cousin taught me how to fight. See mah finger, see mah thumb, see mah fis', you better run!"

My dad was a powerfully built, but sensitive, Jewish writer. He taught me baseball. He taught me to throw and swing a bat, and took me to Vic Tanny's gym with him on weekends. So throwing apples became my primary defense. I never realized you could be *taught* to fight. I figured you just put up your fists. You were as good as what you were born with, as good as the size of your biceps when you made a muscle. The fact that boxing was a sweet science eluded me until many years later. But Bobo had his own way of mixing fists with jive to psych his victims into confusion. Especially if they were white. Nobody taught him this.

Some of the older Catholic school boys in uniform felt divinely inspired to kick my ass after school. They had some religious axe to grind. I stood accused the moment the St. Patrick's School uniforms confronted me.

"Were you baptized?"

"What's that?"

"You'll find out when you go to hell!"

"I ain't goin' anywhere."

"You walk like a nigger."

"I do not!"

My stride apparently had a rhythmic bounce that came from walking home uphill every day. I was boppin'. I knew nothing about religion, mine or theirs. The strange accusations flew by in a whirlwind of self-righteous anger and green-uniformed punches. They kicked my books, which they called "nigger school" books.

So finally I brought Bobo home with me. Bobo crawled along the side of the road, camouflaged by trees and bushes. Sure enough, at the top of the hill I could see the green uniforms waiting. This time I advanced fearlessly.

"Hey, Bagel! How's nigger school?" said the boldest, blocking my path. He kicked at the schoolbooks in my hands and grabbed my collar. Like a panther, Bobo lunged out of the bushes with snot hanging from his nose, pushed his face against the white boy and recited a poem:

> *Ah got the time*
> *You got the bread*
> *Take yo' money and bus' yo' head*
> *You are a cracka*
> *Ah am a nigger*
> *Fuck yo' mutha and pull on the trigga.*

The big white kid gave pause. Bobo might have even been smaller, but they'd never encountered his like. They'd never encountered any colored kids before, period. Bobo pummeled him while his assistant bullies froze. Even after the kid was beaten, Bobo kept returning to the defeated carcass for an extra last kick, striking out at something much deeper than this particular kid whom he'd never seen before. The St. Patrick's kids never laid their hands on me again. They only gave me dirty looks from a distance.

7. Your Son Ain't No Angel, Either

BUT BIG WILLIE REMAINED A PROBLEM. Apparently, he had some time to reflect in his burr-headed skull since the day we went nigger chasin', and decided that maybe I needed some of his firecracker medicine, too. His mother, the old hag Mrs. Wilshire, sat out on the front porch's worn-to-shit couch with the flea-bitten, chained-up dog. Poor Negro households had lived-in furniture, but the Wilshires' furnishings were worn beyond anything I had ever seen. She stared at me pop-eyed, always looking like she just woke out of a stupor. I had on my father's shoes and hat again, looking like an idiot.

"I thought Pop told him don't be comin' 'round here n'more."

"Aw, shit," said Willie, "Pop ain't been 'round for days."

Big Willie Wilshire, the neighborhood's whitest white kid, related his nigger-chasing conquests to his brothers and some other boys playing mumbley peg in the yard. "You shoulda seen them niggers run," he boasted of the episode in the car. "Make 'em jump, make 'em dance, firecrackers in their pants." Boy's inhumanity to boy.

Willie Wilshire's firecracking escapades came to a screeching halt one day, when a whole pack blew up in his face. A tetanus infection resulted from the gunpowder, and he lost his two front teeth. And so he developed what henceforth resembled mad-dog fangs on each side of his mouth, with sharply irregular teeth in front. There were no Tommy Toothbrushes at the Wilshire household. Dentistry of any kind did not figure in the family budget. But no mind. Common sense would have taught a lesson to anyone else, but not Willie Wilshire. Willie went right back to the firecrackers.

And such was the case as he still sniggered in the midst of relating his firepower. Suddenly he fixed on me. He lit a punk with a match, then lit a fuse. Then he tossed a lit cracker on me. It bounced off before it blew, but he followed with another and another.

We're circling in a slapstick comedy chase, me stumbling in the oversize shoes. Another kid joins in, throwing firecrackers at me. Other white kids are whooping it up. I hop, skip and jump like a darkie. My own eyes bug out. My feets do their stuff, but cannot shuffle off to Buffalo in my daddy's shoes. They refuse to run.

Three years older, Willie Wilshire pins me down and punches my face. He does this with a sadistic sense of duty, like he's just taking care of some final business of the day that needs to be settled. With his butch-cut astronaut crew, freckles and maniacal eyes looming over me, I am living in the moment. I am utterly defenseless. This at an age when a bee sting or skinned knees were world-changing events. The violation of each punch in the face is so shocking, the entire world turns upside down. Like drowning.

But Willie comes to a merciful stop. I am profoundly humiliated and stunned. It's not the first time this has happened. I stumble home crying, with a bloody nose and lip. Like some beaten, underage Civil War casualty.

A bigger, stronger tyrant who lords his size over someone smaller lying prone on the dirt—another enemy offering early lessons in how vicious the world could be. An astonishingly rude awakening.

As I coaxed my father to beat up Big Willie Wilshire, we took a walk to the Wilshire's front door. It felt like being on enemy territory, but with Hercules at my side. I was fearless standing beside my father, his formidable size and stature enhancing my own.

The patriarchal pappy of the clan, Jacob Wilshire, opened the door. He stood there unshaven in overalls.

"Mr. Friedman," he said, chewing his cud. "Your son ain't no angel, either."

And that was that.

8. We Need a White Boy

I LEARNED MY FIRST DIRTY WORDS from Bobo. If you were overheard saying a dirty word in school, you could expect an irate swat from the teacher's yardstick and a trip to the principal. Saying one at home got me a trip to my room. But then, with my newly educated eyes, I recognized in my father's own novel—which I could now pick out words from, here and there—the word "shit." I ran to my mother.

"Look, it says that dirty word here! In Daddy's book!"

That night my parents had a little heart-to-heart with me. You mustn't ever say such words out loud. But it was okay to write them in a book. For big people. Somehow, I didn't buy it.

The big world out there in Glen Cove was a cauldron of insanity. My parents provided my only bedrock of sanity and security. At least I think they did. If I had been left only with our nanny, Mrs. O'Leary, I would have gone insane. And from the colored section, I always returned to a lovely home. But I kept my parents busy.

"Josh—*you've done it again*," was my father's stock line, if he came to collect me from trouble. Months might go by, in which I was presumed to have matured. But sure enough, I'd hear the chilling refrain, whilst some store owner held me hostage for stealing candy: "Josh, *you've done it again.*"

Our principal, Miss Tiger, made a personal visit to our

house one evening. All trouble aside, she assured my folks how pleased she was to have me attend South School. There would be more of a racial balance in the future, she promised, ever so delicately. It was important that I stay. For now I'd be their token white.

My father believed men took care of the Big Picture—earning a living, political decisions, war, things of that nature. Matters of kids' education were best left to mothers. After his initial decision to have me attend South, he stayed out of the way. Meanwhile, my parents kept imagining they saw more white kids at my school. If they saw a white face even remotely in the vicinity, Mom might say to Dad, "See, there are white children everywhere."

"And more coming soon," my dad reassured her. But the only other white child destined to attend South was my brother, Drew. He was two years younger, and he became the second white kid at South. There were two first-grade classes; Drew began in one upstairs with Miss Grogen, who had been my teacher. Within a few weeks he was transferred downstairs, to Miss Volpe's room—the slower class. Perhaps some kids in Volpe's class were mildly retarded due to a lifelong bad diet of Ring Dings and Hostess Twinkies. But there was Drew, right at home. Where he strangely proceeded to draw his teachers on the desks—naked.

My dad flew in for the 1963 March on Washington, in a show of solidarity with Negro brethren at a time when maybe every extra body meant something. He went to *walk with Martin*. A victorious Civil Rights movement was by no means certain. He confessed astonishment now that while in college he'd never even noticed or considered such things as there being no Negroes on the basketball team. Such things weren't on the radar of whites back then.

But during the Kennedy years, my folks took a strong position on social progress. Before they enrolled their first child in a Negro school, an even more liberal friend of theirs extolled how grand an opportunity this was. Why, young

Josh would be a "leader" when he grew up. The friend even lobbied my parents to send me there.

A few years later, when the same liberal friend had a daughter, she was put in a Skinner Box—a radical experiment devised by behaviorist B.F. Skinner, wherein the newborn child spent her first year in an isolated box, protected from germs, society and her very parents' loving touch—not to mention Negroes.

9. A Knot Is Not a Noose

"**Y**OU REALLY A NIGGER, RIGHT JOCK?" asked Jeffrey Lincoln. "You a light-skin nigger, you really one of us, right?"

"Yeah, that's right," I said, convinced this was true.

Jeffrey gave the impression he was better off than the other kids. He always complained that his momma made him take a bath on Sundays, and he was known to have more than one pair of underwear. The other boys marveled over the birthday presents Jeffrey claimed to have gotten. "Ah got me a bicycle and a train set and a domino game for *mah* birthday."

"Hey, y'all see *King Kong* on TV last night?" he once asked, so I figured he had a TV. He curled his eyebrows in astonishment. "Man, it would take a *thousand* toilet papers to wipe King Kong butt!"

We'd been planning to hang out at his place, without Bobo. I'd never been there and expected it to look like a toy store. We set out after school one afternoon, and Jeffrey led me farther into the colored woods than I'd ever been before.

Some old drunk emerged from behind a shack and poleaxed me with his stare. "Yo' daddy hate niggers!" he shouted. Jeffrey led me on.

"Ah ain't no fuckin' bum!" continued the old man, raising his fist. "Uncle Sam is mah daddy . . . and my barber."

"When we gonna get there?" I wondered.

"Just upside that hill. That's where I stay."

His place looked like a haunted house, but this was no make-believe spook house at Coney Island. He really lived there. It was a crooked, boarded-up shack. Alongside the house was a small gathering of middle-aged colored women passing around a homemade jug of rotgut. It was in the vapor of their sweat. A 250-pound woman was sitting up on a porch preaching while her audience listened attentively. She was ranting on about Limpy, Bobo's uncle. Uncle Limpy was the rakish owner of a body shop whose main source of business came from car wrecks that he himself was in.

"Someday the Lord is gonna strike that Limpy, you wait and see, he's gonna strike him down. The Lord or somebody gonna strike him, because you cain't go through life cussin' and fartin' at everybody, everything you see, you just cain't do that and escape the Almighty's wrath. Or do you think I'm a mo-ron?"

"He a shit-heel and a heathen!" came another woman. They passed the jug.

"You can't go about stealin' everybody money. That nigger cussed out God Almighty himself, then broke mighty wind, yes he did, right befo' mah eyes," continued the leader. "I tole him he should go straight to church to beg forgibness fo' his soul, and that Limpy bent down and said that the Lord could kiss his shiny Black ass. But the Lord ain't gonna kiss Limpy Black ass. Or if he do kiss it, then that nigger knows somethin' I don't know and wanna find out about pretty quick."

"You right, Legertha, you right!" echoed the sisters, all of whom were whipped up to a man-hating frenzy.

"When I axed him ain't you s'poze to be runnin' yo' bidness at the shop, he just up and flashed me all his money and said he don't need to work cause he got his ways. But ah know what his ways is. He a fartin' man. And a thievin' man. And ain't one thing a fartin', thievin' man is good fo', and that's laying 'round the house and fartin', then goin'

out thievin'. I swear, that Limpy got the devil in his bones
and his bowels. There is somethin' wrong with that nigger,
somethin' done gone wrong deep down inside his intestine.
Am I right or am I a mo-ron?"

There were grunts of amen amongst the ladies, as they
passed a jug. Two women came into view carrying shotguns
with a rope of squirrels slung over their shoulders. The
larger one stopped in her tracks and bellowed, "Just a
minute, Mr. White Cracka! Where the hell do you think
you is goan?" All the colored women took notice, and I froze
under their haughty gaze.

"He wid me," said Jeffrey.

The woman who had been lecturing the mob stood up.
"Why you bringin' this white shit over here Jeffy, ah'm
surprised at 'chu!"

"Momma, it's okay cause he mah fren," came Jeffrey.
"Besides, he really one of us, he a white nigger."

"He a nigger, my ass! He got no bidness up hyeah—"

"Momma, he just come to play—"

"You buttin' in! You buttin' in to what ah was sayin'. Ah
tole you never to talk back to me, heathen! Shoo, the fibs
that chile can speak."

"What we goan do with this cracka, Legertha?" said the
woman with the shotgun and squirrels.

"Why don't we whup the tar out of 'im," barked a voice
from the mob.

"Hell, ah'll blow off his fuckin' haid!" came the large
squirrel woman, motioning with her gun.

"It be all right by me."

I went limp with a sickening fear. This was the wrong
place to be. I felt their bottomless hatred and anger. The
preacher woman wobbled over and knocked me down.
The force of her fat arm wasn't too hard, but I knew I'd better
hit the dirt. I was on my own now. I didn't move. I didn't
know where to run, and if I tried, the big lady was sure to
shoot me down. On the ground I was at their mercy.

The Black ladies encircled me and began to clap their hands and hum some supernatural progression foreign to my ear. Some of them swayed their hips, child-bearing hips that had all once fallen prey to the rapscallion Limpy. And then they did a two-step, shifting corned bare feet toward me, then dancing back. It was a nightmare. I strained to see Jeffrey, but he had disappeared behind the army of Black ladies. The preacher woman started in a sermon-like voice:

"You chained us hand and foot and took us from our mother land to live in slavery and disgrace."

"Hallelujah!" cried the rest.

"Bound by chains you made us toil in the cotton fields from sun-up to sundown. You dressed us in rags and made us eat the lefover scraps and slop not fit fo' a hog. Lord have mercy on our souls!"

"Amen, the Lord have mercy," chanted the chorus.

"But . . . I didn't mean it," I mumbled.

"What 'chu say?"

"I didn't do it." My colored accent disappeared, and I felt whiter than I ever felt before. Right then and there I wished I was colored so bad I just looked up to the sky and prayed, if the Lord really exists, prove it to me and make my skin Black right now, strike me with a bolt of Blackness. Make me, if not the Blackest nigger in the world, at least a fine shade of brown. The preacher woman went on to blame me for everything from the slave trade to the recent assassination of Medgar Evers and the bombing in Birmingham, killing four of their young.

"And to this day you continue to commit social injustice upon the colored people."

"But I'm one of you. I'm a light-skin nigger." My words came out muffled with my face in the dirt.

"That's right, choke, go ahaid and choke!" came another voice from the pack. I saw someone's old-lady shoe kick me in the head.

"We want 'chu to hate us!" came another voice.

A bucktoothed lady with a lisp added, "Thaths right, thucka, an we wanna kill yo' momma and yo' poppa and all yo' kind." The shotgun barrel was pointed my way as the other women cleared away from me. Then the tribe of monsters closed in, about to snuff me out. I heard black crows in the distance, seeming to join the chorus against me. I wished I could be one of them. Or I wished the ground would open and take me in. I cried to be back with my family, in the safety of my bedroom, amongst my toys, with my guinea pig Sitting Bull, things that seemed so far out of reach. I had trespassed into hell, and learned my lesson good. Still, there was no shot.

"If he think he a nigger," came the sober voice of the squirrel lady, "ahmma get some rope and lynch his ass." The squirrel ladies seemed more businesslike than the others. They set down the day's hunt and untwined a frizzy rope from around their shoulders.

"C'mon, Mr. White Cracka," said the huge woman with the shotgun, shoving and smacking me off into the woods. "Ah got somethin' for ya."

Jeffrey's momma held him at bay. I saw his eyebrows curled with helpless concern.

"Teach him good!" yelled one of the ladies. The whole pack laughed as the two hunters led me off to my little white boy's fate.

"Give him a nigger hit! Give him a nigger hit he won't soon forget!" screamed another. The two squirrel hunters led me down a dirt path. They were on a mission, they knew their business and spoke not a word till we reached a clearing. "Stop right hyeah."

One of them hitched up the rope around a tree branch about eight feet high. The other tied my hands behind my back. I stared blankly as they fashioned a makeshift noose. They tied it around my neck.

"Got some good rope lovin' for ya," she said. "Jus' the way you did to us."

My ideas on death stemmed from pictures I saw in my favorite magazine, *Famous Monsters of Filmland*. But they never portrayed the grim reaper as a big fat colored lady. The two of them who led this death march were scarier than Dracula or Frankenstein—whom I secretly believed were my guardian angels. But neither had yet come to my rescue. Real monsters roamed the earth. The lady who tied my hands behind my back snorted like a rhino through her massive nostrils. They pulled the rope up as high as they could around the branch, which lifted me off the ground . . . but just barely.

"That's right, peckerwood, choke, go ahead and choke! Kick them little laigs, kick em!" And, oh, how my little legs did kick. Luckily, I could still touch my toe to the dirt every other moment as I bounced from the neck. Each time I touched the ground I was able to equalize the pressure on my neck and catch my breath. Sort of like coming up for air to prevent drowning. They were too stupid to tie a proper hangman's noose. Or maybe they were too smart. They merely tied a loop around my neck. Finally, they walked off.

My nose was running and my mouth foamed with spittle. But I kept touching ground. It was twilight, getting darker. I dangled in this pathetic situation, bouncing, dangling, touching a piece of the ground, gasping, catching my breath. I didn't know how long I could hold out. It seemed like a half hour before Jeffrey found me, cutting me free. His expressive eyebrows were hunched up in a look of incredible worry.

"Run, Jock, run! Run!" Jeffrey ordered. So I did. I ran, as I'd done before from enemies, up the hill past the point of being out of breath. I imagined if I turned around the colored ladies would be right behind, grabbing for my neck. When I finally reached my back porch I was gasping nauseously. The colored ladies were nowhere in sight. I began to feel the warm safety of home sweet home, and it never looked so sweet. I promised myself that I'd never go down to

Glen Cove Avenue again.

I was too embarrassed to tell my parents how I got the rope burn around my neck. I made up some story. They questioned me relentlessly, but I maintained I tumbled down a hill. Then I became furious. The next day I figured to track down the squirrel ladies and kill them with my imitation stiletto pocketknife, the one I had ordered off a Bazooka Bubble Gum wrapper.

And so I brought the knife to school, but decided maybe I'd hunt them down tomorrow. Or the next day.

10. Mrs. O'Leary

ASSISTING MY PARENTS IN OUR upbringing throughout childhood was a nanny of sorts, Mrs. O'Leary. She would present problems far worse than colored school, or the white kids who scorned me for going there. She was a huge, unsmiling menace, and we hated each other from the first day she arrived. Remarkably, she would mellow with age. After a decade living with us, we loved her. But the years moved slowly for children.

Mrs. O'Leary had come through a babysitting agency, primarily to take care of newborn Kipp, my youngest brother. The second time she babysat for us, I clung to my dad's leg, begging not to be left alone with her again. O'Leary's voice turned sweet as an angel's, bewildered as to why the boy would panic so?

"Well I *never*," she spoke with genteel humility, starting to weep, turning to leave. My parents apologized, pried me off their clothes with love and affection, and inched their way out the door for a fabulous night in the city. The MG sports car rumbled out the gravel driveway.

On cue, O'Leary folded her arms and backed up against the door. "Let's see how *smart* you are," she admonished, a vengeful scowl on her face, "now that Mommy and Daddy are gone." She crooked a finger in my face. "I don't like you any more than you like me. But, oh, you'll mind what I say. You *won't* climb the refrigerator, you *won't* roam the house, you *won't* wander outdoors. I don't give a *damn* what your parents let you do. While *I'm* in charge, you'll sit in the foyer till bed, where I can mind you."

I'd never had a stranger enter my home and dictate a whole spectrum of rules and regulations. I didn't like it.

The good, sweet-old-lady side to O'Leary only manifested itself when our parents were around. Our father was a writer, with a magazine editorship by day in the city, and our mother an aspiring actress. They led hectic schedules. If I awoke any weeknight, I heard the comforting staccato flurry of typewriter keys from the kitchen table downstairs. It was the rhythm of the night. Mrs. O'Leary often found him early in the morning, slumped out cold over his Royal.

By the time I was in second grade, brother Drew and I were left in the care of O'Leary half of the week. She was reliable, mature, cooked meals, did dishes, mopped floors. She did a good job with her primary charge, Kipp. Soon she was given the bedroom downstairs for her three-day stays. Which eventually became four, then five days.

She achieved some notoriety within our parents' wide New York literary circle. Everybody wanted "a Mrs. O'Leary." But God forbid if anyone mistook her for the *maid*—she became deeply offended and would shoo herself off to the bedroom and slam the door.

Furthermore, she didn't fancy the spook house Drew and I rigged up in the basement. Luminous skulls flew on fishing lines. Dummies, stuffed with old clothes, sat stiffly on a love seat. Drew and I crowned their necks with monster masks all the way from Don Post Studios in Hollywood, California. Ordered exclusively from Captain Company, *Famous Monsters of Filmland*'s mystical mail-order back pages. She just couldn't make sense of the concept, and would knock rubber bats out of her path as she trekked to the laundry room.

O'Leary arose at dawn, donning one of her rotund,

flowered muu-muus and two dainty pink woolen slippers. She'd had the slippers for years. Her thinning blonde hair was particularly frizzy in the morning, though her eyes were clear blue. Few teeth in her head were her own; a set of upper dentures floated in an Efferdent water glass by her bedside. She rarely bothered with them in the morning, when she could be holy hell.

When the teeth were out, she mispronounced my name "Jrosh." My colored friends mispronounced my name "Jock." So I was Jock to the colored kids, Jrosh to O'Leary and Bagel to the Catholics.

Alone in the kitchen, she prepared a breakfast for herself of Cracker Barrel cheddar cheese, with equal parts slices of salty butter on Wonder Bread. Once, when whole wheat bread was brought into the household, O'Leary refused to have any part of it. "I've been eating white bread for years," she declared patriotically, "and it hasn't hurt me." Embarrassed to chew in front of others, she only ate in private.

In the morning, Drew and I could hear the *pssst, pssst, pssst* of her pink slippers, like sandpaper against the floor. Her arthritic legs bent under an ever-fattening rooster-like frame. "Puh, puh, puh," she breathed, climbing one stair at a time, the poor woman, waddling toward our bedroom if we overslept to wake us for colored school. She mopped her brow with a handkerchief as she reached the top of the stairs, using the same handkerchief to mop up around the sink, the breakfast table, even to dry dishes. If Drew or I complained about the rag, she marched right off to her room and slammed the door.

Evening was similar to morning. Supper was at 5:30. My brother and I never knew whether we'd encounter the Good Mrs. O'Leary or the Bad. More often than not, it was the Bad. I was first to brave the kitchen one night, when we returned from our outside play.

"Good evening, Mrs. O'Leary," I began, like a little gentleman, testing the waters. O'Leary banged some pots and pans and didn't turn. She'd prepared her specialty, a tuna casserole. Her anger was distant, aloof, impossible to crack. Her bad moods were set in stone. Yet, when she started the day in a foul temper, it was automatically considered to be me who was "in a mood."

"Oh, boy," I said, sitting down at the table and forking in a mouthful. Still no reply from O'Leary. I threw up my shoulders in defeat. "This casserole is delicious . . . but I hate it!" I spit a mouthful back on the plate. I knew O'Leary was my enemy for the evening, so I had nothing to lose. And since I met Bobo, I could be holy hell.

Kipp was always kept separate from us in his highchair in the kitchen. Brother Drew arrived for supper in his brown overalls. He emitted hog-like grunts whenever exerting physical effort. "Your brother's in one of his *moods*," said O'Leary to Drew—her first words. She went to fetch Drew's plate, scooping a spatula full of casserole. She brought over his glass of milk, immediately ingratiating herself with Drew this evening. She often tried to befriend one of us and freeze out the other, establishing "sides." Drew would now represent the sympathetic ear, to which O'Leary would broadcast her attack against me.

Drew dug into this tuna casserole quietly, forking out a tomato slice from the bowl of vinegar in which it floated. Another specialty of O'Leary's was a tomato-vinegar salad that clashed with our obligatory glass of milk.

"How is it, dear?" she asked Drew.

"Good."

"The Professor thinks it's *lousy*. Hah! He don't know what put him here."

I was known as "The Professor" because O'Leary thought I was too big for my britches. A precocious smart-ass, something a woman of her standing found unacceptable in a kid. Any time I doubted her word, she branded me The Professor.

Drew stared into his food as he ate. He grunted. O'Leary watched. He was the model of good behavior. I was ready to carry on a one-way conversation only so long. No one would speak to me. Exasperated, I went into my trusty old scatology routine:

"Mrs. O'Leary, your tuna casserole gives me *diar-rhea, con-sti-pation, diar-rhea, con-sti-pation, diar-rhea, con-sti-pation!*"

It was like a football cheer, my mantra, as I danced around O'Leary, who went numb and blank. I then fell to the ground, laughing. Drew strained to hold his laughter, having been officially aligned with O'Leary this night.

Finally, O'Leary would turn in defeat to Drew: "I fail to see any *humour* in The Professor's actions. Those are bodily dysfunctions. When you boys become young men—if this idiot here ever does—your brother will feel *ashamed* when he looks back to this."

One thing I did share with Mrs. O'Leary was the true origin of the red ring around my neck. I told her I got hanged. She took this silently, but looked heavenward and made the cross of the Father, Son and Holy Ghost.

11. Dare to Dream

WHAT DO YOU WANT TO BE WHEN *you grow up?*

I don't wanna be me a garbage man.
A janitor.
A maid?
Laundress, like mah momma.
Shoeshine man!
A cook.
Ah don't know, a maid, ah guess.
A fighter!
Garbage man!
I wanna be a flyerman, like Smokey Bear, so I can blow the flyer out!
A teacher.
Dish washer.
A singer!
Household maid.
Cab driver.
Elevator man!
Night watchman.
Fighter!
Yeah, me too. A boxer like Cassius Clay.
I wanna be me a doctor, so I can look at people feet.
A porter, I guess.

. . . I wanna be in the Beatles.

Hey Bobo, what you wanna be when you grow up?

A nigger. Kick white people's ass.

12. Drake O'Leary

A '56 THUNDERBIRD, BADLY DENTED, pulled into the pebble driveway, careful to avoid our maze of toy car roadways. Out hopped Drake O'Leary, Mrs. O'Leary's son. His presence always broke the tension. He never disapproved of my hair. He was currently a clam digger in Oyster Bay, and he visited his mother every month with a new fiancée.

"How's ol' Sitting Bull?" asked Drake, fond of the guinea pig.

"Fine!" screamed Drew and I.

Drake was a rugged, hirsute longshoreman type in his late 20s. He sometimes brought a pail of clams he'd dug himself. This time he slipped Drew a magazine, with a secretive wink and a "Shhhh." Sure enough, a stiff maiden sat back in the car. Drake hoisted us onto his shoulders. He was in exceptionally good spirits.

"Hello, Lu," he nodded to Mrs. O'Leary's best friend, visiting that afternoon. "Mother," he intoned, with great flourish, "I've brought someone special for you to meet." He set down a small bouquet of flowers for Mrs. O'Leary, something my father would receive a florist bill for next month. He kissed his mom on the cheek then went back to the car, Drew and I nipping at his heels. Drake opened the door and a blonde stepped out.

"This is Suzette." Drew and I stood looking at the ground.

"Josh! Drew!" roared Drake. "Where are your *manners*?" He was quite concerned with matters of etiquette and often admonished us about proper salutations.

"Hi," I said.

"Pleased to meet you," nodded Suzette, a delighted smile over her face.

"Manners!" whispered Drake, out the side of his mouth to me, as he escorted Suzette to the patio. I saw the switchblade sticking out of his jeans back pocket, which Drake often used to pick his fingernails.

Drake presented the new woman to O'Leary, who held her emotions like a mortician. Despite her name, Suzette, who was a student at the Grace Downs Charm School for Girls, didn't speak French.

"Well, Mother, what do you think? Isn't she a living doll?"

Drake sat the woman down, several years his junior, and began stroking her hair. Drew ran off grunting to the bushes. Suzette blushed, made eyes back at Drake, but didn't say a word. She let men do the talking. O'Leary and Lu lit up tense cigarettes and seemed to keep their beers out of view. Drake, his eyes gone ga-ga, began smooching the woman loudly, right before the two old dames. "Ain't she sweet as sugar?"

Drake did handyman jobs around our house for a flat $50 a week. It was duly noted by my parents that Drake "had a piece missing." He was bad at intersections, twice smacking up our family car, and got arrested in bars, always blaming "colored people." He was overeager to perform menial chores. "Shine your boots, sir?" he would ask. "Wax the car?" I'd heard my father remark that Drake was perhaps "a little too anxious to shine boots."

Occasionally O'Leary's hard face went soft before Drake—her handsome boy, this big lug of an Irishman. But not tonight. There was a threatening undercurrent in Drake's charming voice, as though he were instructing all present that maybe they should all love Suzette, lest he reach for that switchblade in his back pocket.

Occasionally, Drake stayed overnight. I overheard odd behavior late one evening. Drake began to call O'Leary "Mommy" in a whiny voice. His mother put him up in her room, usually during a crisis. He would share her single bed and don one of her oversized nighties. They were huge, transparent pink negligees that hung loosely over Drake when he went to the kitchen for a beer.

The next day, O'Leary would send me out with her negligees, instructing me to take them to the French cleaners "so they don't end up in the nigger warsh."

O'Leary had three sons, just like my parents did. The middle O'Leary son's picture hung on her wall in the small maid's room she occupied. He had died in the 1940s as a boy. It was a sepia-toned portrait of a 12-year-old, Drake's older brother. Whenever Mrs. O'Leary spoke of the event, cloaked in mystery, she instantly cried.

Even more mysterious were the whereabouts of her long-gone husband, from whom she had acquired her surname. It was apparent that something dreadful happened long ago. She went white with silence whenever I asked.

Drake had started a family or two, then deserted them, leaving behind a few kids—Mrs. O'Leary's grandchildren. Sort of like Uncle Limpy, the trails of kids he left behind seemed more like litters. O'Leary had ex-daughters-in-law, nieces and nephews, all with their own hard-luck stories. She dreaded personal phone calls. Often they were cries for help from a single mother, left to fend for herself. Christmas was a time of particular grief for O'Leary, whose own grandchildren went presentless. She resented the elaborate toys Drew and I received, like the battery-operated Robot Commando or Hasbro Cyclops.

"Everybody! I've bought Suzette an engagement ring," announced Drake, with delight, holding aloft her finger.

"How precious," growled Lu. But Mrs. O'Leary looked deflated.

It was then that O'Leary's eye, still supervising her charges, spotted little Drew behind the bushes. She ordered him out and made him pick up something he had dropped and kicked behind a shrub. It was a tattered copy of *Playboy*, the girlie mag. She made him hand it over.

"You sneak. A dirty magazine! What would your *father* say?"

"My father wrote a story in it," retorted Drew.

"Don't be smart!" said O'Leary.

Drake shook his head with a sly reproach. "You boys. Now that takes the cake. What'll become of your p's and q's?" He swung an arm around Suzette, and they left abruptly.

Later that night, he returned alone to stay with his mother. And through O'Leary's door, in the wee hours of the night, could be heard, with chilling clarity, the admonition:

"Don't bite Mommy!"

13. Even More Rules

THE RULES AT SCHOOL WERE sometimes worse than the ones Mrs. O'Leary imposed at home. And like any other school, rules were rules. Or maybe they were more rigorously enforced at South. Here was school, like all others, where the law of the land dictated you be present between 8 a.m. and 3 p.m. on weekdays. This was enforced by powers much bigger than you. You sat in your seat most of the day like a plant. You didn't answer a question out loud; it could lead to detention. And when we were held for detention, the colored girls looked at me and Bobo like pariahs, as *they* got to leave at three o'clock like good children. They didn't dare even touch us; we might be contagious, because we were *bad*.

Everybody else raised their hands. When the teacher asked a simple question, all hands shot up, waving frantically, everyone panting "Ah know, ah know!"

"Hey, Miz Grogen!"

"Hay is for horses," corrected our teacher.

"'Scuse me, can I go to da baffroom?"

"You may not. But you may be excused to the *lavatory*."

It was impossible for a kid to prove he really had to pee. You had to be granted the benefit of the doubt. Sometimes our old teacher came charging into the boy's room. So you'd better be in there at the urinal whizzing away. Often, permission was refused with a flat N-O. But when Bobo had to piss, he just up and walked out of the room.

One time the teacher left the class unsupervised for half an hour, taking some of us with her for dental tests. When we got back, Sabrina was sitting at her desk sobbing, soaked in piss. There was a pool of it on the floor. The girls explained that Sabrina had her hand raised to leave the entire time but didn't dare leave her desk. She finally couldn't hold it in. Colored girls were told to sop it up with paper towels and napkins. Sabrina repeated the same blunder again. The girls who cleaned it up never seemed to mind much, giggling and wiping up every drop as though practicing to be future cleaning women.

Strict as our first and second grade teachers were, they taught the colored kids to read. At least most of us. Nothing was going to stop them from this noble mission, certainly not Bobo. If it required the thwack of corporal punishment upon our butts, then Mrs. Grogen held her yardstick aloft— the teacher's sword of discipline. Oh, how the jelly under her chin and her arm did quiver as she held it aloft, daring Bobo to disrupt her class once more. She smacked it down upon his desk.

And then we went back to the daily repetition of the alphabet: *"A say ah, ah, ah, B say buh, buh, buh, C say cuh, cuh, cuh . . ."*

It wasn't long before the colored girls, more advanced than the boys, were singing "The Name Game." When Bobo repeated the song to them, he used the one name you weren't supposed to:

> *CHUCK!*
> *Chuck, Chuck*
> *Bo buck*
> *Bonana fanna fo fuck*
> *Fee fy mo muck*
> *Chuh-uck.*

Besides Bobo, the only other boy who sometimes wore fancy
threads was Torrence, in our class since first grade. He
always sat in the back of the classroom in a world of his own.
He never fought. Torrence wanted to be a doctor so he could
"smell people feet." After he confessed this aloud to the class,
he ducked his head under the desk, kicking his legs up and
down, with an embarrassed giggle. But the teachers liked
Torrence because he sang like a nightingale. Bobo called
him a "pussy," and every time he passed his desk it was
Bobo's custom to smack him on the head. The sound was
loud and crisp against his shaved baldness. Yet Torrence
would shake it off and continue singing as though nothing
happened. He had a voice like Diana Ross. Sometimes we
played "Wipe Out" on the back of his bald head.

Music class was held once a week. The music teacher,
Miss Bonk, wore red lipstick that looked ghoulish against
her pale, doughy face. The only songs we sang were patriotic
hymns, performed in a near monotone. Songs like "God Bless
America" and "Take Me out to the Ballgame." Written, of
course, at times when Negroes were either disenfranchised
or not allowed to play pro baseball. Again, Bobo stormed out
of music class and disappeared, which broke every rule in
the book. I don't know how he got away with it. He never
learned the national anthem.

   At the end of every session with her ghoulish lips aglow,
the music teacher thundered out the opening piano chords
of "The Star-Spangled Banner." Her voice cracked at the
crescendo as Torrence reached "the rockets red glare" in
falsetto. Her double chin vibrated with patriotic emotion.
I imagined those bombs bursting in air and through a haze
in the heavens saw that our flag was still there. Torn and
bullet-ridden, but still there. The colored kids sang with
pride, but knew little of shining seas and purple mountains'
majesties above the fruited plain. These were the last days
of unquestionable pride in America.

During second grade, an announcement came over the school intercom:

"Faculty and pyu-pils, may I please have your attention. . . . A terrible thing has happened. . . . It has just come over the news that President Kennedy has been shot. Please stay calm and wait for further announcements, eh?"

Her voice trailed off asthmatically. All of a sudden teachers were scurrying about and screaming. TV's were turned on, the ones only used when we watched the astronauts lift off. Teachers were crying; they seemed frightened. But we hadn't really studied presidents yet.

"Who he? He a whitey? What they go mess wid him fo'?"

Parents streamed in to South School that day to get their children. Maybe some of the kids might get assassinated too if they walked home alone. Maybe the country was finished. Big mommas grunted and snorted into their handkerchiefs. I'd never seen that many Black people cry. It seemed to me like they had something stuck in their throats.

The killer was caught the next day, and his name was Oswald. The name, which we'd never heard, had an ominous, evil sound. *Oswald.* His shadowy image looked like something out of *Famous Monsters.* A terrible boogeyman who killed our President. Then we were deprived of children's television for three days.

14. Get a Haircut!

BUT SOMETHING OCCURRED TWO months after the assassination that made me the happiest I'd ever been. It began like this:

"You look like a Beatle bug."

"A what?"

"A Beatle bug." Colored kids suddenly started calling me Beatle Bug. Then I saw teaser spots on TV that said The Beatles Are Coming. "I Wanna Hold Your Hand" and "She Loves You" came over WMCA on my Silvertone transistor radio. At first I was mystified. By the second hearing, intrigued. But by the third time I heard "She Loves You," it all hit like a hurricane. I watched *The Ed Sullivan Show* and was mesmerized. *Meet The Beatles* spun magically on my new record player for hours each day.

Since I was white and had long hair already, the colored kids thought I looked just like a Beatle. My mother bought me new Beatle boots at Thom McAn, turtlenecks, and let my hair grow even more like theirs. White parents in my neighborhood were appalled. "Get a haircut!" yelled strangers from cars. I had a moptop.

"Get a haircut!" I heard that barked at me a hundred times behind my back. From a passing cop, a fireman, a white friend's father who stood blocking the front door. And from our gym coach at school. He was a thick-necked tough guy with a whistle chain around his neck. He was quick to smack heads together or pinch you hard. Little kids though we were, he seemed to convey you're in the Army now. In the gymnasium, he taught the boys and girls to play something called "Brownies and Fairies." It involved one team sneaking up behind the other, then a chase and tag. Another favorite, Dodgeball, involved throwing a hard red rubber ball at other kids, eliminating players from a circle. But when the coach would demonstrate, he'd throw the rubber ball with enough force to knock a kid back. He referred to us as "'boons"— short for baboons.

"All right, all you 'boons, form two lines for Brownies and Fairies."

"Hey, Coach, was Babe Ruth colored?" asked some kid. A look of astonishment came over the coach.

I received a personal reminder at the end of each period: "Hey, Friedman, when are you gonna get a haircut? You look like a 'boon."

Colored folks couldn't care less about my hair. Only white people were offended. The principal stopped me in the hall and asked when I planned on getting a haircut. And most disturbingly, the pretty new teacher we all inherited the next year would call me "Josephine." But my devotion to the Beatles only grew stronger, as they kept pushing the envelope further. Every time you saw them, their hair got a little longer—and lovelier. So I'd dare to grow mine longer. But the Beatles were way across the ocean in the land of England, far out of reach of gym coaches, principals and rock-throwing whites.

Barbers were also angry at the Beatles. The news reported incidents of gym coaches taking boys by force and cutting their hair. South School's gym coach only threatened to give me one. (Thirty years later I would catch myself barking to a Black kid on the street, "Hey, pull your pants up!")

I tried to keep up with Bobo by getting bad grades. My

mother's attempts to shape me up were futile. "The Beatles did their homework and got good grades," she pleaded.

"No they didn't!" I shot back, a smartass.

15. Summer of '64

WE SPENT THE SUMMER OF 1964 far away from the colored kids, in Fair Harbor, Fire Island. The summer provided an abrupt change, a chance to be white again. I played with freckled, lily-white children on sand dunes by the ocean. None of them knew or cared where I went to school. I stared across the ocean for hours, imagining England at the other end, where the Beatles lived. We took a sand taxi to Ocean Beach for the local premiere of *A Hard Day's Night*. Mrs. O'Leary came along to Fire Island, to take care of Kipp and torture me and Drew.

Far from this idyllic setting, events transpired that became known as "the long, hot summer of 1964." Negro youth swarmed upon whites-only lunch counters in cities like Jacksonville, Florida, demanding service. They firebombed buildings and tossed Molotov cocktails into the mayor's campaign office. All the major Civil Rights groups focused on the racial battleground of Mississippi. They embarked on voter drives and "freedom schools," which included Black history for the first time. Frederick Douglass, Sojourner Truth, Rosa Parks, Emmett Till—these subjects were not yet taught. Slavery wasn't mentioned in American schools any more than the Third Reich was in German schools. A thousand mostly white volunteers, many from elite colleges, descended on rural Mississippi. Northern agitators were at it again, trying to destroy the Southern way of life. White Mississippians considered it another Northern invasion of the South. Among the casualties were the infamously murdered young Civil Rights workers Chaney, Goodman and Schwerner.

In the South, it was whites who introduced violence into the equation. But when the Civil Rights movement came North, it took on a different demeanor. They weren't sayin' *honey chile* and *hi-de-ho* and *shufflin' off to Buffalo*. In the North, Blacks were loud and sassy, talked back, rioted, looted, robbed. Black ghettos became cinderblocks, and there were riots that summer in Harlem, Bed-Stuy, Rochester and Philly. Malcolm *hates* whitey.

Also unbeknownst to the kids of South School, there had been loud protests about "racial imbalance" in New York City education. The Citywide Committee for Integrated Schools—a coalition of Civil Rights and labor groups, white liberals and Puerto Ricans—worked together to arrange boycotts. They emptied the schools of half a million Negro kids for two days in February and March of 1964— right after the Beatles hit town. Leading the New York City charge toward integration was the Reverend Milton Galamison, of Brooklyn, and his sidekick, Mrs. Annie Stein, a white Jewish parent and organizer—both given backbone by the sociological studies of Black psychologist Dr. Kenneth Clarke. They had this concept that "the only way a Black child can learn was to be seated alongside a white child." (This concept gained no momentum by my example, and the idea was eventually repudiated.) Rev. Galamison was the co-speaker at the Audubon Ballroom when Malcolm X was assassinated the next year.

We didn't know Malcolm X, where Mississippi was, or how to spell either. But coming back to school on September 7th was an abrupt reentry. Mississippi might have had the meanest whites in America, but New York surely had the angriest Blacks. Back in Glen Cove, I couldn't fathom why everyone was so angry. I had no idea what Bobo did that summer. But he came back to school a little more worldly. Emmett Till's nickname had also been "Bobo." Burn, baby, burn.

16. Miss Grimsby

THIRD GRADE. OUR TEACHER WAS
Miss Grimsby. A smartly coiffed young lady torn between
education and a singing career. It was well known she
once appeared on *The Lawrence Welk Show* singing
"White Christmas." And so, a tradition began where
South School would present her in the auditorium on a
snowy December morn.

"Pyu-pils—*our own* Miss Grimsby," announced
Miss Margaret Tiger, our principal. Miss Grimsby, dressed
in her Sunday best, came out smiling angelically with
a church pianist accompanying. She opened with a few
Christmas hymns, went into "Silent Night," then closed
with her signature piece, "White Christmas." Miss Tiger
stood to the side of the stage, arms folded, swelling with
such pride she looked like she was about to burst. Just like
Sergeant Carter when Gomer Pyle went into his operatic
croon. Christmas could never be so white at South School
without our own Miss Grimsby.

Offstage, and out of sight from the principal,
Miss Grimbsy was a gum-smacking broad from Brooklyn
who spent her Saturdays at the beauty parlor. The sloppy
outline of her Playtex brassiere showed through her dress.
She wore flesh-colored stockings, and her heels rose a little
higher than schoolmarm standard. Because her skin was
alabaster white, the blackness of her eyebrow pencil and

false eyelashes were especially pronounced. Several beauty marks highlighted with black pencil seemed absolutely pornographic. If it was perfume she wore every day, I couldn't tell. It may have been her own intoxicating scent.

Twice a year, Miss Grimsby threw a dance for her third grade-class—right before Christmas and Easter vacations. These were the only dance affairs ever at South School. Kids became self-conscious about their clothes.

"Ah told mah momma, ah don't care what kind of pants you make me wear, so long they ain't *baggy*," declared Jeffrey.

"Why can't I have a purple suit like Bobo?" I asked at home. "I don't want *baggy* pants." My mother said Bobo's suits may have looked flashy, but they were cheap. They were from Grant's Department Store and they'd soon fall apart. I waited for Bobo's suit to fall apart, but it never did. And I never saw any boy-sized sharkskin suits at Grant's, or anywhere, nothing that looked like Bobo's.

"Dahhh, you got *baggy* pants!" ridiculed Bobo, strutting to school in his Cuban heels and his purple Continental sharkskin suit. It fit so snug, it seemed tailor made. I looked down at my chinos, horrified. I had thought they were pretty tight.

"They baggy," said Bobo, and I was crushed.

Some of the girls, smartly attired in Sears Catalog school wear, chimed in: "Baggy pants, baggy pants, dahhh!" They wore sweaters and charm bracelets. They put their noses in the air at the sight of boys in rags. And the boys—excepting Torrence, Bobo and myself—were in hand-me-downs and rags.

Especially huge-nostrilled Mumsy. A frayed rope around his waist held up his trousers. They rose above his ankles, had holes, and were big-time *baggy*. On the morning of our third-grade dance, he came to the schoolyard with a prized possession.

"What dat?" Jeffrey asked.

"Here go mah record," said Mumsy, showing everyone a scratched LP that had long since lost its cover. "For the dance."

"What kinda record?"

"It's a boys' record. You play it."

'You ain't play a record," explained Bobo. "You *fly* a record."

"Nuh uh," said Mumsy, starting to drool. "You play it. It's got music. It's a boys' record, it got music for boys."

"*Boys'* record? What the hell you talkin' about, music for boys? You s'poze to fly a record. Ah show you," said Bobo, reaching out.

"Nuh uh, dis here *mah* record," recoiled Mumsy. "Ah only got one record."

"Well, ah show you how you really play a record. You make it fly." Bobo coaxed the record out of Mumsy's hands. "Now, you watch how it done." He wound it backhand and let it sail like a Frisbee to the end of the school yard. It hit the pavement and went to pieces. Mumsy walked over, retrieving the pieces, and began to cry.

"You done broke mah record."

Bobo shrugged without a care in the world, and walked off.

17. The Sneak

THE NEXT NIGHT, FRIDAY, MY MOM left before dinner to meet Dad in New York. They wouldn't be returning until Sunday. When I came down for supper, O'Leary was friendly as pie. Tonight, she was in a snit toward Drew. Drew seemed to have lost his appetite, and O'Leary held him at the table to clean his plate, while I ran upstairs to watch TV.

After the Smothers Brothers and *Honey West*, I came downstairs. Drew was *still* held prisoner at the supper table. O'Leary sat before him on her stool.

"Oh, he'll clean up every drop," she announced, arms folded, lording over some weird proceeding. Seated across the room was her best friend, Lu. Lu had just arrived from a big afternoon at the beauty parlor—the most exciting event in her life. Her hair was in a fresh beehive. Lu was even bigger and fatter than O'Leary in a muu-muu. She wore pink cat's-eye glasses on a chain. She was a waitress at Henry's Confectionery Luncheonette, moonlighting as a babysitter at the same agency O'Leary had come from. She was in her mid-50s, the same as O'Leary, and lived in town with her ailing daddy. The poor woman was an old maid.

"Lu loves you kids," O'Leary would say, before her bosom buddy arrived on a Friday night. "She's just crazy 'bout you boys." But Drew and I feared her. O'Leary liked to exercise her babysitting power before Lu, show she didn't "take crap from these kids."

"How about that Mary Mondelli, she still stealing your tips?" asked O'Leary.

"She's Italian," said Lu, taking off her coat. "They can't help it when they see coins. They love shiny stuff."

Drew sat at the table, cowering before them.

"Oh, he'll clean up every drop," she repeated, to her audience of Lu. Drew appeared deaf and dumb. "He'll eat it once he fetches it back on his plate." And then, with a terrific swipe of her arm, she smacked Drew's dinner plate off the table. I watched the Jell-O shake under her arm. Drew's beef liver rolled under the radiator. "Fetch it!" she ordered. Lu shook her head, a burst of mocking laughter and cigarette smoke coming from her lungs. She filled an ashtray with red-lipsticked Benson & Hedges butts.

Drew, grunting softly, dutifully reached under the radiator to sweep his roll and half-eaten liver back on the plate. He walked back to the table and sat down before his meal in silence.

"Look at him. You'd think he'd know I was onto his sneaky tricks by now." I watched my younger brother's hell, and only felt relief it wasn't mine. O'Leary was *my* "friend" tonight. She made a point to ask if I wanted any dessert, cupcakes were in the pantry.

"Look at him," she repeated, sarcastically grinning at Drew, but directing her comments to Lu, as though Drew wasn't there. "The *Sneak*. That's what he is."

Lu shook her head. "Pathetic."

"Tried to hide his supper behind the icebox. Plays innocent. But, oh, I'm always watching, watching," she continued, pointing to her eagle eye. "Ain't that right, Sneak?"

Drew shook his head, signifying No.

O'Leary let out a cackle. "No? There's only one thing worse in this world than a sneak. And that's a liar. Not only is he a sneak, but a lousy, no-good liar. A *sneak* and a *liar*!" Her diction was like British aristocracy, Oliver Hardy admonishing Stan Laurel. "Oh, he thinks I don't see. Sneaking about, into things that aren't his business. What are you hiding, Sneak?" O'Leary swiped his plate off the table again. "Pick it up! Gets too big for his britches, needs to learn some table manners. That right, Sneak?"

Drew held his head down over the table, motionless. I couldn't quite figure why O'Leary considered my younger brother to be such a sneak. He never misbehaved and led a quiet existence. His worst crimes involved running downstairs in the morning and dumping out brand-new cereal boxes on the floor to get the prizes—with me cheering him on. It never occurred to him that piles of wasted cereal on the floor might be traced back to him. But he was three years old then. Perhaps he was a sneak for the same reason I was a professor. Lu sat in quiet agreement with O'Leary, shaking her head. Mrs. O'Leary provided Lu with plenty more anecdotes concerning Drew's sneaky ways. The time he hid his food, or tried to cover up a broken toy. "That right, Sneak?" she would say. "Sneaky as a Jap."

"Pathetic," chimed in Lu.

The two ladies finally gave up on Drew and went to the back porch to watch TV. Drew was released to the backyard where they could still observe him. It was twilight and crickets were chirping, fireflies appearing. Lu carried her bloat with a graceful strength, and she moved fast. When she sneezed, it was a huge dainty sneeze, like a 250-pound kitten. When they strolled off together, their rear ends waddled like the backs of two old Volkswagens.

The two gals scanned *TV Guide*. Their favorite program was *Alfred Hitchcock Presents*. O'Leary read aloud the listings, classifying each program as a drama, melodrama, variety show or comedy, and noting which were in color, even though the TV was black and white.

They sat on wicker patio chairs, their huge flanks billowing over the edges. The chair seats were sagging.

O'Leary's hindquarters had already caved through two chairs. She set out two Pabst Blue Ribbon beers, one of the social occasions when she had a drink in the open.

As usual, Hitchcock would walk out on a set somewhere in limbo, a few props set up. O'Leary immediately mimicked his monolog, her bulldog face twisting into drunken, double-chinned expressions.

"*Gootevening* ladies and gentlemen"—stops to suck in some breath—"On tonight's programme. . . ." Lu was in stitches, but O'Leary kept a straight face, pretending not to notice. Strangely, in age, build and facial resemblance, O'Leary could have been Al Hitchcock's very sister. Once the melodrama began, they opened their beers with a can puncher and shot the gab. It was that rascally Hitch they'd been romantically interested in, and once the episode started, they stopped watching.

"You can only blame the parents," said Lu. "It's the parents that spoil them rotten."

The gals had established, as a matter of course, that Drew and I were "spoiled rotten." O'Leary kept track of every new toy we'd received and its price. The masterful monster masks, from Don Post Studios in Hollywood, were $35 apiece (ordered from the back cover of *Famous Monsters*—the latex they were made of would disintegrate in twenty years). Perhaps the most baffling expense that truly inspired the gals' awe was the cost of boarding my treasured guinea pig Sitting Bull one summer at the vet when the family went on a trip. It cost fifty cents a day, for two months.

"You'd have to be a *nut*," said Lu, shaking her head.

"You know, Lulu," O'Leary said, "those Appleby kids across the street were easy to mind. Those parents knew how to raise kids right. They never misbehaved, they minded, never climbed furniture. Timmy and Jane were in bed by eight o'clock . . . not like these *brats*," she said, with a crackling burp. The mundane shortcomings of children took on the importance of worldwide events.

Drew and I overheard their conversations as we carved new roadways outside in the gravel. Kipp was already asleep in his baby bed. We had Tonka trucks making pit stops at gas stations, with Warriors of the World riding them, winding through colored neighborhoods on their way to the city. We became nearly oblivious to the derision coming from our elders.

"Tell Lu what you call that crap in the basement," shouted O'Leary.

"It's a monster house," I said, ambling over.

"If that doesn't take the cake," she said to Lu. "Can you imagine parents letting kids take over the house?"

"Tickles me fartless," said Lu.

18. The Dance

MISS GRIMSBY'S CLASS CAME TO order with the morning Pledge. Everyone stood to the right of their desks, hand over heart, facing the flag that hung at the front of the room. Bobo remained seated, grooming for the dance that afternoon. He worked his fingernails with a file while the rest of the class recited:

> *I pledge allegiance*
> *To the flag*
> *Of the United States of America*
> *And to the republic*
> *For which it stands—*

"Albert Francis Monk! Stand up and say your pledge!"

Stopping cold, Grimsby grabbed her yardstick. She stood haughtily, hand over hip, in a slow boil. Then she smacked the yardstick down over his desk.

"What're *you* laughin' at, Josephine?" she inquired, turning to me. Miss Grimsby dished me out a daily dose of humiliation. A Beatle haircut was subversive to the likes of Grimsby. She nicknamed me Josephine, after Josephine the Plumber, the butch Comet Cleanser TV pitchwoman. All the colored girls laughed.

"Dahhh, dahhh, there go Josephine!"

"That's enough!" ordered Grimsby. This was only

Miss Grimsby's second year teaching little booger-eating children. She ruled by the yardstick with a short temper. "Okay, Bobo, stand up. Let's hear it. Alone."

Bobo stood up. But he just stood there.

"Let's hear it."

Bobo put his hand to his chest. He looked up at the flag dreamily. Then he pulled out his file and went back to his nails.

Just when her anger flared to the breaking point, Bobo got his laugh. She was the straight man in this act, and she broke character, cracking up. I hardly ever got a smile out of her. But then she quickly regained composure, smacking her yardstick for order in the court. Affectionate to violent from one moment to the next, she ruled by this yardstick with a whip-like motion that ricocheted off a desk or a misbehaving fanny. For refusing to say his Pledge, Miss Grimsby ordered Bobo under her big oak desk as punishment. There, in the twilight, alongside her stockinged legs, he was "punished" for an hour. Bobo sat huddled like an imbecile while she crossed and uncrossed her legs, adjusting her stockings, dangling her shoes. Occasionally he let out a yelp from under the desk, when Grimsby would kick him. I tried to be bad and dreamed of being sentenced to the same punishment. Alas, I only got sent to the back corner, made to sit like a dunce facing the wall.

Grimsby spotted me chewing gum. "You look like a cow chewing its cud," she ridiculed, performing a broad pantomime of a chewing cow. Then with the crack of a yardstick upon her desk: "Spit it out, Josephine!"

After hours, Miss Grimsby herself chewed gum. She was an educational civil servant. One who admired Jacqueline Kennedy and astronauts like John Glenn, whom she taught us about. She was the first to teach us the New Math—updated formulas for the old arithmetic. She kept a small box of gold stars in her desk. The highest honor Miss Grimsby bestowed was a little gold star applied to the day's best homework. Usually a beamingly proud colored girl was the recipient. I didn't receive many. But when I did, I stared at it in my bedroom, thinking about how she had licked it with her own tongue and spit and affixed it to my very own homework. Even me, Josephine the Plumber. I may have removed a couple and licked them back. And while Bobo may have witnessed the mysterious glory between her legs under that desk, the closest I would ever get was to swap spit with the dried molecules of saliva on the back of golden stars she licked on the front of some homework.

On the day of the dance, the class learned the magic of making butter—part of our Christmas holiday celebration. Bobo was released from under Grimsby's desk. Paired up two to a desk, we stirred bowls of heavy cream.

"Wow!" shouted voices from each team as the stirred cream transformed into butter. "Wow!"

Jeffrey and Bobo, who both had the tightest slacks, churned their butter at the back of the room. They looked up from their bowl, snickering at other boys' clothes.

"There go Mumsy baggy *raggy* pants! Who your tailor?" Bobo and Jeffrey hit the floor in hysterics.

Miss Grimsby had Torrence, the singer, go around the room with a salt shaker, sprinkling some into everyone's butter bowl. As he rounded Bobo's desk, Bobo slapped the back of his head while wearing a sharp ring. Torrence let out a shrill feminine screech and said, with much head soreness in his voice, "Ah don't mind y'all whompin' me upside the haid so long you don't use no ring." So Bobo apologized, removed the ring and smacked him with his bare hand. Torrence smiled and continued his rounds as the salt fairy, singing current Impressions' hits.

Most kids left school during lunch hour. Others sat in an armory-type recreation room. On days I brought lunch, I really felt big, my mom having packed a sandwich and apple into a little lunch pail. The stores were filled with new lunch pails at the beginning of the school season. They were square metal boxes with TV set dimensions, usually with white characters licensed from TV. The colored kids had no Negro action figures whatsoever on their lunch pails, not that anyone even considered those things for a second. Not until later, when a Harlem Globetrotter suddenly debuted on a lunch pail. Some kids had generic plaid thermos-colored pails or just paper bags.

I was empowered, feeling the presence of my mom there in the Lone Ranger lunch pail, all the way down at school. In the lunch room, the clashing scents of fifty ripe lunch pails opened at once. Bologna and mayonnaise, cream cheese and jelly sandwiches, apples that fell from local trees. Any kid could buy a half-pint of "health-giving milk" for a penny.

Torrence sat like a little gourmet on the cafeteria bench, spreading out a ham and cheese sandwich, even stuffing a napkin into his collar. His meal looked the most appetizing just by the way he spread things out and daintily applied his own mustard and tomato slices. He taste-tested the mustard from the tip of his pinkie, then shimmied in his seat, pleased. He sang while he chewed, wiggling his butt in the chair. Others, with wretched leftovers, watched in amazement. Torrence's mother worked for some catering business, and he got choice samples.

After lunch, the big event. Here was a favorite activity from the outside world, breaking the grim formality of school. Such a dance was the only time when Miss Grimsby dropped her yardstick. And she made peace with Bobo.

Someone plugged in a record player. Scattered across the floor were James Brown 45s and different versions of "The Twist." I brought my Beatle 45s. This wasn't exactly Grimsby's music, but she happily conceded to the times. We pushed all the desks to the back.

"Okay, class. Are you ready? Let's dance!" The colored kids went into a frenzy. I danced with Sabrina, with Pamela, even with Fat Emily. Isaiah drooled. Mumsy danced with James. Torrence cake-walked, clapped his hands and danced alone, beatific.

"Here go the Sideways Pony," trumpeted Bobo, demonstrating some lateral moves, way ahead of the rest.

"Hey, Bobo, do da Mashed Potata," challenged Jeffrey. Bobo shoved Jeffrey out of the way and tore into it.

"Do the Locomotion!" challenged Jeffrey.

"Here go the Locomotion," went Bobo, chugging around the classroom like a train.

"Now do the Boogaloo."

The Twist was everybody's favorite, and Grimsby let her hair down, ready to take the dance floor herself. She got cuckoo for the first time. Wow! *Miz Grimsby au go-go*. Our teacher kicked off her heels and faced down Bobo, still a foot shorter than herself.

Then something unusual took place. During the next song, Bobo Monk and Miss Grimbsy danced together. Their eyes were upon each other. No one else seemed to exist. When she started twisting the night away, she shook her hips in a way we never saw a teacher shake. Then she did the Peppermint Twist. The girls went bug-eyed, they never thought she had it in her.

"Oohh, Miz Grimsby!" She went down low, twisting her fanny in rhythm. The colored girls continued to squeal.

"Oooooh, Miz Grimbsy! Miz Grimsby!"

"Hold on, hold on!" shouted Bobo. He went to the hi-fi and turned up the bass to full.

Grimsby's eyes locked on Bobo, her man-child dance partner. He danced like his hero, James Brown. A proud, undulating little Black Man. She was charmed. Next came a slow dance: "It's a Man's World." They danced at a distance from each other, but still seemed connected.

"Bobo 'n' Miz Grimsby, Bobo 'n' Miz Grimsby," whispered the colored girls. I wished I could break in as dance partner, but this could never happen. I was Josephine.

At the end of the slow dance, Miss Grimsby quickly regained her composure. She slipped back into her shoes.

Minutes later, Bobo began flying Sabrina's 45s out the window. Sabrina became hysterical. Grimsby went for her yardstick and whacked Bobo's butt.

At three o'clock, outside the school, the colored girls were all a-buzz, showing off their superior spelling skills:

> *Bobo and Miz Grimsby*
> *Sitting in a tree*
> *K-i-s-s-i-n-g*

After the dance, Grimsby was light as a feather, not her usual self. It was snowing lightly. Jeffrey asked for a ride home in her convertible. We followed her out to the teacher's parking lot, where she waved Bobo and Jeffrey over for a spin. The two bald-headed boys hopped in, Bobo in the front seat, Jeffrey in the rumble seat. This may have been their first time ever in a car, any car.

Grimsby cranked open the roof of the car. She wore a scarf around her hair, and sunglasses—suddenly very Jackie Kennedy. I felt crushed as my pals jumped in without me. But then Grimsby gave me a pitiful hangdog look.

"You comin', Josephine? Get in the back."

The whole car smelled just like her subtle perfume. Made me euphoric.

"Hey, Miz Grimsby—" came Jeffrey.

"Hay is for horses," corrected our teacher.

"Miz Grimsby, you drives dis car fas?"

"I do not. You don't want me to get a speeding ticket, do you?"

"Naw."

"Where you live at?"

"None of your beeswax."

"Hey, Miz Grimsby . . . You got a boy fren?" came Bobo.

There was a pregnant pause. Private lives of the white teachers were private, and therefore mysterious. The professional line outside the classroom was never crossed.

But just what kind of grown men did Grimsby date? Clean-cut choral singers with crew cuts from *The Lawrence Welk Show*? Hirsute 'boons like our gym coach? Would she consider Drake O'Leary? Uncle Limpy?

She sighed and left the question unanswered, as if to say who needs men? And then, she did what she most enjoyed, besides teaching. She began to sing. First a few absent-minded bars, then full throttle. "White Christmas" and songs of its ilk sounded like chalk on a blackboard to our ears. We were only attuned to Motown, Beatles, Kinks, Rolling Stones, James Brown. We sat in her car like idiots as Miss Grimsby sang her signature ballad, a light snow flurry emphasizing the lyrics. I was too intimidated to say a word, and embarrassed as hell when she looked me square in the eye, emoting. But I still wished I could someday give her a ring from the A&P gumball machine. The expensive, five-cent machine.

We drove to Carvel, the company that invented soft ice cream. There was always a fresh, cold smell at the counter from the silver soft serve machines. Bobo and Jeffrey ordered vanilla cones, I ordered a chocolate, and Grimsby ordered something called pistachio, with a Rum Baba Nut Cake to go. Pistachio was the third choice of flavors you could get. Bobo, Jeffrey and I didn't know what the hell it was, much less be able to pronounce it.

"All right, who didn't get?" said Grimsby at the counter, handing our cones over her shoulder.

"Ah din't, ah din't" cried Jeffrey.

"Here you go, Sport," she said, making sure we all were happy.

"Don't you get any on the seat!" warned Grimsby, as we jumped in her car. But it was hopeless. None of us could manage our ice cream cones properly, with gobs of it dripping down the cone and onto our pants.

"Here, lemme show ya," said Miss Grimsby. There was a certain trick to licking the beehive of ice cream in a circular rotation, so that it remained on the cone. And then she did something odd. The teacher took Bobo's cone and licked around in a circle, the same tongue that licked a gold star on the day's best homework. Bobo and Jeffrey had never received such a star. But now, she swirled her tongue around Bobo's large vanilla cone, demonstrating the proper technique for handling Carvel ice cream. "Like so," she said, with a final flick of her tongue. This was better than a gold star. Bobo took back the ice cream, a bit flustered, and went at it like Grimsby instructed, rotating the cone full circle.

"Now, you got it," she said. "See that, Josephine? Jeffrey? Got the knack?"

Always the teacher, Grimsby was expanding our horizons outside the confines of the classroom.

19. Things I Believed as a Child

THAT WHEN THE EMERGENCE OF color TV was ballyhooed in the early '60s, I thought it literally meant colored *TV—some new television set that just broadcast Negroes. When I discovered this wasn't the case, I was gravely disappointed.*

That Mick Jagger was Alfalfa of The Little Rascals, all grown up.

That there was one hair on the back of your head from which all your brains would spill if pulled.

That a bruised banana was Man's Best Friend, because my father had told me so once when I refused to finish one.

That Mrs. O'Leary was actually the Bette Davis character from What Ever Happened to Baby Jane?

That I Love Lucy *was a straight drama. I didn't know it was supposed to be a comedy. I thought it was about the unfortunate travails of some hapless housewife, accompanied by an unwarranted laugh track, incongruous with the action.*

20. My White Neighborhood

NEW DEVELOPMENT HOMES WERE encroaching on my white neighborhood, distinguishable only by the different color they had been dipped in on the assembly line. A few stately English Tudors represented an older Long Island, with finely aged crab apple trees spread across their lawns. We lived in a beauty.

Directly across the street lived a God-fearing Catholic family. There were three kids, roughly the same age as us. The Applebys often warned that I'd "burn in the flames of hell for eternity" unless I immediately switched over to their religion. They wouldn't let me enter their home unless I got baptized first. Mrs. Appleby always had my mother walk around the side of the house to the backyard, where they sat outside sipping lemonades. No Jews were allowed inside, but the backyard was okay. I wanted to get baptized just to see what in heaven went on in there.

Cardboard nativity scenes glowed in their front yard each Christmas. The birth of Jesus had an enchanting, warm glow, with a string of light bulbs across the snow—and we did get snow *every* Christmas. The display helped guide Santa Claus to our hamlet. Being secular, we only celebrated Christmas. I was confused by Chanukah. The only Jewish holiday we celebrated was the Seder, held each year at my grandparents' in the Bronx. It revolved around food, and was my only brush with Jewish religion, because the prayers always began with the youngest boy. And that was usually me. *What makes this night different from all other nights?*

But the Applebys didn't like Santa coming to my house, because he wasn't supposed to visit Jews. So they were confounded each Christmas by the bounty Santa had left Drew, Kipp and me.

The three Appleby children were half-crazed in their fervor to keep a record of the sins I committed. Mrs. O'Leary was Catholic, too, but she never talked religion or worried about my sins. But the Applebys reminded me of them, both mortal and mundane ones. Like bringing colored kids into the neighborhood. God's Law was so unforgiving that they assured me one slip-up would send even themselves speeding into hell.

Down the street was Bobby Mortimer, exactly my age. He was good for sleigh riding and had the best baseball glove in the neighborhood. His father bore a striking resemblance to Yogi Berra. Bobby was the type of boy who would stick a fork into one of his fifty salamanders for no reason, in a sudden spastic motion. Fish tanks in the basement contained lizards and reptiles, a hobby his parents encouraged so Bobby wouldn't get too lonely.

Bobby's father was Exalted Ruler of the Glen Cove Elks Lodge, one of those mysterious fraternal orders for middle-aged veterans. What was so exalted about him? On Friday nights, for an after-dinner treat, Mr. Mortimer took his son down to Garvies Point, the town dumps and cesspool. They would sit and watch raw sewage dripping out pipes into open pits. They laughed, they pointed. Once in a while Bobby invited me to come along. When we arrived, I happily joined in, whooping it up at the gushers of shit. Having an adult lead the charge, an Exalted one at that, whilst laughing at shit gave official sanction to the practice. Any grown-up who laughed at this was a hero in my book. But it was more than recreation to Mr. Mortimer. This was an exquisite pleasure that seemed to rejuvenate him after a hard day at his lumber yard. As the flow started to die down, he wiped the tears from his face, out of breath. Suddenly it started flowing out again and Mr. Mortimer yelped and cheered while waving his Elks Lodge cap, as though it were a spouting oil field.

Then there was, of course, the troublesome family that provoked the ire of all who lived nearby. Smack in the center of the neighborhood was a ghastly junkyard of a house looking as though it were blown out of the colored section in a hurricane and dropped between the highest priced of homes. Totally out of place—even illegally so, had zoning regulations been enforced—it caused people to rubberneck when driving by. In it lived the impoverished Wilshires.

From my bedroom I heard the lungs of Big Willie's mother, Mrs. Wilshire, in the distance as she cursed her children through the night. She was an elephantine woman with bulging varicose veins and a mustache. Jacob Wilshire, the frequently unemployed head of a small gardening operation, would show up on front doorsteps demanding to mow people's lawns. He was known to have knocked down garden statuary in fits of anger when refused.

Always among the Wilshire clan were cousins, aunts and other assorted kin that came from Appalachia or somewhere to visit for weeks at a time. Families were outraged when ant-like squadrons of them trampled into backyards with buckets and stripped down apple trees, cleaning out the long-awaited fall bounty. Afterward, apples were seen mashed against telephone poles and littered along the streets with one bite taken out of them.

Their front yard was dirt, not a blade of grass in sight. A rabid-looking hound was chained to their front porch to ward off colored people. The Wilshires claimed that before they got the dog, "the niggers" broke in at night and stole all their food. Why they were targeted was a mystery, because the Wilshires appeared to subsist on a steady food chain of crackers, and nothing but crackers. Saltines were the primary groceries in the pantry; sometimes varieties like Ritz, oyster crackers or zwiebacks for holidays. Why didn't "the niggers" break into the Mortimers' around the block, with a refrigerator full of lamb chops? Whenever I entered the rat-infested domicile, Mrs. Wilshire assigned someone to stand guard by the pantry to make sure I didn't steal any crackers.

At supper time, seedy Wilshire children were seen on the streets anxiously munching fistfuls of crackers, their eyes darting about to make sure no one would grab away their dinner. Neighbors occasionally saw a hungry face peering into their kitchen window. They'd offer food. But the Wilshire child would snap back with vicious insults.

I never recall seeing colored kids go hungry. Only the Wilshire children. They said their nightly prayers in nighties, on their knees, three to a bed. *Now I lay me down to sleep . . . and if I die before I wake. . . .* Two fears distressed their dreams, as their heads slumbered upon pillows: rats and niggers.

Yet there was one particular crisis in which the whole neighborhood considered the Wilshires an asset, and that was when my colored friends turned up in the area. The toughest, bone-whitest gang in town, the Wilshires lurked like alley cats, 24-hour sentries on the lookout for mice. No one was more anxious to chase out colored kids than the Wilshires and their clan.

21. Aunt Nellie

"**P**SST," CAME AN URGENT WHISPER from the basement of Babes' apartment building on Cecil Avenue. A wrestling match played loudly from the TV. "C'mon down. Got thigarettes for y'all."

"There go *Hecha Momma*," said Bobo. Bobo and Jeffrey called all big fat colored ladies *Hecha Momma*—which, in fact, was local kidspeak for mythical pancake icon, Aunt Jemima. Mumsy was downstairs smoking on a couch. Hecha Momma urgently handed out cigarettes to Bobo and me.

"Go on. Take a puff. *Take a puff!*" said the huge-nostrilled woman. She was Mumsy's Aunt Nellie. I contemplated the Winston she assigned me. It was the same brand Fred Flintstone sponsored. Cigarettes provided instant cachet into the adult world.

"Go on, take a puff!" I didn't know whether to blow into the filter or draw out the smoke. She was so sweet in her encouragement, her voice so sugary, I tried to oblige. But she was diverted by the wrestling show on TV. A match between white wrestlers Gorilla Monsoon and Hard Boiled Haggerty. Aunt Nellie thumped back before the Philco in a squat position, her big hammy haunches just like the men she was watching. A package of cornstarch lay on the couch, which she periodically wet a finger into then licked off. When the 500-pound Monsoon got his opponent in a headlock, she jumped up and down like a lunatic.

"Whomp his butt, whup his ass!"

My cigarette went out due to improper technique. "Here go another light," she said, striking a match. "Dat's it, dat's it." Bobo and Mumsy sucked at their cigarettes like pros. I tried to hold my own.

"Take a puff!" she demanded. I coughed fantastic. Aunt Nellie doubled up snorting with laughter, slapping her hammy thigh.

"Fine tobaccos," said her boy Mumsy, exhaling the smoke through his huge nostrils like smokestacks.

*"Win-ston taste good like a—*puff puff—*cig-ar-ette should,"* sang Bobo, with a luxurious sigh of smoke. He and Mumsy lay on their backs with drunken smiles.

"Oh, y'all such big men!" said Nellie. And then she looked at me dreamily. "I just love white folks," she said. "I really do." This gave me the creeps. But Nellie *loved* white people. She was probably the first Negro woman to *give up* her seat to a white on the bus since the custom ended a decade before with Rosa Parks.

Just moments ago, I hadn't known whether to blow or suck.

And then, someone knocked upstairs. Aunt Nellie grabbed our cigarettes. "Put it out, put it out!" she panicked. "Put out them thigarettes!" Nellie Leech stomped the butts like a rhino upon the dirt floor. Much like the wrestlers on TV. But it was just Jeffrey at the door.

"Where Mumsy at?"

"He right here."

"Hey, Mumsy, c'mon down to Lincoln House."

"After he drink his tea," said Aunt Nellie, suddenly maternal. She prepared a special, down-home hog's hoof tea for her sickly, smelly nephew. A simmering pot on the stove was filled with pig's feet. It stunk. "Would yo' white fren like some tea? It make you grow strong, just like G'rilla Monsoon."

Mumsy was an only child and stayed with his Aunt in the basement underneath the white-brick apartment building on Glen Cove Avenue. The wrestling match was over quickly.

"Wha'chu do today, chile?" asked Aunt Nellie, stirring the pot on the stove. "You go to school?"

"Yeah, I go to school," said Mumsy, patting his textbooks on the table. "Did some readin' and some 'rithmetic today."

"Ooh, mah baby learnin'!"

Mumsy hadn't been to school, and he never read anything in his schoolbooks. Yet the books, hand-me-downs from previous school years, looked dog-eared, and well-studied by previous kids.

I choked down a sour sip of hog's hoof tea and gagged. So this was the elixir of the mysterious Mumsy. No wonder he stunk.

"Straighten yo' eyebrows, chile," Aunt Nellie instructed her nephew before we left. She was most concerned with this particular grooming touch, running her fingers over Mumsy's thick brow. No matter where he was all day besides school; or that he never bathed, he smoked and didn't know the difference between a urinal and a toilet. As long as his eyebrows were straight.

"And Jock, you straighten out them brows, too. You cain't go out like that!" I never saw anything crooked in my eyebrows, but Mumsy's aunt always did. I rubbed down my eyebrows.

"Y'all have fun. And Mums—don't you go near them train tracks, now!"

She figured we were headed for Lincoln House. Since Mumsy was poor as can be, he received some extracurricular guidance at Lincoln House, the barn-like community center for Negro children. There were no windows, and the surrounding grounds were barren.

But even though they solicited three-dollar donations door-to-door from white neighborhoods (and raised thousands), Lincoln House wouldn't admit me. I once followed Mumsy there, but some man blocked me at the entrance. I heard laughter and noise. I wondered what went on inside.

"Oh, they got pies and games and stuff for boys and girls," explained Mumsy. I had never tasted Lincoln House pie, baked exclusively for the poorest colored kids. I felt I was missing something.

22. An O'Leary Christmas

YOU COULD ALWAYS COUNT ON A white Christmas in Glen Cove. And when it snowed, I played with white kids. You didn't see many colored kids sleigh riding, throwing snowballs or building snowmen. Maybe they didn't have warm enough coats.

The morning after a snowstorm, cars and roads were buried. Trees were blanketed, branches sagged under the weight, pine cones sparkled. It was a whole 'nother world outside. Commerce came to a halt, and families were snowed into their homes. The grocery store called Foods on Back Road Hill hung a sign that said CLOSE. To a boy venturing out into this heavenly white stillness, it was paradise. A total whiteout.

Robert Moses, who built the parkways opening up Long Island to the masses, believed that Negroes did not like cold weather, or cold water. The temperature at Jones Beach pool was kept extra cold to keep them out. Coney Island's Steeplechase pool did the same. For centuries, slaves had it drummed into them that they couldn't swim. Especially those near rivers or bays, where they might entertain thoughts of escape. They were told they would sink. And they were probably told the snow was dangerous, too.

Before the snowplows encroached and car tires were fitted with chains, before rock-salt trucks came by to melt down the roads, the first signs of life in the deep were children. Kids dragging sleds, knee deep through the snow. Any hill was fair game. Every white kid had a Flexible Flyer sled. The one with the red eagle trademark, wooden seat slats, and a steering bar.

When colored kids went sleigh riding, they used cardboard boxes. It looked more fun than riding a sled. When I tried cardboard once, it discombobulated. Your ass and the box parted ways, taking a spill in different directions. With a sled, you always had a long march back uphill, dragging its weight by string. The deep fluffy snow was powdery at first. You had to pack it down for an hour before it got good.

Finally, after hours outside, you were overcome with snow fatigue. Your gloves were wet, buckle-up snow boots filled with snow, your red cheeks were freezing, your hands and feet nearly frostbitten. Sometimes I was convinced I had frostbite on the trudge back home. I was met by Mrs. O'Leary, who prepared hot chocolate with melted marshmallow on top.

"Here's what I did with my boys," she said, tucking my hands under her flabby arms. And my hands were so cold, I gave in to my better judgment. I allowed her to flap her underarms over my hands. And amazingly, they did warm up fast.

Before each Christmas, Mrs. O'Leary hung a wreath of mistletoe from the ceiling. When she caught one of my brothers or me underneath, she exacted payment of one kiss. The kiss came from cold lips, accented by her billy goat beard, a scratchy, invisible stubble on her chin. We closed our eyes and gritted our teeth in discomfort. O'Leary's display of affection seemed oddly romantic instead of grandmotherly.

I begged for a red Schwinn Phantom bike for a year. Captain Kangaroo endorsed them. I didn't want a Sting-Ray with a banana seat to pop wheelies and look cool; I wanted a cruiser, for distance and speed. Three-speeds and ten-speeds were for older kids. My mother drilled me a thousand times to look both ways before crossing a street. I thought of Big Willie Wilshire and his lack of such parental warnings. He never looked both ways and ran through intersections at top speed.

The bike became my proudest possession and ticket to freedom in the outside world. Pushing the limits of kids' travel boundaries, I had wheels.

My parents went to San Juan for a week during Christmas vacation. The morning after they left, there stood my brother Drew outside the front window, shivering in his underwear. He stood patiently waiting to be readmitted into the house.

"He had it comin'. The *sneak*," said O'Leary, in case I had any questions. And don't even think about letting him in. And by the way, can I fetch the milk bottles on the back porch? Drew's head bobbed up in front of the living room window. He was in his white jockey shorts, shivering, holding his arms around his sides.

I went out the back door for the bottles in my underpants. The door slammed behind, door-slamming being one of her trademarks, and she locked it. I joined my brother in the snow. We waited a moment, gathering our wits. I'd never been outside in my underpants, and what if someone saw me?

We knocked at the front door. No answer. Then we ran around to try the back. Ten minutes later we caught sight of O'Leary in the living room, just going about her merry way. I knocked. "Pathetic," she said, with a cackle, shaking her head. For the next half hour, we shivered outside, more terrified someone in the neighborhood might catch us in our drawers than we were of the cold. We ran in place, trying to stay warm.

Then we tried running around the house, knocking on windows. But she played dumb, singing to herself, *tra-la-la-la.*

Finally, we saw the front door open. No O'Leary there, just an open door. We tiptoed in and I went for my

Louisville Slugger in the closet. I made my way through the rest of the house with the bat.

"Look at The Professor," O'Leary said for Drew's benefit, breathing heavily. "He's taken a bat to one of his elders." Her eyes became more hateful than ever before. I'd committed some terrific crime against an adult.

"When my parents come home I'll get you fired this time!"

"Your parents aren't coming home. *They're dead.*"

This was, perhaps, the most terrifying moment of my life so far. I went into some form of shock. Mrs. O'Leary let out a hair-raising, high-pitched cackle. I was convinced more than ever she was Baby Jane, from *What Ever Happened to Baby Jane?* with Bette Davis. I held the bat aloft.

"You dare, Josh, *you dare!*" she spat, like a nasty little girl. O'Leary grabbed a frying pan and held it aloft. I raised my bat higher. One Hank Aaron Louisville Slugger versus a frying pan. I raised the bat over my head. She raised her frying pan. And we circled each other like this—a circus-like routine that had occurred a dozen times before. Truth be told, Mrs. O'Leary had never physically struck me or Drew. Her brand of terror was strictly psychological, but it was scarier than any monster movie. Pushing, shoving, yes, but amazingly I never knew her to carry out a violent threat. Nor did I to her.

"I ain't takin' any more crap from you kids," said O'Leary, growing tired. She threw down the pan and hobbled off to her room.

When my parents did arrive back from the Caribbean, my brother and I ran out the drive and leapt upon the car. It was as if the little MG was the Allied Forces come to liberate us.

"Fire her!" I demanded, as my father hoisted me upon his shoulders.

"What do you mean, fire her?"

"No, really, she could have froze us to death. She threw

us out in our underwear."

"Right now?" came our dad, jolly and ready to dedicate the rest of the weekend to his sons. "You guys feel pretty warm to me."

My mother said I sounded like the King of Exaggeration. O'Leary had turned friendly a few hours earlier, cooking up a pot of chocolate pudding and letting Drew lick the spoon. But I was still livid.

"Okay, okay, we'll have a little talk with her," our parents relented. But Mrs. O'Leary had already puttered off in her old jalopy and wouldn't return until sometime next week.

23. Miss Grimsby's Date

AFTER CHRISTMAS VACATION, BOBO and I went to lunch at Henry's Confectionery. Mrs. O'Leary's pal, Lu, waitressed there, and she seated us several booths behind Miss Grimsby, who sat with a gentleman caller. Our teacher's back was to us. She didn't notice we were there.

The gentleman wore a neatly pressed workman's shirt bearing the trademark Port-o-San on the breast pocket. A vacu-van with the same logo was parked outside. A pitch-black tank squatted on top with a yellow hose encrusted with the business at hand. He seemed like an exceptionally clean, though hirsute, grease monkey, with a Brylcreem pompadour. I noticed his gold tooth and pinky ring as he delivered a pitch. Was Miss Grimsby buying an outhouse or something?

But the date wasn't going well. Grimsby spoke curtly between popping french fries into her mouth, annoyed. He was not polite society or *Lawrence Welk* material. I felt embarrassed for her. What kind of judgment did our fair teacher exercise with men? We slunk down in our seats, trying to eavesdrop.

"I run a successful franchise," the man explained. "People gotta go, right? I drive the truck what drains the thrones at construction sites. Come home Friday, scrape the doo-doo from under my nails, shower up, slap on some aftershave, slip into my Sunday best . . . and I'm all yours, Toots. . . .

So . . . a teacher at the *colored* school?"

"I'm an *educator*," Grimsby corrected the man in the shit biz.

"Readin', 'ritin' and 'rithmetic and all?"

"That's right. I teach third grade. They're my kids."

All of a sudden, we were her kids. We were the substance of her life as she held her ground against the Port-o-San man. Everything considered, it was hard to imagine that the quality of education at South wasn't up to speed with the white school the Wilshires attended. Maybe better. The Wilshires could barely read. South had a similar white curriculum, white teachers and Dick-Jane-and-Sally readers. We learnt us the same readin', 'ritin' and 'rithmetic.

"Lemme ask ya," said the man. "Are those kids any smart?"

"Their reading skills are on par with the national average."

"Wouldn't you rather teach regular school?"

"All children are regular, Mr. Clyde, and I'm happy to teach at South. In fact, I'm needed here more."

We needed her, she needed us. The white teachers at South School, with the possible exception of the gym coach, were indeed colorblind. His eyes looked sincere, and he seemed to plead his case:

> *Don't judge a book by its cover*
> *Or this man as a lover*
> *The moonlight up above shines through the loo*
> *Though few may find inspiration*
> *In my hose o' sanitation*
> *When it comes to lovin', mama*
> *Let me show you all the things*
> *This doo-doo man*
> *Can do*
> *Your doo-doo man*
> *Your doo-doo man*
> *Can do*

He muttered something and Grimsby suddenly lost it.

"You're not gettin' *happy hands* outta me, mister!" She protested in her best Brooklynese, standing up with her pocketbook. "Not on your life, Clyde!" If she'd been holding a yardstick, she would have cracked him. Premarital relations were unthinkable.

"Toots, I ain't asking to compromise your virtue," pleaded Clyde. "My apologies. I mean that sincerely. . . . How 'bout a little peck on the cheek?"

Bobo suddenly leapt out of his seat to Grimsby's rescue.

"This mah teacher," he said. "and mah babes, too."

The man was dumbstruck. "Who the hell're you?"

"Bobo Monk," he said, knocking the man's coffee off the table. The Port-o-San greaser grabbed Bobo by the collar, thrusting him up against the wall.

"Let go of my pupil!" came Grimsby.

"*Hangh?*" came the man. "This little baboon?"

"That's right, Mister," said Grimsby, "he's my pupil. Let him go."

The man released his grip, cursing as he patted coffee off his shirt. Grimsby reached out her manicured hand to Bobo, who debonairly took it. She yanked him out of the diner. Back to school they headed without me, hand in hand, Grimsby towering over her savior. School was the one arena where she had total control. Life may have been awkward outside, but she was mistress of the universe in third grade. I saw Grimsby give Bobo a thankful kiss on the forehead once they were outside. The man remained at the table stewing.

"Don't that beat all," he said.

Lu came over and took care of our check.

If she considered dates with guys like Clyde, I wondered, would she go for a clam digger like Drake or a fender bender like Uncle Limpy? If I introduced her to Drake, he might bring her over to the house. Then I could show her my guinea pig and monster magazines. That might be better than being under her desk. Almost. But it wasn't grown men she was after.

A week later I began to see less of Bobo after school. He was involved in extracurricular activities with Miss Grimsby. I noticed, for instance, he came to school with impeccably manicured fingernails, so he'd no longer need to file them during Pledge of Allegiance. It was rumored Grimsby had taken him along to her beauty parlor in Oyster Bay for a manicure while she had her hair done. Paid for on her civil servant's salary. Fat Emily's mother, who did nails there, told the girls. Bobo demanded to have his hair conked. The white proprietor, Mr. Romeo, never heard of this.

"You know, *the process*, like James Brown and Uncle Limpy," Bobo explained. But Grimsby threw a fit from underneath the hair dryer and screamed, "Absolutely not."

By this time, all the colored girls were buzzing with gossip that Bobo and Grimsby were sitting in a tree, k-i-s-s-i-n-g. Maybe she was going out of her way to help him like a social worker. Bobo didn't mention a word about it. Supervision at Bobo's home was nil. Nobody amongst the impoverished Monk family questioned Bobo's whereabouts. The kindly Mrs. Monk, often bedridden, had her hands full with Bobo's younger brothers and sisters. She was delighted that some nice white teacher had shown a personal interest in her boy. Yes, she could take him bowling on Friday night and to the movies on Saturday. Mrs. Monk probably even dropped a few nickels in Miss Grimsby's palm when she came to pick him up. But the colored girls were talking. Did Miss Tiger know her Christmas nightingale had taken such a keen interest in her most illiterate third-grade pupil?

"They was holdin' hands at the Cove Theatre," whispered an indignant Pamela to the girls in class.

"*Oooo*," sang the girls.

"And then, it was dark, but . . . they was k-i-s-s-i-n-g on the balcony, yes they did."

All the girls went bug-eyed, laughing.

"What dat movie?" asked Fat Emily.

"It was a *good* movie. *Roustabout* with Elvis."

"Oh, he good."

Where Bobo had once presented the teacher with an apple, he now brought her a box of chocolates from Henry's Confectionery—though it was an already opened box, with missing chocolates, surely stolen. I imagined Grimsby shucking the education life, running off to Acapulco for a foreign wedding license. There they sat at poolside, an imbecilic confused grin on Bobo's face as they sipped piña coladas, Grimsby pausing to whack him every so often with her yardstick. Just where rumour and innuendo collided with fact was hard to gather. He was more than just the teacher's pet.

"Hey, Bobo," asked an incredulous Jeffrey in the schoolyard. "You see Miz Grimsby titty?"

"*Yeah*, ah see her titty. More 'n that. An' fine titties, too."

"Wow!" came Jeffrey, stuttering with amazement, his voice jumping an octave. "Damn, Bobo, you-you-you-you crazy!"

24. Drake on the Job

DRAKE BEGAN A NEW JOB. CLAM diggers couldn't work in the winter. Mrs. O'Leary went to pick him up in her poor old jalopy with bad brakes. Every time she bought another used auto, it became her "poor old car." Drake was living temporarily in an extra room in our basement. She brought me along to some huge manufacturing plant in Hempstead. It was always a kick to see Drake. A whistle sounded at 4:30, and factory workers streamed out of the gates.

"That's Drake!" she said. A mob of men came through the distant gate. "I can tell his walk."

"How can you tell, Mrs. O'Leary, he's a mile away?"

"Oh, I'd know his walk anywhere. He's my boy."

Sure enough, the tiny figure emerging from the distance, whose walk seemed indistinguishable from hundreds to me, was Drake.

"To know somebody just by his walk," I said, of O'Leary's trick. "Wow, that's magic."

O'Leary was not so much proud as relieved whenever Drake held down a job. He became her workingman. The apple of her eye. She held her breath every day that he maintained employment. It was like watching a tightrope act.

"As soon as it gets warm," said Drake, "what'ya say we go clamming?" He winked at me. He always promised to take me clamming in Long Island Sound, something I looked forward to for years. It never occurred. But it was flattering to be taken seriously by a grown man, to have him as a friend. I sensed he still thought like a kid. Drake would bring a magnificent bucket of clams to our house. Littlenecks and Cherrystones. He'd rake over a hundred of them from the mud in Oyster Bay, where they were so plentiful they weren't even considered a delicacy. But they were. I struggled to open clams myself. The procedure was complicated, but Drake snapped them open expertly with his switchblade, from the joint behind the thick end of the shell. If you found one slightly open, something was wrong and you chucked it out. It took a real man to eat a clam fearlessly, said Drake; they weren't for sissies. You'd get nearly drunk on magnificent Long Island Cherrystones from Oyster Bay, which Drake washed down with a cold beer.

This afternoon, however, he sank down in the front seat of the car.

"You know, mother," began Drake, "every man has a right to earn a living for his family. To earn his daily bread."

"His daily bread," repeated Mrs. O'Leary.

"Now a man who's a real man—he eats red meat, fish or fowl. One of those every day. And these foods don't come cheap nowadays."

"Right you are, Drake," she agreed. He was gamey, but smelled of an honest day's work. Drake always splashed on extra helpings of Old Spice aftershave, emitting a pleasant manly scent no matter how hard he'd worked. Drake mopped the sweat from his brow. He had his own white monogrammed handkerchiefs, with the initials "D.O."

"I work alongside the colored. Just part of the j-o-b. Now a man is a man, white or colored. They have their right to earn a living, too. Isn't that so, Mother?"

"That's right, Drake."

"They don't bother me. I don't bother them."

"Good. Let's leave it at that," said Mrs. O'Leary.

"I stay out of their way. They should stay out of my way."

Mrs. O'Leary gave her son a beer in the front seat and reminded him that *Wild, Wild West* was on at eight, his favorite show. Drake punched a can opener over the Rheingold and took his first sensual, deep swig. Even Mrs. O'Leary and I derived satisfaction watching Drake the workingman drink an ice-cold beer, which he richly deserved after his labors—whatever they were.

Drake downed the beer ferociously, then crushed the thick can in his grip. And then Drake did something strange, moving his jowls, which were covered by a five o'clock shadow. But no words came out, as if he were carrying on an imaginary argument. He stopped to mop his brow again. Then he began jabbing his finger at an invisible foe. Though she kept her eyes on the road, a touch of anguish appeared in Mrs. O'Leary's eyes, the ongoing pain of being full-time mother to this grown man. She feared nothing so much as those late-night phone calls from a member of her troubled family, from a hospital or a county jail pay phone, where Drake was given his one dime for a call. And he always turned to her.

"*Goddamn nigger bastards*," he grumbled to himself, through clenched teeth.

"You say something, son?"

"It's the *niggers*, Mother. They're at it again."

"Now, Drake, I don't want to hear that kind of talk from you anymore."

Drake held his peace from then on. When we got home, he sprang from the car, and went down to his space in the basement, unheard from all night. A week later, the job was over. Once again, an altercation to do with "colored guys." Just part of the j-o-b.

25. Visiting the White Crackers

LIKE MRS. O'LEARY, DRAKE WAS always cordial to the colored kids. Kids were kids, and he was practically one of us, part of the kid world. I could almost imagine Drake standing dumbly in line with my class, filing into the lunchroom. Not all the grown-ups in my neighborhood were that way. When Bobo, Jeffrey and Mumsy came over, we usually stayed in my yard, but not always.

One afternoon after school, we went on a botanical expedition to the Applebys' front yard. Mrs. Appleby's mint bushes ran along the side of her house. I picked a few mint leaves for everybody to sample.

"Wow!" said Jeffrey, grabbing handfuls. Then Bobo dug in and Mumsy followed, stuffing their pockets with mint leaves. In the process, they stomped flowers and plants into the dirt. I went to the sidewalk praying that the Applebys weren't home. Sure enough, a window shade parted and the late-afternoon sun revealed several horrified Appleby faces. They started to scream in unison. Colored kids on the flowerbeds!

Bobo rolled over backwards throwing a handful of mint leaves into the air. We ran like bats outta hell across the street and through my front door. We sped past Mrs. O'Leary, up to my bedroom and flopped down on the floor. Mumsy wasn't with us.

"Where he at?" asked Jeffrey.

"Don't know."

"You see him, Bobo?"

"Nope."

"What if they ketch him?"

"Shhhh," warned Bobo, looking out my bedroom window. It was open and we cautiously peered around the edge. We had a bird's-eye view into the Appleby's front yard.

"There he go!" declared Jeffrey in a tense whisper. "There go Mumsy!"

Flustered in the mint-leaf confusion, he climbed up a tree on the Appleby's front lawn. He continued to climb higher. Then he froze, about two stories high up the mighty oak, befouling the rarefied air of squirrels and birds. High enough to break his neck or get killed if he fell. I knew well the terror of scaling trees with abandon, only to freeze near the top. Easy to jump and grab hold of a higher branch, then pull yourself up. But once you scaled three or four branches, then looked down, you were in for a rude shock. You can't slowly pull yourself back down—you have to drop your body and hope your legs catch it right. And if you look up, well, that was even scarier.

Sure enough, a couple of the greasers from down the block heard the commotion. Then Big Willie Wilshire followed behind on his brakeless bicycle. The Appleby children came out and a small crowd formed under the tree. Big Willie and the greasers started to hurl crab apples up at Mumsy.

"Git down!"

Mumsy pulled his weight up another branch, and then another. *Mumsy be up a tree, three stories high! Hey, Mumsy, what you be doin' so high, when your lip hang so low?* The branches deflected the apples from hitting their target. But the apples splattered against the bark like applesauce. Autumn leaves of sunburst red and yellow fluttered down.

We heard a siren in the distance. Sure enough, the sound of big white trouble. A Glen Cove Fire Department ladder truck pulled up to the curb. There was a second driver at a rear steering wheel. Mr. And Mrs. Appleby emerged and pointed out Mumsy up on his perch. Even from the distance of my window, we could see his nostrils flaring. Two firemen stepped out of the truck, in thick rubber boots and coats with their engine company logo. There may have been no Negro firemen or police allowed in both Glen Cove departments, but the white ones came to the rescue of colored people.

Although we were safely hidden in my room—and Mrs. O'Leary had seen us scamper upstairs—no one spoke above a whisper. We watched Mumsy's predicament unfold. More people gathered in the presence of the fire truck, and a cop car showed up. The firemen squinted their eyes through the sun at Mumsy.

"All right, Son, c'mon back down now."

Mumsy maintained a neutral expression.

"Who, me? Ah cain't," he yelled, frozen with vertigo. I'd also gotten stuck in many a tree, losing my nerve.

The captain, who was taking notes, tucked his writing pad under his arm. "Didn't you hear what the nice fireman said? Get down from there before I come up and get ya!"

"Ah'll give 'em back, all of 'em," said Mumsy, pulling mint leaves from his pockets. They rained down on the spectators. More Wilshire brothers in torn undershirts stood back contemplating the situation like vultures. I knew that if the cops weren't around they'd have Mumsy down to the ground and crucified within minutes. Only Mumsy's smell could save him. Nobody could bear to wrestle him. All of a sudden, the ladder on the truck began to turn on a gurney. It unfolded, telescoping toward Mumsy, getting longer, and started to snap through twigs and leaves. A fireman climbed up.

"Leave me be, please, just leave me be!" begged Mumsy.

The fireman on the tower ladder reached up and grabbed an ankle. With a yank Mumsy fell on his stomach to the branch below. "Okay, leggo," he puffed, "ah'll get down myself." Mumsy held onto a branch kicking his legs until he gave way. The fireman had cherry-picked himself a Mumsy off the tree. Strange fruit. His huge nostrils opened and closed with each breath as the ladder began its descent. He looked at all the white faces surrounding him. The firemen led a terrified Mumsy onto the truck tailboard. We saw the glint of his bald head reflecting the last rays of sun in the back seat.

Then Mrs. O'Leary charged outside to the rescue. It was the good Mrs. O'Leary. She conferred with the firemen, telling them Mumsy had just been playing, he was pals with her boy Josh across the street. She loved men with official standing; they were her superiors. She displayed an unusual quality of charm around working men. If they were Irish to boot—and some of the firemen were—she instantly affected a perfect brogue.

"You good men needn't worry, I'll mind these kids."

The firemen, who felt an instant rapport with Mrs. O'Leary, were relieved to get him the hell out of the truck, their faces crinkled like little girls' from the stench.

Big Willie Wilshire ran and grabbed a textbook that lay near the tree.

"That's mah 'rithmetic studies—give it here!" demanded Mumsy. Mumsy never studied anything as he hardly ever came to school. Yet the book was in terrible condition. Big Willie Wilshire ran off tearing pages from it.

Mrs. O'Leary raised her hands. They were wings of protection to Mumsy, who came underneath the protective shield of Mrs. O'Leary's old-lady underarms of quivering jelly. She *nah-nahed* at the Wilshires, foiling them before they could get their clutches on Mumsy. She knew they hated colored kids. "Sorry, boys, you'll have to scram. *Skedaddle!*"

Then she served us all milk and cookies in the den.

26. Vic's

MY FAVORITE STOP IN GLEN COVE was foreign to Drake and Mrs. O'Leary: Vic's. Our dad bought Don Diego cigars there, which he smoked while unfolding his Sunday *New York Times* or *Herald Tribune*. Drew and I acquired our monthly issues of *Famous Monsters* and *Mad* from Vic's magazine stand. That's where you got them. Every month a new pile of *Famous Monsters* magically materialized on the wooden boards at Vic's. I didn't know how they got there. These were treasured alternatives to the mandatory *Highlights for Children* and *Jr. Scholastic*, provided at school or the dentist's office. Vic and his sister Florence were old newspaper dealers with dark circles around their eyes. They'd been running the stand forever. The creaky wooden floorboards had their own special smell of fresh newspapers, cigars, comic books and Topps baseball cards. A chocolate lollipop, jaw breaker or hard plug of Bazooka cost a penny.

Amid musty aisles of toys in the rear was one shelf that fascinated me. It was crammed with lowbrow Times Square pranks. Stuff that made you feel warm all over. Stuff that you could use. Whoopee cushions, handshake buzzers, severed rubber fingers, masks, Aurora monster models (which, combined with Testors Glue, will probably stay together for centuries), and a perennial favorite: plastic vomit. The package said "Ooops!" on the outside. Fortified with plastic vomit, I thought I could take over the world.

The whoopee cushion package illustration said it let out "a real Bronx cheer." Why this sound was unique to the Bronx I didn't know, but I figured it must be a place famous for farting. Either that, or the razzing Yankee fans gave to visiting teams.

Mrs. O'Leary thought these treasures were inappropriate and couldn't understand why my father let us have them. My father saw no harm in it. But higher up on the shelf there were items out of reach to kids. Old Vic stood guard whenever I eyed something up there. I sensed the forbidden fruit was stacked at the top—something off base that Vic was ashamed to carry but kept in stock for juvenile delinquents, like the greasers down the street. I saw a urinating statue and nudie "French decks." Real contraband, but somehow available at Vic's.

"You don't want anything up there," said Vic, shooing me away.

The wooden stairway leading upstairs, where Vic and Florence still lived with their mother—who must have been a hundred—were lined with Warriors of the World. The two-inch hand-painted warriors cost a whole dollar each. Drew and I always chose a new warrior for our collection. We could only get one at a time. The stairway was also stocked with toys of a generation ago, like Charlie McCarthy and Mortimer Snerd dummies encased in their original see-through boxes, now yellowed and coated in dust. Jerry Mahoney, however, was my main dummy, operated by New York ventriloquist Paul Winchell, who had his own local TV show. Vic's ancient mother, who'd never been seen, was somewhere upstairs. We were afraid if she peered around the staircase it would scare the hell out of us. We nervously picked out a Warrior, then hurried back down the stairway.

Famous Monsters made icons of Boris Karloff, Bela Lugosi and Lon Chaney, Jr., thrusting their 1930s and '40s work into the present moment. The magazine was my guide to the lineage of Frankenstein films. As if they all made historical sense, from the original Universal movies through the 1960s. The storyline grew convoluted as it wound from film to film. After the first two, *Frankenstein* and *Bride of Frankenstein*, original director James Whale proclaimed, "the rest were made by hacks." He was absolutely right.

The face of the monster, first sketched by director James Whale, came to its iconic realization through the brilliant makeup of Jack Pierce, another *Famous Monsters* mag hero. Though chilling, the image of Frankenstein from Universal Studios was comforting and calming, eye candy of sorts. Pierce's master creation, though following the same makeup blueprints, changed from film to film—or maybe it was because Karloff aged five years between each film. Like Bela Lugosi, he was nearly 50 when he first played his greatest and handsomest role. The relationship between the Frankenstein makeup and each actor's face was unique. The facial structure of each actor who took their turn—Karloff, Glenn Strange, Bela Lugosi, Lon Chaney, Jr.—betrayed the makeup. While Karloff's was most beautiful, due to the structure of his actorly face, Glen Strange was the most "dead" looking. Lugosi's and Lon Chaney Jr.'s turns were hack work. Both of their double-chinned features defiled the Frankenstein mystique. Any actor who took on Jack Pierce's classic makeup became a blend of himself and Frankie. As such, I would hallucinate other people's faces in Frankenstein makeup, including teachers, Mrs. Wilshire, Mrs. O'Leary and Uncle Limpy.

I took pride in memorizing dates of horror films. He's created in the original 1930 film, and dies in the explosion of the castle, but he survives under the wreckage at the onset of *Bride of Frankenstein* in 1935. Then by 1939, in *Son of Frankenstein*, he is thawed out from some iceberg, though it's not clear how he got there. By the time he meets Abbott & Costello in 1948, he's shipped from Europe by crate to McDougal's House of Horrors museum. And why did 1958's *Frankenstein 1970* even bother to have the monster's name in it? When the gothically overwrought Hammer Films in England revived the cycle in the 1960s, the whole storyline had long since tested my ability to suspend disbelief. Christopher Lee made a terrible monster, the makeup a disgrace, and he'd already upset my steadfast belief in Lugosi as Dracula. I always assumed every movie was the official lineage in the ongoing saga of Frankenstein's survival. I didn't realize that any cigar-chomping huckster could procure the Frankenstein name from public domain. By 1966, they had him fighting Jesse James, something that disturbed me, because I just didn't believe it. It was on a double bill with something called *Billy the Kid Meets Dracula*, which I refused to see. The monster's reputation was drained of every ounce of dignity, turned into a cycle of drivel to milk out every dime any third-rate hack could bleed from the name Frankenstein.

I went to the movies with Bobo, Jeffrey and Mumsy—making up the extra change needed from my pocket, since they never possessed more than a few nickels. Though it wasn't required (like it was south of the Mason-Dixon Line), colored kids seemed to stake out the balcony seats. From the back rows of the balcony, you could hear the projector whirring. Bobo could block the light beam with his hand, interfering with a projection from Hollywood.

Whenever a Negro person appeared onscreen at the movies, Fat Emily, Ada Potata and Pamela laughed and pointed derisively. But when I saw Negroes in movies, I wished the camera would veer off into the alternate universe of the maid or the porter. Follow them home, away from white people, as they soaked their corned feet in Epsom salts so they'd be ready to jump and shout at church on Sunday.

Sometimes there were Saturday creepshow matinees, tailor-made for me. Bobo, Jeffrey and Mumsy acted scared, cracked jokes (*Could Cassius Clay kick Frankenstein's ass?*), screamed and threw popcorn like kids. But I identified with Frankenstein on a profound level, and wished to know him personally, almost as much as the Beatles. I felt like Frankenstein, an outcast amongst the villagers, whom people threw rotten crab apples and firecrackers at, wanted to hang or stone to death. But Frankenstein was stronger than a hundred men, and I sure could have used him on my side. I wondered whether I, too, was one of the walking dead, and tried endlessly to will his appearance, as though our destinies were somehow intertwined. He never arrived.

I had real monsters to deal with.

27. Dancing on the Levee

IF THE PRINCIPAL WAS UNAWARE that one of her teachers may have become intimate with South School's most troublesome pupil, she had other things on her mind. In observance of the tenth anniversary of the *Brown v. Board of Education* ruling by the Supreme Court outlawing segregation in public schools, a delegation of NAACP members descended upon Glen Cove. This was unprecedented. Northern agitators bussed down South for Civil Rights marches and voter registrations. Poor colored folks from Mississippi, however, did not charter bus trips to protest conditions in New York. Except in the case of South School, which received such a visit. Miss Tiger, our principal, was under siege.

Tiger singled me out of class that afternoon. On Monday May 18, 1964, my presence was required at the school board meeting in the auditorium. I was told to sit in the back row. I didn't have a clue about Civil Rights or racial politics, but she intended to make some kind of an example of me. Twenty-five Negro Civil Rights foot soldiers from the South sat with their arms folded, in opposition to officials of the Glen Cove Board of Education. The delegation wore suits, ties and vests and held their heads loftily.

Truth be told, they came from a society encumbered by Jim Crow laws. In North Carolina, where many South School parents came from, for instance, the law dictated:

Books shall not be interchangeable between the white and colored schools, but shall continue to be used by the race first using them. . . . The state librarian is directed to fit up and maintain a separate place for the use of the colored people who may come to the library for the purpose of reading books or periodicals.

There had been hundreds of such laws, written into state statutes throughout the Old South.

The NAACP sat on one side of the auditorium. The white school board members sat on the other. The NAACP's local education chairman, James DeWitt Anthony, was top agitator in charge. Anthony exuded education from every pore. *Magna cum laude* in Latin and French from Howard University, minoring in English and Education. Air Force lieutenant in communications, stationed in Europe right after the Korean War. Then went on to Harvard Law School, with a stop at the Sorbonne. He was currently an Assistant Attorney General and litigator in matters of habeas corpus for the State of New York. Anthony wore thick black glasses, carried a briefcase and wore his tie tight at the collar, somewhat like Malcolm X, so that his eyes and neck veins bulged. He took the lectern:

"Ten years ago this week, we achieved our landmark Supreme Court ruling—*Brown v. Board of Education.* Today, we've come here to help you observe it and to help you remember it. It's time for the board to make it plain whether it deplores the cancer of segregation. Segregated education is inherently inferior."

"Amen!" shouted his entourage.

"Your comments will be noted by the board," said the school board chairwoman, a Mrs. Tuthill.

Miss Tiger twitched uncomfortably. She portrayed herself as a staunch Civil Rights advocate. You'd have to be to run a colored school, and there was no doubt about that.

But she was white, her teachers were white and the school board was white. Yet that wasn't the NAACP's primary complaint. Incredibly, their charge was that there weren't *enough* whites. Children, that is. The NAACP's charge was "*de facto* segregation."

James DeWitt Anthony continued in stentorian tones, like Frederick Douglass: "The life of the American Negro has had an angry history, but its present and future in this democratic country is his hope to make Americanism work. Our Negro graduates—where are they? Not from South School."

Reverend Baker, pastor of the local First Baptist Church, stood up to interject. "Mr. Anthony. We can't allow you by innuendo to denigrate the teachers of this here school. Miss Tiger and her faculty are bustin' they britches to do the best job they know."

"That's right!" came a lone female voice from the rear. A paltry representation of South School parents were sitting off in the back, wearing their Sunday best.

"Thank you, Reverend," continued Anthony. "But I must direct my inquiry to the principal and the school board only. Is it true, Miss Tiger, that only two percent of your South School students enter the academic program after they leave?"

"What academic program?" asked Tiger.

"The middle school program."

"Only two percent? Absolutely not true!" countered Tiger, smacking her clipboard.

"I have spoken with parents of this community," said Mr. Anthony, "and been told that their children are not taught things that other schools provide. I have been told that two children were demoted a grade for being late. And I have been told that children here must sit quietly with their hands folded after lunch, when other schools allow a time of playground activity."

Tiger became apoplectic. "We provide outdoor activity

every day!"

"Then why is the playground closed in back of the school?"

"It was closed due to a health hazard from the dumps. Our children play in the front."

Dr. O'Kane, the Superintendent of Glen Cove Schools, held up a sheath of papers before the assembly. The Superintendent of Schools seemed scarier than the police chief. He was the boss of all principals. I always wondered what kind of trouble you'd have to be in to be brought before the Superintendent, as opposed to the principal. He could hire and fire mere principals. And then, I'd heard there's even a higher authority than the Superintendent, something called the New York State Board of *Regents*. There were eight Regents, and they sat at some dizzying height of authority. They had an official seal that you saw on schoolbooks. And the boss of them was someone called the Chancellor. I imagined him as sitting atop a throne or a chariot, or perhaps being carried on the shoulders of the Regents, like Haile Selassie, the Emperor of Ethiopia. God knows the punishments he could mete out, if you were sent to him.

The Superintendent spoke:

"Other towns on Long Island were cited for having *de facto* housing and school segregation problems. But charges were dropped against Port Washington."

"Yes!" said Mr. Anthony. "*They* moved toward equitable districting of Negro pupils in the public *schools*."

"And you dropped your complaints against Great Neck's Spinney Hill School."

"Yes, Mr. Superintendent. Spinney Hill's Negro school has been shut down. Great Neck has integrated. Only Glen Cove remains a disgrace. Glen Cove will not allow South School's children to invade their lily-white schools. White families will not allow their precious children to be bused into South, not over their dead bodies. Your mayor-supervisor has made sure that you, the local school board, maintains autonomy, denying the State Education Commissioner the power to order school districts to integrate. To hell with any Supreme Court decision. To hell with the law."

"We are in compliance with the law," insisted Miss Tiger.

"Where is the integration promised by the law?"

"We have an integrated body of pupils," insisted Tiger.

"Integrated body?"

"And we're working on expanding it," said Tiger.

"Where are the white children in this school? For the impoverished Negro child to emulate and copy as role models? Present one."

"You betcha," said Miss Tiger. "Josh! Step down, son." I stood up, clueless as to what all these adults were fussing over. I was scared.

"*This* is your example of segregated education?" said Anthony. "This lone mop-headed white boy? *He* is the example our Negro children are expected to follow?"

"Sit back down, son," said Tiger, giving in quickly.

"I am furthermore aware," charged Mr. Anthony, "that South School provides no emphasis in its curriculum on the Negro's history and contributions to culture—"

"Mr. Anthony," interrupted the principal. "The children are aptly made aware of George Washington Carver and his invention of peanut butter."

"Peanut butter?!" Anthony shot back.

"He a faggot!" came someone from the audience.

"Every textbook I perused while visiting the library had pictures of Negroes dancing on the levee," continued Anthony, in his charge. "These are examples of inferior education. Anti-Negroism."

"Your comments will be noted by the board," said the chairwoman, like a broken record.

Then Dr. O'Kane, the superintendent of Glen Cove Schools, defending his principal, stood up from the front row.

"Mr. Anthony, I've examined the texts in question and seen the illustrations of Negroes dancing on the levee. These books are all we have to work with. But Mr. Anthony, I ask, just what does dancing on the levee indicate to you?"

"Why," said Anthony, considering his words, ". . . they're celebrating the arrival of King Cotton."

"Amen!" shouted the delegation.

And then, Jeffrey's momma, Legertha Mae Lincoln stood up, as if in church. She had a red dress and Sunday hat on, so unlike the clothes she wore the day I was lynched. "Mah pappy sharecropped," she said aloud. "Ah picked cotton as a chile. It was hard and foul. Ah didn't want mah babies to pick no goddamn cotton!"

Mr. Anthony continued: "That's right. And you didn't send your children to this school to dance on the levee. Those Negroes in your illustrations are celebrating a bumper crop for Master!"

"*Hangh*?!" screamed Miss Tiger, growing apoplectic.

"That's right! So that all could reap the bounty. All but the Negro. So they can pick and cull the harvest for shipment on down the Mississippi River for all of Dixie to rejoice. But the Negro had no share in cotton's bounty. Never has and never will. That's what dancin' on the levee means to me, Mr. Superintendent!"

"He ain't shittin'," came Legertha Mae Lincoln, from the side of her mouth. And then louder, "Stuff that in yo' corncob pipe and smoke it, muthafucka, with peanut butter, too!"

Miss Tiger gathered up her notes, her sweater, and stuttering incomprehensibly to herself, walked out. Her arms were too short to box the NAACP.

28. Long Island Gals

I ESCAPED TO THE LIVING ROOM floor beside my hi-fi player, ecstatic over the Beatles' *Something New*, the third LP. O'Leary hobbled in, bursting my bubble.

"Jazz is comin' back, Josh. Just you wait and see." She often made this pronouncement. Rock 'n' roll's days were numbered. Any time now the noise I listened to would fizzle out, and the world would return to real music. Some watered-down Dixieland she'd heard on *Lawrence Welk*. Her favorite songs were "Baby Face" and "By the Sea."

"They *made* their money," she reasoned about the Beatles. "Now they should go back home and let *our* boys make *their* money."

Always the patriot, O'Leary reminisced over her childhood in Oyster Bay, playing with the grandchildren of Theodore Roosevelt. Sagamore Hill, Roosevelt's 155-acre estate, was now a picturesque National Historic Site. When she took me there, I would stare at a glass case that contained a lock of Abraham Lincoln's hair in a tube. There was also a lock of Washington's hair. Both had belonged to Roosevelt. She often sat in Roosevelt's lap when she was five, over at Sagamore Hill. Before her rear end blew up to ten times the size it was then. Several useless wicker chairs remained on our patio with busted seats. At least once a year another porch chair gave out as Mrs. O'Leary's arse plunged through.

"I'm a Long Island gal," she said, alluding to some Mayflower-type lineage of Oyster Bay fisherman. "Me and Lu, we're *real* Long Islanders." She hoisted her first beer of the evening.

"Aren't I a Long Islander, too?" I asked.

"Not exactly," said O'Leary. "You see, Josh, a Black man is a *Negro*. And a Black woman is a *Negress*. Your father is a *Jew*. And your mother, a *Jewess*."

"Then what does that make you, Mrs. O'Leary?" I asked.

"*I* am a *woman*!" she cried in breathless tones, then stormed off to her room and slammed the door.

29. Bloodgood Cutter

*S*PEAKING OF LONG ISLAND, CONSIDER
the strange life of Bloodgood Cutter (1817–1906), Long Island's
farmer "Poet-Lariat" and world traveler, who befriended
Mark Twain. He was quick to foreclose mortgages on widows
and orphans, holding an open Bible in his hands while
admonishing strangers. The stock from whence Mrs. O'Leary
and Drake sprung were raised on Long Island potatoes, onions,
clams and oysters. Their forefathers lived by the potato. Until
the Irish Potato Famine of the 1840s, when starving masses
sailed for America. The ones who settled near Glen Cove
switched their dependence on potatoes to clams and oysters.

Glen Cove was 200 years old in 1868. A glimpse of
Glen Cove in the century before Mumsy appears below, written
by Bloodgood Cutter:

The Bicentennial Celebration at Glen Cove
May 24, 1868[*]

My friends, we have assembled here,
To celebrate the two hundredth year
Of this your pleasant dwelling-place,
And to thank our ancestral race,

---

[*]   Joan D. Berbrich (ed.). *Sounds and Sweet Airs: The Poetry of Long Island* (Port Washington, NY: Ira J. Friedman Division/Kennikat Press, 1970).

For choosing this location grand,
As any in our common land

Here you have a fine water view
With all its privileges, too.
Oysters and clams grow on your shore
You have them brought fresh to your door;
Then they are a delicious treat,
But canned, they're hardly fit to eat.

Last summer we had them on the ship,
While on our long excursion trip;
I did not fancy then their taste,
So quantities did go to waste.
Then, if you want salt water fish,
Can have the kind just as you wish;
Or if you want the splendid trout,
Go to your ponds and fish them out.

Here you have bathing-places good,
Where you can enjoy the briny flood;
In summer citizens here come,
To bathe and enjoy your rural home.
For bathing in the briny swell,
You know they generally pay well;
That is a great advantage too,
And benefits many of you.

For you to appreciate your home,
Around the world a spell should roam;
If in the East a spell you rove,
You'll long to get back to old Glen Cove.
Is above all supremely blest;
And to our ladies I can say,
They're highly favored every way.
Your tables at our fair does show

Fruit and vegetables as grand,
As any in our favored land.
And here you have a fine steamboat,
Faster than many now afloat;
In going to the city great,
She almost flies through Hell Gate strait.
You find it very healthy too;
And as you pass each point of land,
The scenery is very grand.

It is equal to Naples' Bay;
And 'tis by far much safer too,
For no volcano here hurts you.
Is generally with knowledge stored;
With society of this kind,
There's great improvement of the mind.
That will repay the farmers' toil;
Your onions planted in the field,
It seems enormously do yield.

Here too you have great water power,
That grinds your grain into fine flour;
Your mazena that's manufactured here,
And your starch goes most everywhere.

On that I think do of times feast;
I think I saw the boxes stand,
In Alexandria the grand.
To me indeed 'twas quite a treat,
To see there Glen Cove food to eat;
As through strange places I did roam,
It pleased me to see things from home.

In Cairo I went in a store,
And many boxes there I saw;
In fact, in what great place you go,
Glen Cove mazena they do show.

With all these blessings at command,
You need not seek another land;
But here you should contented live,
And thanks to the Almighty give.

Two hundred years have passed away,
And as to our fathers, where are they?
Old Father Time has laid them low,
And with us all 'twill soon be so.

30. Shoeshine Boys

MUMSY LEECH WAS A LONER. HE would wander along the train tracks, and sometimes I'd see him with a raggedy shoeshine kit in tow. He knew a man named Shine Man Shuggs, who was Aunt Nellie's former sweetheart. Shine Man oversaw a revolving gang of shoeshine boys at Penn Station. Shine Man issued footstools, polish tins and rags for any industrious colored kid willing to work. His cut was a dime from every shine.

"This my shine kit," said Mumsy, proudly carrying a raggedy box, like some treasure chest. The box held the worldly accoutrements of a professional shine-your-buckle man, filled with filthy rags, a brush and smeary tins of Kiwi polish.

I had fantasized about running away from home, but never had the balls to carry it out. What lay out there for a nine-year-old kid? Endless amusement parks, freedom from school and a deferred bedtime? Pinocchio tried this and got turned into a donkey. And what to wear? Mumsy claimed all you needed was a good undershirt to keep you warm in winter. An undershirt alone, and nothing else. We were warned of dangers, but didn't quite know what they were. We didn't know homosexuals existed.

But armed with ten bucks, the most I'd ever had in my pocket, I embarked on a bold journey to New York City. Mumsy knew how to negotiate the Long Island Rail Road

ticket counter. Kids' tickets were sixty cents each at the
Glen Cove station. An impersonal female clerk issued
two, without suspicion. Everybody was warned about the
Truant Officer, looking to arrest kids who played hooky. But
I suspected he was just an imaginary boogeyman. He never
went after colored kids.

If caught, I'd be in BIG trouble. Two nine-year-olds
alone—although Mumsy might have been ten, nobody was
sure. My worst punishment could be a day's banishment
to my bedroom, tortured by the screams of kids playing
Ringolivio on bicycles outdoors. A suffocating jail sentence.
Mumsy, however, lived without supervision and could blow
with the wind. A smelly little colored kid who could travel
into the city by himself. This showed a degree of worldliness
beyond my own.

The Long Island Rail Road was the ultimate choo-choo
train for boys. Sometimes you boarded one of the older,
rickety cars and got bounced around like popcorn. It took
about an hour into the city from Glen Cove, with all the
stops. And each stop brought you closer to Gotham. I'd taken
this trip a hundred times with my mother. But this time
I rode with Mumsy. At every stop, the pit of my stomach
dropped another notch as the distance from home increased.
While Mumsy sat oblivious, I gazed out the window like
Dorothy hallucinating en route to Oz. I didn't see witches on
broomsticks. But the route offered glimpses of Long Island's
"Gold Coast" of the Gilded Age, where 19th century robber
barons built thousand-acre estates. American castles hidden
in wooded regions of Glen Cove. They were now abandoned
ruins, historical parks or private schools.

The Gold Coast was the polar opposite of
Glen Cove's colored section. Fantastical mansions built
by F.W. Woolworth, the DuPonts, and seven Pratt family
estates, heirs of Standard Oil. The manors had coats of arms
with names like Winfield, Welwyn, the Braes, Pembroke,
Beaupré, Poplar Hill, Malmaison. (The colored homes also

had names, at least to me: Lincoln House, Bobo House, Mumsy Place, Limpy Shack.) J.P. Morgan's estate was now a convent for nuns. Killenworth, formerly the manor of one George DuPont Pratt, became the retreat of the Russian delegation to the United Nations. Khrushchev would visit. Some, like Mr. Mortimer, believed the Russians were using this estate as a base for spying on the Long Island arms industry; companies like Grumman.

This had been Great Gatsby country. One home, jutting over a cliff, was the locale where Cary Grant was kidnapped and taken in *North by Northwest*. Manors were interconnected by bridal paths, without fences or boundaries. Fox hunts became obsolete by the 1950s, as second- and third- generation heirs of the robber barons assimilated into oblivion.

Long Island was 118 miles of exquisite earth, rock and pebbles that materialized 18,000 years ago, in the waning millennia of the last ice age. After World War II, civic power broker Robert Moses opened up this pristine land to the people. He invented the concept of the parkway, built bridges and expressways from city to Island. The dawn of suburban sprawl. Levittown was the first enormous undertaking of assembly-line housing developments for returning World War II GIs. (Blacks were restricted from Levittown until the '60s.) Nassau County was no longer a European fiefdom for the super rich, like Newport. The land was opened up to teeming urban masses from the Bronx, Queens and especially Brooklyn, that whole borough with an inferiority complex. An urban migration of Jews, Italians, Irish, Polish, Puerto Ricans and Negroes. There went the neighborhood. Where manors stood were now suburbs of *Long Gileland*, school systems teeming with mentally disturbed teachers, racial unrest, upward mobility run amok . . . pizza parlors and delicatessens with bagels and lox. The Gilded Age gentry, like an affected English aristocracy, would not recognize the North Shore of Long Island now. The Coast was no longer

Gold since the Goldbergs moved in.

But Mumsy and I were unaware of this. Glen Cove was still an outdoor paradise for boys. Old roads went up at nosebleed angles, with gothic cliffs and angular hills, all there for exploring. We might spend an hour climbing trees and jumping down dirt embankments early in the morning, before school.

Mumsy sat like a blind man as we bounced in our seats. It wasn't long before the train crossed over the Nassau County line. The next twenty minutes provided a travelog through Queens. A place so unrelentingly ugly, so displeasing to the eye for mile after mile, that it was beautiful. Con Edison smokestacks, soda bottling plants, hubcap-strewn cobblestone side streets. A massive graveyard stretched out into the horizon, far as the eye could see. I couldn't believe there were that many dead people in the world. In Queens, the elevated subway—heaps of rusting metal—still remained, having escaped sale to the Japanese; its Manhattan counterparts, the Third and Sixth Avenue Els, were dismantled and sold as scrap iron before World War II, only to come back at us in bombs at Pearl Harbor. I figured Flushing, Queens, was famous for toilets. Forest Hills, Jackson Heights, Jamaica, and finally, Astoria. Industrial billboards for Swingline Staplers, Silvercup and Fink White Bread. Just who was this Mr. Fink, and where did he come off challenging the mighty Wonder Bread, that whitest of white breads? The bread that Builds Strong Bodies 12 Ways. Once-quaint rows of two-story brick dwellings aged into grim domiciles—postwar dream homes, built under the GI Bill, when Queens was still a working-class promised land.

People had strange, tiny backyards with no privacy— always an expressway, service road or railroad peering right in. Everything seemed sullen and overcast, even on a sunny day. In warmer months, little rubber swimming pools appeared under clotheslines. Were these people not entitled to some privacy? Hanging to dry, the shit-stained boxer shorts of a million working Joes, side by side with the bloomers and pantaloons of their varicose-veined wives. Yet each backyard represented someone's little piece of America. Somebody's tiny slice of the pie. Oh, what poor inhabitants dwelled in this deadened, gray borough. Did anyone ever have fun here? Were people happy in Queens?

There, in Astoria, Queens, as the conductor bellowed, "Last stop, New York," was the Yoo-hoo bottling plant. I imagined a million gallons of cheap chocolate water flowing through tanks under Yogi Berra's billboard endorsement. The port of entry to New York City was forever pockmarked with Yogi Berra's head. Was it possible Yoo-hoo made you look like Berra? Smell like him, blemish like him, acquire a *deese-dem-and-dose* philosophy and grow hirsute? Would a bellyful of Yoo-hoo enable you to squat on your haunches for nine innings? Or would Berra have been better utilized as a pitchman for Turkish squat toilets?

Queens represented the ass-end of the Industrial Revolution, the rusted iron bones of the robber barons. As the squatting captain of the Bronx Bombers, no face seemed more New Yorkish than Berra's. His grimy five-o'clock shadow reflected the working man's Bronx. Just as Ralph Kramden's represented blue-collar Brooklyn. The Yoo-hoo sign *was* 1950s New York; just like the end crawl of *The Honeymooners,* picturing Brooklyn's moonlit skyline, backed by the intense crime-jazz theme, "Melancholy Serenade," by Jackie Gleason & His Orchestra. Before the train submerged into total darkness under the East River, careening and squawking like a cart in a Coney Island spook house, I saw Berra toast his bottle of Yoo-hoo. And that, boys and girls, meant Welcome to New York.

There was a moment of heightened anticipation when the train stopped. Because the instant the train door slid open, the underground bowels of the city hit you square in the face. The black-and-white smell of grime and hot-dog counters and Con Edison steam vents. Subterranean Manhattan. "No Spitting" signs warned of $25 fines. Yet there were stains on the landing where a million violators had rudely ejected their chewing gum. "Phil D. Basket," the cartoon Sanman, represented a public-relations campaign to catch litterbugs, brought to you by the Citizens Committee to keep New York City clean. Sanmen, shorthand for sanitation men, were New York's Filthiest. The glamorous profession, we were warned, that awaited me and Bobo and Mumsy and Jeffrey.

The masses emerged into the ironworks Penn Station, a magnificent gateway to the empire of Gotham. It was soon to be torn down. The destroyers did their work insidiously, over three years. The public was unaware of the deconstruction taking place around them. Only afterward could New Yorkers take the full measure of their loss. Penn Station was the greatest of New York's architectural losses, the sacrificial lamb that triggered the landmarks preservation movement.

An exposed steel-framed train concourse. A purgatory of descending platforms, the heavenly light cascading through clerestory ceilings. It was like entering Mount Olympus or Oz or, more to the point, the Roman Empire. Incoming travelers on one level, outgoing on another. Train tracks lay below stairwells, deep beneath the city. I wondered why this destination was called "Pennsylvania Station." Wouldn't some folks figure they got off in the wrong state?

Walking fast among thousands, through turnstiles, Mumsy and I ascended an iron stairwell to the concourse. If you didn't step off the escalator at the last second, you'd be ground into spaghetti. There stood the Savarin coffee shop with its winding marble counter, with bronze and leather stools.

Pomade-haired young colored ladies in white frocks beckoned from behind the Nedick's hot-dog counter. They made surreptitious appointments with Long Island Rail Road commuters. Balding white men in starched shirts and ties sweated profusely as they arranged illicit rendezvous with the colored hot-dog waitresses. The counter ladies were hookers. And smiling broadly in a Nedick's hot-dog cap behind the counter, like a Pullman porter at your service, was the young actor-to-be, Morgan Freeman, his first job fresh from Mississippi. This I was to learn many years later, but the face was unforgettable.

"Hello, boys, what can I getcha?"

Mumsy and I ordered hot dogs and orange drinks at the counter, and felt welcomed by the smiling counterman. The hot dogs were fantastic, served on thin cardboard trays.

Though sooty with decades of city grime, the roof made the three-story cathedral look like some sort of heaven streaming down through the iron girders. So that people upon entering might feel godlike themselves. Everyone arriving in New York would feel something important. Everyone, perhaps, but the shoeshine men.

But even they acted like they kept the world shiny in the grand scheme of things. The main shop in Penn Station was Shine King, where men as black as the shoe polish they buffed labored full-time in do-rags. Commuters sat upon thrones with their *Herald Tribune, Journal-American* or *Times*, snap-folding the pages into place as only New Yorkers do, like the way they folded their pizza slices. Ashtray stands were provided for cigars. Rare was the lady customer. Women just didn't look appropriate with their legs hoisted over shoe stirrups at face level with hard-looking Negroes stooping at their feet.

Off from the main waiting room and concourse, in an antechamber by the subway, stood a gaggle of boys with shoeshine benches. "Shine?" they shouted in unison as potential customers strolled past. Each shoeshine boy smiled a little harder to snag a commuter, at the ready with a rag. These were city boys from Harlem. They were scrappier than us, and butted each other out of the way to nab customers. They knew how to negotiate on the streets, and even underneath.

In the center of this action was Shine Man Shuggs. Old-timers like Shine Man Shuggs were going out of style. They no longer popped boogie-woogie rags. The old-time rhythm left their hands at the onset of arthritis. The joy was long gone from when shining shoes was like some minstrel show tap dance. Creeping into the profession was an angrier breed whose technique displayed more defiance, in the way of "spit shines."

But the boys were ragamuffins with razzmatazz. I heard one lay down the oldest con in the game:

> *Mister, bet I know where you got dem shoes.*
> *You do? Where?*
> *Gimme a nickel if ah get it right?*
> *Okay, I'll give you a nickel.*
> *You got 'em at the bottom of yo' feet.*

A few boys shouted their own *shine-your-buckle* raps:

> *Spit on yo' spats, if ya like it like dats!*
> *Buff yo' scuff, if ya wanna look tuff!*

Currently at fifty cents, shoeshines remained an authentic Big Apple bargain, worth every penny. The customer felt the sheer energy that went into it. At Shine King on the main concourse, men made $15 a day in wages, but most of their earnings came from tips. Of course, a little extra pop of the rag, for show, didn't hurt. They said tips could reach over $50 a day. Although tips were better at Shine King, Shine Man Shuggs' boys could top twenty-five bucks before evening's rush hour.

Shine Man himself did dozens of shines a day in his black smock. He learned his craft from the crème of the

Brotherhood of Sleeping Car Porters in Chattanooga, Tennessee. I'd heard Aunt Nellie say that he was the original "Chattanoogie Shoeshine Boy" (*He pops a boogie-woogie rag, The Chattanoogie Shoeshine Boy!*). But there were probably as many Chattanoogie Shoeshine Boy impostors as there were older Black men claiming to be Stymie of The Little Rascals.

"Yes, suh. A shine give you self-respeck, make you look fine to the ladies, show you got style," said Shine Man Shuggs as he finished with a customer. He wore a painter's smock with hundreds of black stains. His rolled-up sleeves revealed arms that were wrinkled and leathery, as if he'd become an old shoe himself. Well-insured white men were everywhere, always in need of a rush-hour shine.

But I didn't buy it—how a measly shoeshine gave you style and respect. Were grown women stupid enough to be more attracted to men with shiny shoes? Was that all they were looking for? And did men really require a shoeshine for their self-respect and pride, whatever the hell that was? Was that really important to a man's character? Or was that ever-present shine a smokescreen covering up a litany of imperfections and flaws? Shouldn't people be *more* suspicious of someone whose shoes always shined, like Drake O'Leary or Uncle Limpy? Underneath Limpy's shiny Cuban boot heels were socks with holes in them. And Drake, whose golden initials were monogrammed into his hankies, used those Egyptian-cotton handkerchiefs to wipe clam juice off his switchblade.

Mumsy introduced us, and the Shine Man took notice of me. "So, you two railroad men come in from Glen Cove?"

"Mr. Shuggs, this here mah white fren. He wants to work."

"Lord, Mumsy, you sho' stinks like a dead dog. When you take a baff?"

"Ah ain't take no baff."

"Well, that's for sho'. Now why you wanna waste mah

time with some cracker boy?"

"He ain't waste nobody time."

"Well, this here a little nigger's job. Ain't no cracker ever be shinin' shoes 'round heah, no way, no how."

"But he good."

"Well, let's see now. Can he pop a rag?"

"Yeah, he pop a rag."

"Can he hustle? This ain't no reg'lar job now, it's a hustle."

"Yeah, he hustle."

"Can he hustle with muscle?"

"Yeah, he got muscle, mo' than me. Show 'em, Jock."

I rolled my sleeve and flexed my skinny arm.

"See there, Mr. Shuggs," said Mumsy. "He hustle just like a nigger do."

A heavy old Black woman hobbled over to the stand.

"Ah got miseries in mah feets," she moaned to no one in particular, taking a load off on the chair. "Shine me up, Shuggy."

Mr. Shuggs went to work, narrating for Mumsy and my benefit.

"You see, every shoeshine man have his own secret techniques," Mr. Shuggs instructed. "Whether you rubs the paste in by yo' finger or with yo' rag."

He dabbed his index and middle fingers into a mysterious tin called Ox Blood. "Now me, I'm a man who use his hand. This way you get the feel of the leather, skin to skin."

As he buffed his rag, the woman's dull old-lady shoes began to take on a hot shine.

"It's a lot of people who look down on it," he said. "But it ain't about what you do, it's how you do it. You try," he said abruptly, handing the rag over to me, after he had already worked one shoe to a finish.

"Mr. Shuggs don't 'low no spit," said one of the boys.

"That's a disgrace," said Mr. Shuggs.

This was a big moment that I hadn't expected. I was

under the spotlight, nervous as hell. The old Black lady looked down on me reproachfully. She had a heady smell of Comet and ammonia and Mr. Clean.

"I want me a nigger shine," protested the lady.

"You hush!" ordered Mr. Shuggs. "Now go to it, Son."

I went at it, careful not to miss with the rag and get polish on her flesh-colored stockings. I found my rhythm fast.

"Son, you all right. You done found your callin'," he chuckled. "Yep, you done found your callin'."

This was an exciting vocation that reaped instant coin, better than a paper route. To the shoeshine boy, people were just shoes. Up walked leather loafers or wing-tipped Stacys or soft Italian stomps, sometimes even women's pumps. As a matter of fact, more ladies stopped by Shine Man Shuggs' operation than at the better-equipped Shine King shop. Here, women could sit floor level with a boy taking care of them, rather than compromise their modesty high up on some stirrups. And you could still look up their skirts.

But there was no way I'd ever be allowed to pursue it, not until I grew up. My parents would never allow me into the city. Mr. Shuggs' small fraternity of shoeshine boys eyed me suspiciously. I had invaded their turf as a white dilettante. I wasn't some poor slum kid who needed change.

Mumsy opened his shoeshine kit and was hard at it, hustling with the other boys. Whiskbroom, polish and paste.

> *Mumsy shimmy and shammy*
> *Flip, flop and fly*
> *Mumsy giggle and wiggle*
> *He pop that rag and polish that scuff*
> *Make them business mens look tuff.*

After an hour or so, an odd formation of humorless Black men wearing bow ties and tuxedos all marched over. They put their shoes up on each boy's stanchion. Shine Man Shuggs looked none too happy. One of the boys took a wet polish rag to begin. The man reached out to grab the boy's forearm, preventing the shine. The boy looked up confused as the rest of us froze.

"We bring greetings from the Honorable Elijah Muhammad," said the tuxedo man.

"The honorable *what?*" came Mr. Shuggs.

On a far wall, I noticed posters of "Dashing Dan," the Long Island Rail Road's "route of the dashing commuter" logo. Dashing Dan was a suburban white man with fat thighs and paunch, waving a briefcase and umbrella on the run, as he checked his watch for a train; his counterpart was a 1940s hot-tomato, Dashing Dottie.

"We are here to enlighten and educate." The man handed Mr. Shuggs a card, which he squinted at cluelessly. All the tuxedo men held books that said *The Holy Qur'an*. They seemed programmed, almost robotic.

"What example are you teaching these boys? To play the role of the servant?"

The boys in question went back to their work, letting Mr. Shuggs handle the intrusion. These kids were pros, part of the rhythm of Penn Station, where all the world streamed through. They'd seen it all.

"What the . . . these are mah boys. They workin' for me. Not only do they earn money," declared Mr. Shuggs, "but it's a craft. They take pride in what they can do."

"They see the way you carry yourself. An old Black man stooping to shine the white man's shoes."

"Y'all say you don't like the way ah carry myself?" he said, growing indignant. "Now, you listen here, Mister. I been feedin' my famblie since I was knee-high to a jackass, and my boys be feedin' they famblies, too. You cain't wear no flashy threads or zoot suits 'round here. Or no monkey suit y'all got on your ass. No, Suh. You needs a smock and a rag and can of polish. *And* a smile."

"Surely, there's no need for a smile . . . this is a job for freed slaves. Shining somebody else's shoes is an act of servitude that reflects subordination going back a long way. Those who aspire to a lifetime of rubbing the dull leather of the white devils' shoes are no more than *bootblack clowns.* Buster Browns."

"Now, you listen up here, goddammit!" came Shine Man Shuggs. "You know how many mens got they promotion 'cause of the shine I gave? Not only do a shine make you look rich, but it give good *luck.*"

"Our people in the shoeshine business are nothing but rejected and despised members of the so-called Negro race," said the robotic man.

"Up, you mighty race!" chanted one of the men.

"Now, you want a shine or not?" interrupted Mr. Shuggs. "Otherwise, take yo' damn feets off dat stool, and move yo' Honorable Elijah ass on outta here. Goddammit, we workin'."

The men took one long hard look at him, then turned to leave. "Brother Malcolm," said one bow-tie man to another, as they marched off in formation, "I think you failed to persuade him."

31. Yankee Stadium

SPRING WAS THE BEGINNING OF baseball season. Little League. They leveled Ebbets Field for project housing; they replaced the Polo Grounds for projects. But they didn't get Yankee Stadium. This was the funky soul of the Bronx, of an old New York that I sensed was precious, as it slipped away before my eyes, the fruitful Puerto Ricans multiplying, and slumifying the promised land of the Bronx. The Lower East Side had gone from Jewish slums to Puerto Rican slums. The Bronx was where my father was born and raised, right across from Yankee Stadium. And it still was the turf of Mickey Mantle and aging Jews.

At a Yankee game one afternoon. The crowd got excited each time Mantle came up to the plate, regardless that he was past his prime. Pepitone hit two line-drive homers over centerfield that day. After grounding out several times, Mick slammed a homer in his last at bat. It soared skyward, unlike anybody else's home runs, the kind Ruth invented a half-century earlier in this same ballpark. And Dad turned to his sons: "Boys—you've just seen a Mickey Mantle home run. Don't ever forget it."

Of course, we didn't.

The side streets near the stadium were where my father's generation played pickup stickball, an inner city kid's game. It was never played once on Long Island. You hit something called a "spaldeen" with a broomstick. Spaldeens were made from defective cores of tennis balls—the sports equivalent of mustard greens or bacon fatback leftovers for slaves. A narrow city street was your playing field, with curbs as foul lines, and manhole covers for bases. All hits were "up the middle," and you measured home runs by sewers. Sometimes, if spaldeens weren't available, they actually used a soda cap. They pretended the sanitation men were the groundskeepers, when games started after the street sweepers passed through.

The kiosks outside Yankee Stadium sold old Yankee yearbooks and baseball periodicals that were produced locally, somewhere on River Avenue in the Bronx. You couldn't find them anywhere but outside Yankee Stadium, not even at Vic's. They sold a Mantle & Maris scrapbook, and a DiMaggio & Williams one. My favorite was the *Old Timer's Baseball Photo Album* series. Photos of players dating back to the Gay '90s, slapped together scrapbook style. You'd look at their gruff faces and dream about men presented as stars of their day, tops in the 19th century, like Cap Anson and Dan Brouthers. Careers were encapsulated briefly by some great feat they'd accomplished, like an unassisted triple play. A sly, squinty-eyed Ty Cobb on the cover, and inside, a picture of him in middle age, hand upon the retired Babe Ruth's shoulder. There was no mention of how he shouted "You half-nigger!" when Ruth came to the plate in their playing days. Great men of baseball with first names like Tris and Rogers and Honus. The hyped-up captions convinced you each guy was just about the greatest of his era. Everybody was the greatest. Bad habits and shameful episodes didn't exist. And, of course, there were no Negro old-timers.

They sold yearbook fakes from the 1950s, reproductions from hawkers on the street to dupe little boys from Long Island, like me. But the unofficial, unlicensed versions were just as fun, because of their shoddy, illicit slapdash production.

These magazines and scrapbooks had soul. They were smudged with frankfurter grease from the House That Ruth Built, infused by city bus fumes in the old Bronx, where everyone's grandparents lived. Sometimes you'd see bus-fume suckers—city kids trailing after muffler exhaust, richly fortified with digested lead gasoline. The past was greater than the present, old times were better times, old stuff was more exciting.

"Did you save any Ty Cobb baseball cards for me from when you were a boy?" I asked my granddad. He'd seen Ruth play many times. To my amazement, he hadn't saved anything from his childhood on the Lower East Side. He never even considered he'd someday have a grandson who loved old things.

"I can't wait till I'm your age, when my baseball cards and monster magazines'll be really old. Then I can give 'em to my grandson."

"Don't be in such a rush," he advised.

32. Jewish-American Lit

THE WILSHIRE KIDS SOMETIMES referred to colored kids as "burnt toast." They were raised with just a tad of that old-time religion, and their father told them this: "The way I see it, God didn't bake bread to be burnt. When he first made us in his ovens, he forgot to take some of his bread out. And they became burnt toast."

It wasn't always wise to walk along Lindbergh Avenue, where the Wilshires lived. Mrs. Wilshire often sat on the front porch with the chained-up hound. The matriarch of the family would cast an evil eye on me. I walked by with Mumsy one day as she sat on the worn-out couch with another fat lady.

"Hello, Sunshine," she called out to Mumsy, waving sweetly. A look of confusion came over Mumsy. "Why, back home we call all our little niggers Sunshine."

She resembled something my brother Drew and I might have had on exhibit down in our monster house. I felt sorry that the Wilshires' mother was such a frizzy-haired hag with hollow, black eye sockets, and eyebags that practically hung down into her morning coffee. But she was the only mother the Wilshire children had. Whatever was bothering her had built up to a boil.

"I got your father's new book," she said, this time addressing me. "Your father writes like a pig." She spit on the porch and turned to her friend. "His father writes like a pig.

Don't ya think?"

"He writes like a pig," answered the other woman.

"I read that book," snarled big Mrs. Wilshire, referring to my father's newest bestseller. "I had to t'row it out, I wouldn't want it in my house." She turned her head cockeyed to her friend. "In the traish. It had words you wouldn't say in front of a dog."

I knew I smelled trouble the first time I discovered a dirty word in one of my dad's books. And here it was. Mrs. Wilshire grabbed a pitchfork from the corner of the porch. "He writes *gah-bidge*. Whadaya think, I can't read, ya bagel, ya?"

Then she came at me with the pitchfork. My dad's celebrated Jewish-American Lit was apparently not her bag. Mumsy took off one way. I ran around to the back of the house. As far as I knew, she was aiming to stick me like a pig. I guess she thought of me as coming from a family of pigs. Rusty junk was piled high, spilling out of the garage.

"Get 'em, Mary!" came the other porch hag. Her daughter Nancy Wilshire, whom Mrs. O'Leary called "boy-girl," kicked my father's hardcover back and forth with her brothers. They played soccer with it in the backyard dirt.

Mrs. Wilshire began stalking me, pitchfork in hand. "Your father writes like a pig!" she hollered. And I found myself in another strange dance with a grown woman out to get me. She chased me all the way down the street, where she stopped at the sidewalk of my house, hoisting the pitchfork aloft like some angry farmer. "A pig!" she said one more time, lest I forget.

I told my mother, who explained that some people were illiterate morons who couldn't understand what they read. Mrs. Wilshire was one. Sticks and stones can break my bones, but names will never hurt me.

"But she chased me with a pitchfork, Mom!"

She looked at me like I was the King of Exaggeration.

33. Charm School

LATER THAT SPRING, DRAKE DROVE me to pick up Suzette before his Friday night date. She was enrolled at the Grace Downs School for Girls. A "charm school," everyone called it, without a trace of irony.

"What do they do there?" I asked Drake.

"They learn *manners*. Something we all could use a little more of these days."

"A whole school for that?"

"Oh, yes," said Drake, most solemnly. "They study *etiquette*. Anyone can be a slob, Josh, and put their elbows on the table. Being mannerly is a dying art." Drake seemed annoyed by this. "You see, there used to be rules and regulations. Emily Post was a great lady. For instance, when you have company for dinner, you're supposed to set three forks to the left, two knives and a small spoon to the right, over a folded napkin. Each utensil is for a different course. A gentleman never eats dinner with a salad fork."

"Really? Why?"

"It would be uncouth."

"Even for Bobo?"

"Well, no, not for the colored."

Drake's mother, Mrs. O'Leary, had been trying to teach me how to properly hold a fork for years, but it just wouldn't take. I held it like a caveman. But now that he mentioned it, I did notice how Drake always held his silverware daintily,

sometimes with a pinky raised. Except when he ate clams
from the bucket, which he knifed open, sliced under, and
slurped down with cold beer.

Drake could also share a good laugh over doo-doo
jokes—and for this, I greatly admired him. It was a rare and
precious commodity in a grown-up, and one that endeared
him to children. It made us feel he was on our team.

The Grace Downs School for Girls was at Winfield, the
41-room mansion that had been F.W. Woolworth's estate.
A holdover from the Gilded Age. Here was testament to
what could be built if you saved enough nickels and dimes.
F.W. Woolworth, founder of Woolworth's Five & Dime,
was an obsessed nutcase if ever there was one. He built
labyrinthine secret passageways, hidden chambers, and
collected the personal belongings of Napoleon, whom he
was obsessed with. Some of Napoleon's furniture remained
there, as well as a dedicated old servant or two. Woolworth
died in 1919. His tortured family abandoned the manor after
the stock market crash of 1929. It was said to be haunted,
and then some.

J.P. Morgan built an even more fabulous mansion on
the water facing Winfield, something that riled Woolworth
to no end. An attempt on J.P. Morgan's life was made in
1915, when a German intruder broke into the house. He
shot Morgan twice before the butler jumped him and saved
Morgan. Morgan lived on until 1943.

J.P. Morgan's estate was now a convent.
Sisters of St. John the Baptist lived in the 57-room main
house on Morgan's Island. They shared the small island
with former Dodger great, catcher Roy Campanella, whose
family lived in an 11-room ranch home. The only semi-rich
Negro in Glen Cove, he was half Italian and half Black. He
was thus barred from Major League Baseball until 1948, the
season after Jackie Robinson's debut. Campanella had an
auto accident driving home to Glen Cove from his Harlem
liquor store, before the 1958 season. He remained thereafter

in a wheelchair.

Drake's girlfriend lived in the dormitory. There wasn't a Negro among them. The Grace Downs School for Girls apparently had a less than sterling reputation when it came to matters of virtue. Mrs. O'Leary was not happy with her son's track record with women, as he'd impregnated then abandoned several. But something was wrong with those charm school students, according to Mrs. O'Leary. In one discreet class, they even learned about lingerie. Mrs. O'Leary and Lu called them harlots. Whatever that meant, the harlots all wore uniforms by day and changed into gowns by night. Gentleman callers could meet up with their harlots in a fancy waiting parlor by the entrance.

"There she is," said Drake, beaming. "Now ain't she a doll?" He wrapped his hammy but muscular arms around her, and they kissed passionately on the mouth.

"This is for my baby," he said, presenting a box of chocolates. "What did you learn this week, Honey?"

"Well. Here's the one-o'clock foot position," said Suzette, poised in a playful mock air.

"Posture, posture," said Drake.

"And here is how we *glide, girls, glide* across the room, with our heels on an imaginary line, toes just to the outside like so, and our hips forward. The Grace Downs Runway Walk. Very old school. We even had to practice with a book on our head," she giggled, plucking out an old volume from the bookshelf and walking across the room. "If it drops from your head, why, you lose a star."

Drake laughed heartily. "That's okay," he said, still beaming at her. "You see, Josh, Suzette is a young lady who will be going places in life."

I couldn't figure exactly how they taught young ladies to be charming, or what exactly charm was. But it apparently had something to do with personal grooming, hygiene, self manicures, pedicures, shaving their legs, shaping their brows, stuff that made no sense to me. What kind of hairstyle goes with which face, what kind of fabric and colors went with which body shape, which accessories, and how to enhance or hide their assets and flaws. And how to be charming conversationalists.

"Know something about everything, and everything about something," said Suzette. Her expertise lay in the field of floral arrangement.

"Oh, she's a flower all right," said Drake, "the flower of my eye." They beamed at each other. But then Suzette revealed she was frightened living here. Several young ladies, as well as many workers through the years, claimed to be spooked by Woolworth's ghost.

"I'm serious, Drake," she said, grasping hold of Drake's arm.

"Old Mr. Woolworth?" asked Drake. "Now, really Suzette. Why would he haunt such sweet young debutantes like yourself? Unless, of course, someone is demonstrating bad habits—like putting elbows on the table or using a potty mouth."

Drake was of the opinion that swear words should never be uttered in the presence of ladies. Or by ladies. If he heard so much as a *goddamn* when out with Suzette, he took offense, and firmly reminded the offender that he was out of line. I'd seen him go chest to chest over this on the street. "There are *ladies* present," he would say, with no shortage of threat in his voice.

"Even Miss Downs' butler says he's seen Woolworth," said Suzette. "And butlers don't lie."

"And a butler *never* passes wind in front of his employers," said Drake, in all earnestness, issuing future instructions should I take up the profession. Drake's gentlemanly ways betrayed the air of a butler or a chauffeur rather than a squire. But he dismissed Suzette's fear, and wouldn't hear any more about ghosts.

34. The Hexadecaroons Ball?

IN THE OLD AMERICAN SOUTH, THE *"one drop rule" meant that if a person had one drop of Black blood, he was considered to be Black. The idea still holds. That, combined with the three-fifths ratio of counting slaves as people, must have once made for challenging study of fractions in Louisiana classrooms. In New Orleans society, not too long ago, there had been a yearly "Octoroon Ball," for well-to-do citizens who were one-eighth Negro. Quadroons, who were one-fourth Negro, wouldn't have been admitted. Likewise, pitch-black sharecroppers would not have been admitted to a Mulatto Ball. Their social calendar was restricted to back-porch chitlin fries. But practically all Blacks in America might still find themselves classified under one of the following anthropological designations:*

MULATTO. *The offspring of one white parent and one Black parent.*

QUADROON. *One-quarter Black ancestry—a person with three white grandparents and one Black grandparent.*

OCTOROON. *A person of one-eighth Black ancestry.*

QUINTROON. *A person of one-sixteenth Black ancestry.*

HEXADECAROON. *Less common usage for one-*

sixteenth Negro. Look it up.

NIGGER. All of the above.

MACAROON. Dense, star-shaped cookies, rolled in coconut, dipped in chocolate.

35. Sitting Bull Goes to Colored School

ASIDE FROM MY PARENTS, AND A deep, emotional over-identification with the Beatles, I loved my guinea pig more than anything. As a matter of fact, for six years, I probably felt closer to Sitting Bull than I did to anyone else in the world. Guinea pigs had a magical effect on me.

I got Sitting Bull in first grade. An Abyssinian guinea pig with swirls of chocolate hair. A boy and his rodent against the world. It may not sound like a winning team, but don't bet against us. A kid can get just as close with a guinea pig as a dog, maybe closer.

Sitting Bull slept under the covers with me a few times a week. You had to be careful not to roll over on your pig; it was only two-and-a-half pounds. When the guinea pig looked me back in the eye, then jumped upon my chest for a nap— this was happiness. Genuine inter-species communication between boy and rodent.

Sitting Bull's cage was lined with cedar bedding, my favorite smell, forever associated with guinea pigs. He preferred to sleep in a shoebox within the cage, so I was always in search of shoeboxes since he chewed them up every two weeks. The shoebox was also a platform for jumping. A rodential castle. Guinea pigs loved to hide—for them, just sitting under the covers in the act of hiding was a sport.

Each morning as I awoke, I instinctively reached down beside my bed to open the wire cage and take him out. Let other kids have their dogs, cats, lizards, turtles or even horses. Great animals. But I was proud to have a guinea pig. Surely, they'd discover amazing links between guinea pigs and humans that mankind didn't realize yet.

But considering the guinea pig's grandest talent, we began to call him Shitting Bull, as Jeffrey christened him. He unloaded a hundred of 'em in my desk the day I snuck him into school. Our desks dated back decades. Old initials from generations past were carved onto the wooden tops. But there were no dirty words. The bubble gums of Negroes past were permanently affixed to the bottoms of each desk.

It was not a happy trip for Sitting Bull. But a grand time for all the kids, who were in on the secret that Sitting Bull was inside my desk this morning. He began kvetching like an old Jew. A few times he started squeaking, and Miss Grimsby turned from the blackboard suspiciously. I threw a piece of carrot into the desk each time to quiet him.

I brought Sitting Bull out in the lunchroom, before I took him home. A surefire health code violation, if such things were monitored at South. Boy, we really pulled the wool over Miss Grimsby's eyes.

Guinea pigs, more than other animals, were obsessed with eating. Any time a guinea pig hears and sees a refrigerator open, it will squeak like a lunatic before the Great Sun God of Vegetables.

Guinea pigs originally came from Peru, where they were still used as food. So I figured, if Sitting Bull and I ever went down to visit his homeland, I'd have to get him a sign that said:

DON'T EAT ME, I'M AN AMERICAN.

36. The Dumps

WHEN WORD GOT AROUND THAT BIG Mrs. Wilshire died, I cautiously rode my bike to their house. It was a new red Schwinn, one I had begged to have for a year. My mother drilled me all year about obeying stop signs. Look both ways before crossing streets. Stop, look and listen. I had to promise a thousand times. Once I got that bike, the great outdoors opened within my reach. I could even ride all the way to Locust Valley or Sea Cliff and get lost. Nevertheless, I couldn't imagine being on this planet without my own mother. I'd be destroyed. Fearfully, I wanted to see what motherless children looked like.

The Wilshire kids were all out screaming and playing ball on the street the day after their mother dropped dead of a heart attack. Pronounced D.O.A., age 35, at Community Hospital. She'd looked much older. They had blackened, rusty baseball gloves of Ty Cobb vintage. I was amazed.

"Don't you care?" I asked.

"About what?" said John David Wilshire who, at my age, was the most sensitive, thoughtful Wilshire kid. He just shrugged with a lopsided grin and tossed the ball. Their father, Jacob, the unemployed gardener, was now left alone with ten ragged kids.

"Let's go to the dumps!" cried Big Willie Wilshire.

"Yeah, to the dumps!"

A posse of Wilshires and visiting cousins, there for

the funeral, all hopped upon their bicycles like adolescent Hells Angels. I followed the pack on my new bike, all the way to the dumps.

The area was known as Garvies Point, which was once an Indian reservation. It provided the Wilshires with most of their worldly possessions. The Wilshire living room had barely any furniture. The paint was worn down to the wood. It was permeated by the smell of stale urine, the same stench I'd encounter in New York subways many years later. In the backyard were all kinds of useless items stolen over the years, or retrieved from the dumps. Enough hubcaps to supply a taxi fleet. Rusty bedsprings, empty TV frames, even a few manhole covers.

Big Willie was the most manic Wilshire, with a yellow crew cut, freckles, and two missing front teeth protruding. He was at least three years older than me, and still beat me up now and then. When he beat you up, he heaved and cried in some private hell, lashing out at demons far removed from whomever he was battling that moment. But each beating still came as a shock.

A holy terror to the neighbors, he was constantly fighting, stealing, breaking windows with rocks, on an incorrigible crusade of mayhem. Willie Wilshire went cascading down steep hills on his stolen bicycle with no brakes, skidding his mismatched Keds sneakers into the pavement till they smoked. Oblivious to traffic or stop signs, he sped across intersections with total abandon, laughing demoniacally. I was amazed at his luck surviving these crossings. But Willie Wilshire seemed oblivious to my presence today.

I arrived at the dumps with the Wilshire gang. The dumps were sort of an extension of the Wilshire's backyard. Junked cars were a prominent attraction, and you could chuck rocks at whatever remaining windows they had. There were Ford Model T's dating back to the 1920s. The hoods had been opened by scavengers. Inside were dead batteries with rusted battery acid and stale black grease glistening in the sun, that smeared off in clumps if you pressed a stick to it. Poking through rusty engines, Willie Wilshire yanked out old spark plugs and stuffed his pockets. The fenders were so decayed that they'd crumble at the push of a stick. Mosquitoes bred in water-logged tires. But Willie Wilshire brought this stuff into his backyard, his house and even his putrid bedroom.

The Wah Chang Smelting and Refining Co. of America, Inc. stood at Garvies Point. They created new metal alloys. Since the 1940s, tungsten ores imported from around the world were smelted at the facility to produce tungsten carbide powder, tungsten wire and welding rods. These metal alloys strengthened America's steel, and were used during World War II and in the Apollo Space Program. Garvies Point would later be found to contain radioactive waste, and plenty of it. There were no zoning laws, no environmental regulations or enforcement. You could dump anything in the pristine earth of Long Island.

In one section of the dumps were deep landfill ditches. In one ditch I saw the awesome spectacle of an entire cow carcass floating atop stagnant water, a rainbow of gasoline spillage around it. I'd never seen anything look so dead, with its tongue hanging out and flies swarming above. The dead cow could no longer swat them off with its tail. The largest black spider I ever saw crawled up the side of the ditch. I didn't dare come too close to these ditches, which seemed like gateways to Hell. Once Mr. Mortimer threatened to toss his son over. Bobby cackled nervously, and I stood back, praying his father wouldn't try this stunt with me. I'd rather be struck dead than fall in.

Garvies Point, as a matter of fact, could be seen from the playground in back of South School. In the 1950s, the dump generated swarms of flies that infiltrated the school and the Back Road Hill. The playground behind South School was often off-limits to us. Fumes rose from burning piles of raw garbage and an unmonitored sewer plant. It was a hellish attraction, but amazing to kids.

"Rat!" screamed Willie Wilshire. "Git it!"

The gang dropped their bicycles and began hurling rocks with bloodlust. The rat was scurrying over garbage piles, in a panic. Here was the most reviled species on earth, hated by both colored folks and white trash as a species lower and more hated than themselves. The rat represented disease to the Wilshires, and was in direct competition for food. Rats focused on poor people, not rich, and seemed to have a pipeline right to the Wilshires' cupboard cracker reserves.

This rat was fat and slow, and when it got hit it squealed and kept running. Something about the way it waddled away tore me apart. Any rodent was kin to Sitting Bull, my guinea pig. I charged in to its defense. The rat was nothing like the domestic Sitting Bull. The rat was wild by any definition, its survival instincts always on alert from enemies like the Wilshires. Still blamed for carrying the plague centuries before, like the Jews for killing Jesus. Rats didn't ask to be born, they just scurried about trying to survive, just like the Wilshires.

But then the whole mob of white kids instantly turned on me, the defender of rodents, and gave chase. Rocks whacked my back as I ran. Maybe I should have let them get the rat, I figured, running for my life. Suddenly all my concern for the rat disappeared. Now I was their rat. One of them kicked my bicycle in the dirt as I fled. The dumps were a bad place to be beaten up and left alone. It was farther from home than I'd ever been, alone on my bike. And I kept running from my bike, pressing further than my hyperventilating breath could hold up, to where I couldn't run another step—but kept on going, as rocks flew.

Circling around, I saw the fugitive rat. It was an overweight junkyard rat. Probably smarter, by human standards, than a dolphin. The rat turned a moment before going out into the road, where a garbage truck was headed, and looked me square in the eye. His expression was of hideous hangdog dejection, uncannily human, similar to Charles Laughton's

Quasimodo in *The Hunchback of Notre Dame* (photos of which ran often in *Famous Monsters*). There but for the grace of God hunkered I. The gang circled back around. I chased my little comrade out into the road.

"Run, rat, run!" Quasimodo waddled out into the street, huffing, out of breath like me.

A garbage truck rolled by and the rat tumbled under the wheel and was flung out into the air. It hit the dirt road dead. I became hysterical. For all the rat knew, I was the one who chased him to his death. I was staggered by guilt. The Wilshires laughed and jeered.

I circled back and retrieved my bike. I didn't care if they hit me with rocks. I'd get each one back another time, as my rock-and-apple throwing ability was superior to theirs. But the Wilshires were through fighting for the day. I rode home alone, a football field's length behind them. The Wilshire army marched home in ragtag formation, on bicycle and foot, like the Spirit of '76, singing one of their anthems:

> *Walkin' down Canal Street*
> *Knocked on every door*
> *God damn, sonofabitch*
> *I couldn't find a whore*
>
> *I finally found a whore*
> *She was rather thin*
> *God damn, sonofabitch*
> *I couldn't get it in*
>
> *I finally got it in*
> *Worked it all about*
> *God damn, sonofabitch*
> *I couldn't get it out*
>
> *I finally got it out*
> *It was wet and sore*

The moral of the story is
To never fuck a whore

Here was a song that took place on 19th-century
Canal Street. In the *shtetl*-like ghettos of the Lower East Side,
in the shadows of pushcarts and horse-drawn wagons
roamed Bowery streetwalkers. Toothless wretches who
taunted pious yeshiva boys, hoisting their skirts to reveal
a shocking bush of hair. They turned tricks with sailors in
cobblestone alleys. And now, 70 years later, the notorious
whores of Canal Street were remembered and insulted, or
maybe celebrated, in a dirty sing-song by the Wilshires of
Appalachia, who chased rats at the dumps, threw rocks
at me, and sang of whores on the day after their mother's
death.

Through the Wilshires, I heard my first incredible
description of *the act*. And now, by way of the Wilshires, I
already knew of a street in New York City where whores,
hard to find though they may be, performed this act. *Find
'em, feel 'em, fuck 'em, forget 'em,* that was the Wilshire boys'
motto when it came to girls.

"The man sticks his dick in a girl's *line*, then it all foams
up." The foam part was to confuse me for years. But the
whores were gone from Canal Street, buried in potter's
field a long time ago. The once-Jewish Lower East Side had
nearly disappeared. Canal Street was now the province
of Chinatown. The place where, legend had it, there were
opium dens, and firecrackers sold behind the counters of
Chinese laundries. And firecrackers were a more tangible
vice to wayward 10-year-olds than whores.

Long outlawed in New York, firecrackers were a highly
prized vice. You could lose the proverbial eye or finger.
Firecrackers were real black-market contraband. Only big
white kids possessed them. They came in packs of twenty,
looped together by their fuses. They were more powerful than
the fireworks that would come to be legalized throughout

the South decades later. The exotic outside wrappers on mysterious Oriental paper had pictures of leopards and tigers. They had brand names like Tiger's Claw or Pirate. Excess silver gunpowder at the bottom of the pack. Then, if you were really connected, there were cherry bombs, ash cans, and the mightiest firework known to kids, the M-80. The elusive explosive was, of course, only talked about. Nobody had actually seen an M-80. Like heroin or a prostitute, it was something you only heard existed.

And of course, the Roman-candle-type firework that the Wilshires called *Nigger Chasers*. Said so on the package. It zigzagged about the ground, shooting out sparks. The Wilshires were textbook examples of irresponsibility, raining firecrackers down upon kids in the neighborhood from trees. On Halloween—which was the Wilshires' yearly *Kristallnacht*—the Wilshires "egged" everything in sight, slit car tires and blew up pumpkins with cherry bombs.

And firecrackers were white kids' artillery to use against the colored kids.

37. Shoppin' for Clothes

THE KIDS WERE OBLIVIOUS TO THE racial politics coming to a boil behind the relative calm of their school. We were definitely learning our three R's: readin', 'ritin' and 'rithmetic. My grades fluctuated. When they were bad, I was trying to impress Bobo, purposely mocking school. Unlike Bobo, I did worry about my future. Our school grades would follow us the rest of our lives and would determine how successful we'd be in life. This was a fact, adults and teachers would tell you. When Bobo grew up and looked for a job, they'd see he was *lef' back*, and he'd have to be a garbage man. That was the only job my mother could think of to scare me into getting good grades. So I expected to be a garbage man, too. Bobo and I would be garbage men. With Bobo along, the job suddenly seemed glamorous. And this was before garbage men were called "sanitation engineers." (The job turned out to pay pretty well in many cities, with good benefits.)

I imagined us in Continental sharkskin suits and Beatle boots, hauling cans, with girls chasing after our garbage truck. We'd be riding the handles of the truck, laughing, having lunch at Henry's. We'd get to go to the dumps every day to empty our truck. No teachers or school officials or parents could tell us what to do, when to go to bed. And heavyweight contender Hubert Hilton here in town still trained behind the garbage truck each morning. It must have been a cool job.

But growing up seemed so far in the future, it was an eternity away. We were sentenced to twelve years of school, and that was twelve years of hard time. Somehow, I sensed this on the first day of first grade, when we were forced to sit quietly like plants and write our names with yellow pencils.

Bobo seemed to have the system beat, refusing to learn, playing hooky more often, and keeping our own Miss Grimsby under some spell. I went with him to W.T. Grant's, Glen Cove's most modern department store.

"Hey, Bobo!" shouted a colored cab driver at the Cove Taxi stand, outside Grant's on Continental Place. "What 'chu doin'?"

"Shoppin' for mah baby," yelled Bobo, a little man about town. He was going to steal Grimsby a present.

"Hey, lady," he said, flagging down a Grant's saleswoman. "Ah want a gif' for mah teacher."

"Well, that's a fine young fellow. Your teacher must be proud."

"She is. Where the nightgowns at?"

Perplexed, the saleswoman led us to women's sleepwear. Bras, girdles, hosiery. It was mysterious and exciting. All these white girdles and Maidenform bras that hid the secrets of womankind. Bobo acted worldly, as if he knew what he wanted. He felt the materials like a connoisseur.

"Need somethin' sof' up against her titties." The saleswoman choked, covering her mouth with a handkerchief.

Bobo was in his purple sharkskin suit and Cuban heel shit-kicker boots, the same suit my mother wouldn't let me get. He went into perfect gentleman mode. He told the saleslady his momma gave him money to buy this present. He yanked out some cheap pink thing from the bin.

"Now ah need me some underpants."

Well, there was a Pennleigh underwear sale, said the

saleswoman. Any two pairs for one dollar. Or regular 69-cent two-ply cotton briefs.

"Lady, ah want me the Sanforized boxer shorts. Same as mah uncle get." Limpy was a connoisseur of haberdashery, and Bobo knew fabric questions that I didn't have a clue about.

Okay, she said, as she plucked out a three pack, wrapped together.

"My momma said ah got to try 'em, see they fit right," said Bobo.

Well, came the lady, it wasn't store policy to try on underwear. But since he seemed like such a smart young fellow he could go in the changing room. Bobo bowed. He marched into a changing room. A minute later, a pair of white underpants flew over the door.

"This don't fit!"

Then, one by one, pairs of white underpants came sailing from behind the dressing booth into the aisle. "Hey, Jock, catch! Put it back, this one don't fit, either!" yelled Bobo. Bobo had me to play for. A command performance for one. Life was a big show. And I was busting a gut. Any behavior was justified, he would go to any lengths, no matter at whose expense—to get that big laugh. As with any Borscht Belt comic, the high from the laughs was addictive. So you had to keep 'em comin'. What was the difference between Bobo and Jerry Lewis? I couldn't yet differentiate between stage and street. All the world was a stage. Either that or one big insane asylum. It was worth detention, a trip to the principal, it was worth busting your lip in a pratfall, suspension from school—as long as you got that big laugh on the way down. Mrs. O'Leary said of Bobo's antics that the only joke was on Bobo. That he would ruin his life, and I would go down in ruin, too, if I followed him.

The saleslady summoned the manager while Bobo was in the dressing room. He strode out in the next pair and modeled some white boxers before the mirror in his black socks. The manager was angry and demanded he march back in and take off the shorts. So Bobo apologized, "Hey, mister, I'm sorry, just trying to find the right size." He went back in to change.

Then he sailed the last pair of white boxers into the aisle. "Got shit stains!" he hollered. Sure enough, Bobo had wiped a skid mark into the drawers.

With one of Bobo's pants legs still off, we were chased out of W.T. Grant's. They warned us never to come back.

38. The Carnival

LIKE A DISTANT TRAIN WHISTLE, delirious screams all the way down from the Glen Cove Carnival drifted into my bedroom window. Carried by the wind, a ballpark cheer came from far away. I had to be washed, brushed and *in bed* by 9 p.m. That was the law. Sometimes it was still light out, and that killed me. But the colored kids were taking part in some sophisticated nighttime fun that excluded me. Here I was, a rich white cracker who'd been to Coney Island, Palisades Amusement Park, Yankee Stadium, Times Square and Broadway. Yet the grass looked greener in the ghetto. Somehow, I imagined colored folks were having a better time.

And so, I begged Drake to take me to the carnival one Friday night, when my parents were in New York. I begged Mrs. O'Leary to let Drake take me. She finally gave in. Drake drove me and his girlfriend Suzette down in his T-Bird. Mrs. O warned us to be back by 10 sharp, or else.

Every June the travelling carnival pitched tents on the dirt baseball lot between the dumps and my school. Like a parade, it was one of the few public events attended equally by white and colored. I sensed the aura of two-bit corruption, where midway barkers and hucksters tried to sucker the public coin. It was not really family entertainment. I hated the circus, but I loved shabby carnivals. There were times when I entered the fun house, and I didn't want to leave. Somehow, this topsy-turvy environment provided equilibrium from the world of insanity outside. Once or twice, my father had to come in and pull me out.

Down at the carnival, people with hats from mysterious organizations walked about: Glen Cove Lodge 1016, Order of the Sons of Italy; Women of the Moose, Chapter 1115, Moose Hall (Mrs. Wilshire was a member of that one). The top-billed attraction for the weekend was Ed Ferrar & His Jungle Cats, a low-rent circus act. The winner of a "Charming Child" contest would be announced on Saturday, definitely for white people. A display featured the 1964 Betty Crocker Homemaker of Tomorrow—a clean-cut high school girl in the kitchen. It was closed at night.

But most intriguing, beyond the entry gate and open only at night, was a heart-shaped "kissing booth." Shauna O'Grady, the Lions Club Lassie, sat beneath a banner, where kisses cost a stiff fifty cents. "Now that takes the cake," Drake said, bemused. He knew her uncle, a merchant marine barking from his wheelchair by the booth. The Lions Club Lassie was a high school sophomore, in her mid-teens, which sure seemed like a big girl to me. In the back of my mind, I might have loved a kiss from Shauna, but perish the thought. I would have been way too embarrassed to admit it. Ostensibly innocent as apple pie, the kissing booth somehow seemed smarmier than the proverbial Canal Street whorehouses of legend. Shauna sat on a stool in the booth with a practiced smile. For fifty cents, all you really got was a harmless peck on the cheek, raising money for paraplegic merchant marines.

"A great cause," said Mr. O'Grady to Drake, his thumbs tightly behind his suspenders as his eyes darted about. And how was Drake's dear old mother doing these days, he asked. He then recited scholastic achievements of his niece, for Drake to relay back to Mrs. O'Leary, who once babysat Shauna.

Directly across from the kissing booth, I spotted Bobo

and Uncle Limpy, stationed against a candy apple stand. Limpy walked in a bop, his do-rag on, bouncing up and down as if walking uphill. He sure liked his sweets, and bit into his candy apple like a horse.

"Ah won me a *prize*," said Bobo, tossing around a stuffed bear that already began to fall apart. He'd stolen it from some other kid.

"Hey, Jock, what'chu win?"

"Nothin' yet."

Limpy and Drake didn't acknowledge each other, even though each man accompanied one of us. Colored folks gravitated to a shabbier part of the carnival, somewhere in the back. That was where I wanted to go, pulling Drake and Suzette along. They followed reluctantly. We passed a card game that colored men were playing.

"Strictly a Negro's game," came the dealer, from the side of his mouth—just in case Drake was interested.

"His money green. What the fuck do you care?" said a colored lady.

"Strictly a Negro's game," repeated the dealer without looking up from his cards. We kept walking.

I saw a sideshow banner for a Negro fat man. Drake shelled out quarters for us, and we entered the little tent. The guy on exhibit was the fattest man I'd ever seen. He sat upon a wooden bench, both legs propped up on couches. He reached to turn down the volume on a TV, wiping his hands from a greasy drumstick he was eating. The huge outline of his balls strained against the tent-like bloomers he wore. There was a sweet smell in the tent, maybe the smell of calories. He went into his daily spiel in a bored monotone.

"Mah name is Jolly Jackson and ah weigh over six-hundred pound. I was married wunst and had two children. I weighed only three-hundred pound then. Mah wife and kids is skinny. I like to watch TV."

I asked what his favorite TV show was.

"*Petticoat Junction*," he answered.

There were loose chickens in a pen outside, and I asked whether they were his.

"Yeah, I eats dem chickens," he said.

"*Manners*," said Drake, nudging me. "Let the man speak."

"Ah like to watch kites fly, and play jigsaw puzzles. I can't walk no more. And I need to live in this tent, so's they can wheel me out the front. They tell me ahm too fat to fit through any door nowadays. But that's okay, cause I like to watch kites fly and play jigsaw puzzles."

"Thank you, Mister," said Drake. Suzette squeezed in at Drake's side, her arm around him tightly. She seemed horrified. But I thought Jolly was amazing. A list of Jolly Jackson facts on the wall claimed Jolly had once swept an event known as the "Big Negro Pie-Eating Contest" across state fairs in the Southwest. He apparently ate much slower now. I wanted to stay longer but Jolly turned the volume back up on his TV and began watching obliviously.

A salty old colored gent stood at a crackling microphone, guessing people's weight and age. "How many underwears you got home, white cracker?" he asked me. All the colored folks around cracked up. "Fo' pair?"

I shrugged.

"Write it down, write it down on this pad, ah'll guess it right."

"How many do a chile need?" shrugged an old lady.

"I don't like his questions," cracked Drake, getting his Irish up. "And I don't like this spot." From the small colored section of the carnival, Drake herded us back toward the main drag.

Silver whirling machines magically whipped pink sugar into a heavenly cloud of cotton candy. It made the whole night smell great. Drake wanted to win a Kewpie doll for Suzette. He tried his hand at the strongman's sledgehammer, rolling up his sleeves and spitting in his palms. Drake actually had "Mother" tattooed in a Valentine's heart on his arm. He usually kept his cigarettes rolled up in the sleeve. He reared back and pounded the mallet onto the mark, which rang the bell at the top, right up to Popeye. "Now, try 'n' beat that. You wanna try, Josh?"

"Naw," I said, ashamed of my skinny nine-year-old arms, which hadn't started to develop. I was unaware that they ever would, and this was a matter of shame.

But I could throw like a bat outta hell—overhand, sidearm or three-quarters. Defending myself, I'd keep whole gangs at bay with apples. God bless Granny Smith and thank God for crab apples. Survival ammo. When I knocked down some milk bottles on the midway, Drake was impressed. Throwing was my secret weapon, the one thing I could always count on. I could out-throw Drake or any grown man I came up against. If not for speed, then for accuracy, but most of all, for distance. I was able to whip my arm behind my entire bodyweight and fly a rock or an apple a mile. From the back of a little league outfield to home plate. I practiced for hours with thousands of crab apples that fell from the trees everywhere. The milk-bottle game required some extra zip with the rubber baseballs provided, but they went down.

"Boy, you got the stuff," said Drake, and I beamed with pride. "We'll have to go for Mets pitching tryouts."

Fat Emily walked by, the fattest girl in our school. "Fat laigs, fat laigs!" shouted Bobo. "Jolly Jackson yo' daddy!"

Emily pursed her lips and turned her head, hiding her shame behind an air of superiority.

"Now, that's not right," Drake instructed me. Tsk tsk. "Fat girls have feelings, too." This was a kernel of wisdom I'd never forget.

Limpy was still stationed across from the kissing booth. He worked his teeth with a toothpick after finishing a candy apple. A few retired merchant marines in seaman's caps lounged about in wheelchairs. The Lions Club Lassie had probably delivered another 50 smackers in the hour since we'd arrived. She was working like a filly. Her lipstick was smeary and she developed a sloe-eyed grin, trying to feign enthusiasm. She was losing her smile.

"Peck on the cheek, peck on the cheek! Have a smooch from Shauna O'Grady," went the paraplegic barker from his wheelchair, "the Lions Club Sweetheart. The merchant marines give their all at sea, delivering goods to the land of the free."

Would she kiss on the lips? Would she do a French kiss? How about if you anteed up double? Just how far would Miss Shauna go for the merchant marines? And what kind of uncle would put a girl up to this? Drake did his bit by purchasing a box of paraplegic merchant marine cookies for Suzette.

Then Limpy made his move. He pushed off the side of the candy apple stand, tossing his apple core to the ground. He nonchalantly took a place at the back of the line.

Drake took notice and stiffened upright. His lips tightened. "Now, that takes the cake," he mumbled to Suzette, from the side of his mouth. He reached in his back pocket for the switchblade, which flicked open. Switchblades were illegal in these parts, just like firecrackers or brass knuckles. You either had to remake the knife yourself, greasing or removing the latch lock. Sort of like making a gun into an automatic. Otherwise, you bought an automatic switchblade on the black market, one activated by a little black button. Drake began picking his fingernails with his stylish Italian import, while he watched the line. Now I'd seen Drake absent-mindedly pick at his nails with the knife any number of times, when he didn't mean anything by it other than to pick his nails.

"I don't like to see that kind of thing," he said, under his breath to Suzette. "I don't like it at all. It just isn't right."

There were several white fellows ahead of Limpy. The first of them forked over his donation, received his fifty-cent peck on the cheek, and blushing, returned one to Shauna's cheek. Everyone laughed. All in good sport, all for the cause, nothing the least bit unseemly. Moving up in line, Uncle Limpy took out an Ace comb, lifted his do-rag, and gave a jaunty lilt to his processed pompadour. He licked his chops. There were still specks of candy-apple red in his teeth.

"I can't stand to see this. Right in front of her poor old uncle," said Drake. "And what would her *father* think?" The merchant marines glanced furtively at Limpy, who seemed to remain oblivious. He reached into his tight, black, pressed chinos, and sifted out small change, moving his big cracked lips as he counted. The moment of truth was coming.

The merchant marines ceased conversation. You could slice the atmosphere with a knife, as they say. The color drained from Shauna's uncle's face like a tourniquet tightening, and the other old salts in wheelchairs looked to him, awaiting his response. Perhaps he now regretted the folly of the kissing booth, a carnival anachronism long past its heyday. Shauna had already done the merchant seamen proud, she did her bit. It was time to stop pimping out her 15-year-old lips. A mutinous sea-hardy rage came into his old blue eyes. And then it was Limpy's turn. Somebody had to do something.

"Can I speak with you a moment, sir?" asked Drake, assuredly polite, but beckoning with his finger. The knife was no longer conspicuous, and I couldn't tell where it was. Limpy squinted at the big chivalrous Irishman, as if to notice him for the first time. The two worst drivers in Glen Cove came face to face.

"Now listen . . . you've gotta be kiddin'," chuckled Drake, as if taking Limpy into his confidence.

"No, I ain't foolin'. Ah want to pay my money for dis booth."

"Well, it's simple. Your money ain't any good here today," said Drake.

"What'chu mean mah money no good?"

Drake waved to Shauna, who waited on the podium, perplexed. "You okay, darlin'? Take a break, sweetheart, you been givin' out honey all day." Her uncle agreed, wheeling toward her protectively.

"That's Bobo's uncle," I interjected.

"Oh yeah? Bobo's uncle?" said Drake. "Tell you what, Uncle. Why don't you come back Sunday."

"What time, mah man?" said Limpy.

"Sunday, at three in the morning."

Drake seemed pretty cool in hot spots like these. At least when I was around. For a guy who couldn't hold a job, he seemed to naturally take charge of things. And the merchant seamen stood right behind him, albeit in wheelchairs.

"Now what'chu all go talking about Sunday morning, when you know damn well everything be close," said Limpy.

"Oh, yeah?" said Drake. "Well tell you what, my friend. I'll be here."

Mrs. O'Leary couldn't have appeared at a better moment to fetch us. We were late. It was past 10 p.m. She ran her battered station wagon right up to us on the dirt grounds. Bobo grabbed the fifty cents out of his uncle's hand and ran up to the booth. He bowed debonairly, handed the change to Shauna's uncle, then took her in his arms. He kissed her on the lips. At any other time, this act might not have been tolerated. But somehow, at this moment, it didn't seem inappropriate, at least compared to what might have been. Drake and Limpy were still squared, neither man backing off.

"Get in the car, Drake," ordered Mrs. O'Leary, with exaggerated calm.

"Oh, Mother."

"I said, get in the car, Drake."

"But, *Mother*. I'm having a *fight*."

"You get in this goddamn car right now, Son."

Drake was genuinely disgusted, as if his mother had spoiled a big moment. "Hell, she ain't *my* goddamn niece.

What the hell do I care?" spat Drake out the side of his mouth, angrily plunging into the car and slamming the door. Suzette and I followed behind.

I heard Limpy moan tiredly, "Man, I just wanted to get me a little . . . kiss."

"Well, ah got *me* one," said Bobo. "She *fine*."

We left in a trail of carnival dust. Drake leaned out the window and shouted one last cryptic challenge: "Sunday, three in the morning." Mrs. O'Leary drove up to Drake's car in the far parking lot. She told him to get in and drive straight home to our house. He took Suzette's hand without a word and opened the door for her. Then he went to his side, got in, and slammed the door.

Bobo's uncle was a bum, came Mrs. O'Leary. "What a waste," she said, shaking her head. But what exactly about Limpy was being wasted? What was society being deprived of that Limpy might offer, had he led a more respectable life? Would not the United Negro College Fund even concede that hey, a mind is a terrible thing to waste and all, but let's just let this one go and cut our losses. Every human being is unique and brings something special into God's kingdom. But let's be reasonable here. Limpy was not part of the Talented Tenth. I'd once seen him enter a grocery store for some Kleenex and come out with a box of Kotex. Couldn't Mrs. O'Leary just let this one mind go to waste, like a punch-drunk boxer's, and be done with it?

When we got home, Mrs. O'Leary fretted as the night wore on. There was no sign of Drake.

39. Mr. Wilshire's Secret

DRAKE DRANK BEERS AT A mysterious cocktail lounge in town called the Clock Tavern. The Clock stayed open later than any place else in Glen Cove. It was closed during the daytime, but at night the neon clock and crossed cocktail glasses were aglow. Once I heard someone call it a "cheater's bar."

"Don't get him started," Mrs. O'Leary would plead about her son, looking heavenward. "Just don't get him started." So whenever Drake arrived home after the carnival, nobody was to mention Uncle Limpy.

It wasn't hard to get Drake started on that particular subject—a subject that maybe you shouldn't bring up too often. Even he would forewarn, *Don't get me started*. But it didn't take much to get his Irish up. A drinker overheard at the Clock Tavern, say, bemoaning a Black person's promotion. A complaint from some old barfly broad about "colored gals using the ladies room who think their fannies are as good as ours." Drake stood ready to take the ball and run. An awful lot of white people kept some extremely distasteful Negro experiences knotted up inside. At least the white people that Drake knew. Though personally unaffected, he took issue with rising crime and Negro militancy.

Pickpockets, once the scourge of Olde New York, had become quaint and passé. Pickpockets, said Drake, were white. But muggers were "the colored," said Drake, even though the news didn't specify race while reporting on this burgeoning trend. Merciless street encounters where wallets, watches, purses or jewelry were violently extracted. Gone was the finesse and charm of the pickpocket, which seemed like a foxtrot with Fred Astaire by comparison. "Good people can't go into the city anymore," warned Drake, on the dangers of New York. We were an hour's drive away in Glen Cove. But Drake never ventured to New York City, and like his mother, possessed some distinctive pride in being a true Long Islander.

Finely tuned to the winds of Negrophobia, Drake was adept at getting people started.

Go on . . . he would nudge some hesitant palooka at lunch break, lending a sympathetic ear. *Then what?* Some gentle prodding, empathetic concern in his brow. *Don't be afraid to talk. Now let's be honest.* And off went the white coworker, taking the bait, grateful to unload a dire Negro conflict, confirming Drake's worst suspicions. Drake offered a sarcastic smile, gestating into a slow boil as he began to brood through the week.

Mrs. O'Leary washed and pressed his work clothes and prepared his lunch pail every day. "He's a working man," she boasted, happy to shoo him out the door each morning along the straight and narrow.

But Drake had recently met "the man down the street" at his new factory job. The man was disgruntled, having to labor side by side with a certain ethnic group on the assembly line. These people were not only slow on the job and contemptuous, but they didn't pull their weight or reach their quotas. And, according to the man down the street— Mr. Wilshire—they got away with it.

Once on the job, Mr. Wilshire posited, "Hey, O'Leary. What would you do if you saw a hundred of 'em surrounding your car?" Drake didn't answer, but slept on that for weeks. A hundred coloreds could overtake your car even if you floored the engine. Food for thought.

Another day at the lunch commissary, Mr. Wilshire finally *got started*. Drake sat spellbound as he confided the most extraordinary episode. Relating the tale to Mrs. O'Leary in the weeks to come, Drake would turn ashen. From what I overheard, in fits and starts, the event, (abetted by a little modern-day research) unfolded something like this:

Sometime after America entered World War II, young Jacob Wilshire and his older brother, Joe, set out by car to Detroit. Detroit had become the "Arsenal of Democracy." Recruiters toured the South, promising white people jobs and higher wages at Northern war and defense plants. They even exhorted Negroes to head North, where there was pig meat a'plenty for all, supper's waiting in Detroit. Migrant workers arrived in such numbers that it was impossible to house them all. Some began referring to Detroit as the "arsehole" of democracy.

Joe and Jacob Wilshire were both declared 4F in the draft. Might have had something to do with inbreeding, or possibly their illiteracy. Rather than stand around scratching their anuses throughout the war, they left the strip-mining hills of their Appalachian hamlet. They sought employment. Like Drake O'Leary, they never aspired to anything beyond the call of laboring for someone else. They would never seek out their own farmland. But they wanted to add their two-cents to the war effort and make something of themselves. Maybe a job at the Packard plant, building engines for bombers and PT boats. They'd never been on an airplane, but the chance to help build one seemed astonishing.

The Wilshire family car, affectionately known as "Old Nellie," was a late Model T that Joe kept in operating order. Even then, an earlier generation of Wilshires accumulated rusty heaps of spare parts piled up across their swept-dirt yard. For a week both of them studied a Mobiloil road map. They plotted their route. Gasoline rationing slowed them down, requiring more stops to refuel, as they wound through the backwaters, sometimes driving through the same small towns twice. There were no superhighways, just small roads through towns across the heartland. A few times, their tank went dry and they had to sleep by the roadside, waiting on the kindness of strangers. They were young, dumb hicks, and this was their first sojourn into the outside world.

When they finally crossed the city limits of Detroit, a brace of ragged white men approached at the Woodward Avenue stoplight. "Which side are you on?" they asked, to the bewildered Wilshire brothers, who merely shrugged.

"You oughtn't go that direction," warned one of the men. The brothers assumed they were also unemployed migrant workers who didn't want competition. So they continued driving down Woodward Avenue toward a neighborhood called Paradise Valley—more commonly known as the "Black Bottom."

By 1943 the number of Blacks in Detroit had doubled since 1933 to 200,000, and racial tensions in the city grew accordingly. To protest unfair conditions, some Blacks began a "bumping campaign"—walking into whites on the streets and bumping them off the sidewalks, or nudging them in elevators. Local and national media anticipated trouble. *Life* magazine called the situation dynamite.

The brothers saw Black people in numbers they were unaccustomed to seeing. And they seemed mighty riled up. Could they be this angry just because Jacob and Joe had driven into their neighborhood? Had the brothers turned wrong down a one-way street? As their jalopy puttered along, the stares grew more hostile by the minute. It was the most fateful wrong turn of their lives. Suddenly they came upon a hornet's nest of rioters, big-city Negroes who were yelling at them louder than they ever heard Negroes yell down South. Factory and autoworkers in muddy work boots and caps, many wielding tire irons. Some wore Stetson hats, coming from out of pool halls holding pool cues.

The road became impassable. They were burning tires

and looting stores. Rocks pelted the car windows.

"Them niggers was swarmed over Old Nellie in seconds," he told Drake. The car was knocked over.

"We's just lookin' for work!" screamed Joe, the last words Jacob heard out of his brother's mouth.

Calloused Negro hands reached through the broken window of the upturned passenger seat, pulling Jacob Wilshire by the scruff of his neck and the roots of his hair through the broken window. "Get the white man, get the white man!" As he was repeatedly kicked, he saw his brother hit in the head with a rock. They were all throwing rocks. "Hunkie! Hunkie!"

Someone, perhaps a guardian angel, hurled a shopping basket over Jacob's head, which may have saved his life, as he was kicked and pelted with stones. He saw his brother Joe pulled from the car and beaten by rioters. They torched the car, and that was the end of Old Nellie.

"I thought I'd died and gone to hell, and hell was full of niggers," Mr. Wilshire told Drake. On the ground, he caught glimpses of rioters throwing bricks at store windows. He saw other white people, firemen, dropping their hoses to flee. He saw upturned peddlers' carts and heard alarms wailing. Then he heard shotgun blasts scattering the rioters, and got a whiff of tear gas, further convulsing him.

Semi-conscious in an ambulance, he heard a blaring P.A. from a sound truck ordering looters to disperse immediately and return home. Stunned, he sat against a wall in an emergency room, watching other injured arrive. Four-stretcher ambulance trucks deposited casualties every fifteen minutes. He remained oblivious to his brother's whereabouts. Negro bloodies were cordoned off from white bloodies in the waiting area. Through his delirium, he saw a dead rioter, wheeled in on a gurney, covered by sheets, with a Black arm hanging down. He saw another in a ruined zoot suit, caked with blood. The man in the zoot suit staggered and crawled across the corridor. A hospital attendant followed, mopping the linoleum floor to keep up with his drippings, as he left his slime like the trail of a slug. The white gowns of nurses were smeared in riot blood and grease.

The Wilshire brothers had sailed right into what would become known as the Detroit Race Riot of 1943. It happened here in America, during World War II. Federal troops in armored cars and jeeps with automatic weapons were finally called in. The sight of the troops on Woodward Avenue cooled the fervor, and the mobs began to melt away. Thirty-six hours of rioting claimed thirty-four lives, twenty-five of them Black. More than 1,800 people were arrested. A white doctor making a house call in a Black neighborhood was also pulled from his car and beaten to death. Thirteen murders remained unsolved. One of them was Joe Wilshire.

Troops occupied Detroit for six months until Roosevelt felt it was safe to pull them out in January of 1944. Accusations about the causes of the riot that took his brother's life reflected fanaticism of the time. In Mississippi, the *Jackson Daily News* blamed the race riot on Eleanor Roosevelt's labors toward social equality, stating, "In Detroit, a city noted for the growing impudence and insolence of its Negro population, an attempt was made to put your preachments into practice, Mrs. Roosevelt."

Representative Martin Dies of Texas, chairman of the House Un-American Activities Committee, assigned blame on the Japanese-Americans who "had infiltrated Detroit's Negro population to spread hatred of the white man and disrupt the war effort." Hysteria about subversive Axis attempts to weaken the nation abounded. Or was it fomented by the Communists?

German-controlled Vichy radio claimed the riot exposed "the internal disorganization of a country torn by social injustice, race hatreds, regional disputes, the violence of an irritated proletariat and the gangsterism of a capitalistic police."

But to Jacob Wilshire, it was just "the night the niggers killed my brother." Like the Kennedys, who also lost a favorite son named Joe, Joe Wilshire had apparently been the most promising amongst his own clan. A clan with little to offer the world. But he didn't even die for his country. (And he didn't have JFK to follow up, he just had Mr. Wilshire.) He died for nothing. Jacob's ten children, who were off and on my friends and enemies, never got to meet their Uncle Joe. They were only indoctrinated with the legend of his slaughter.

No official from the Arsenal of Democracy ever apologized to Jacob Wilshire on behalf of the city. After a day in the hospital, nobody paid his Greyhound fare back home. Like all white folks, he was clueless about racial strife and strained job markets due to huge migrations of Negroes to the North. He didn't care about poor housing conditions at the Brewster or Sojourner Truth Housing Projects in Detroit. His own family lived in a shit-hole back home. Racial divides would not emerge on such a visible and widespread scale again until the Civil Rights movement a decade or two later. It was unclear what happened to the body of his brother, he didn't even remember, and the family couldn't pay for delivery back home. Needless to say, Jacob would never return to Detroit. He somehow migrated to Glen Cove where, if nothing else, he would breed like a rat, establishing a large brood that would forever be on guard against "the niggers."

I noticed Drake began to make a habit of locking his car doors whenever he left the driveway.

40. Drake vs. Limpy

TWO NIGHTS AFTER THE CARNIVAL, on Sunday, Drake left early for a couple of cold ones at the Clock. He was "in a mood," according to Mrs. O'Leary. Late into evening the phone rang. One of those dreaded calls in the dead of night that Mrs. O'Leary always knew, in the darkness of her soul, was ringing just for her, and not my parents. It was never good news. It might be a nephew or cousin, allotted their one public phone call from the county lockup. Or her bosom buddy Lu, whose father had a heart attack, or one of the sobbing former fiancées Drake had fertilized with offspring. They were like abandoned litters. Her worst fear in life was answering the phone late at night.

I heard her moan downstairs in the kitchen, the tension in her voice. Sgt. Goldstein called from the emergency room at North Shore Hospital. Sgt. Goldstein, the only Jewish cop on the fifty-man force, was Glen Cove's most decorated policeman. He'd been on front-desk duty that night and took the report. Yes, Drake was all right, but there had been an "altercation."

It was a slow night, as always. The Glen Cove police blotter contained small infractions of the kind that might occur in the world of a Norman Rockwell painting. Dog bites were phoned in by doctors; windows broken by a baseball or a stone. Someone's wife received a "vulgar telephone call." The occasional report of a raincoat flasher in a car before little girls didn't generate the same alarm as it would years later. Various and sundry "public nuisance" arrests, never specified, or public intoxication incidents outside the Clock Tavern. It was rarely noted whether such incidents were racially motivated.

The Glen Cove police were efficient, professional and unobtrusive. They were not like Nassau County cops, who seemed to draw more attention to themselves whenever they arrived on the scene. But the Suffolk County police had the most fearsome reputation. Negroes from Nassau County often avoided crossing into ultra-conservative Republican Suffolk County, the eastern half of Long Island, farthest from the city.

All three departments knew the name of Drake O'Leary, enough so that Sgt. Goldstein personally called his mother. He was not regarded as a criminal so much as a nuisance ever since high school. Drake was a greaser in the 1950s, when he had his first car wreck. He had a few rumbles in high school, a couple of switchblades confiscated. The gang of Oyster Bay grease monkeys Drake hung with had long since dissolved. But he still acted like the gang was behind him. Tonight's call involved an accident by the carnival grounds at Garvies Point. Drake and Uncle Limpy crashed into each other.

After they were patched up for minor injuries at North Shore Hospital, a parking lot altercation occurred. Drake was arrested. Arrested along with Limpy Monk were one Worsey Johnson and one Rufus Barnes, both of Glen Cove. Back at the accident scene, three tire irons were retrieved from the front seat of Limpy's car. Drake's car had a bat, empty beer bottles and a switchblade. What were they planning that night, I wondered—to bat each other to death? Over Shauna O'Grady? The men, if you could call them that, were all taken to Nassau County Jail after the hospital. Drake refused to call his mother, so Sgt. Goldstein performed the courtesy.

Drake never could negotiate those turns, didn't navigate well at intersections. Rounding Glen Cove Avenue by my school, he barely missed a battered Cadillac that honked at a red light. When Drake O'Leary got honked by a Negro, he didn't like it. That car wasn't just honking him, but also his dear old *mither*, his dead brother, his deadbeat dad who deserted the family, and the whole frickin' world of decent, upstanding, hard-working, red-meat-fish-or-fowl-eatin' Irish.

"Those colored guys slammed into *me*," Drake announced to the police, when they pried the door open. Uncle Limpy, feigning whiplash, claimed Drake slammed into him.

A fight is an intimate experience, and the arrest records of both men now shared this intimacy. Drake and Uncle Limpy's rap sheets integrated. After a background check on their licenses came through, it was apparent both men were leading causes of car wrecks amongst their respective races. And Limpy had rigged his horn at the shop to honk louder, in order to irritate white folks. They were booked for a hearing before Glen Cove City Court Judge Joseph Muldoon.

Mrs. O'Leary made bail for her son. He was back in court the next week. Exceedingly polite to nearly everyone, Drake became aggravated when he spoke to the judge—the one personage, of all people, for whom he should have exhibited his very best manners. Uncle Limpy and Drake stood with bowed heads before the judge:

MULDOON. Now, why would you two nice gentlemen be out playin' bumper cars in the wee hours of a Sunday night?

O'LEARY. I was on my way to go clamming, Your Honor.

MULDOON. Clammin' was it. At three in the mornin'?

O'LEARY. Yes, Sir. Well, better to catch them asleep, Your Honor. An old fisherman's trick.

MULDOON. O'Leary, what do you take me for, a fool? I suppose it was a school night for the clams, too. Have you not grown up yet?

O'LEARY. I know my business.

MULDOON. The only two drivers out at that time, when the decent among us are in bed, and you both couldn't avoid each other? Mr. Monk, you are a menace to the roads of this city.

MONK. Yes, suh.

MULDOON. I'm revoking your license. Do you understand what that means?

MONK. Means ah cain't drive no more.

MULDOON. If you are seen behind the wheel of an automobile during the next year, you will be sent back to jail.

MONK. Yes, suh.

MULDOON. That's a $60 fine each, payable to the clerk within thirty days—or else thirty days in jail. Disturbin' the Peace. Both licenses revoked for the remainder of one year. O'Leary, I don't want to see you in my courtroom again. And stay away from the colored. Case dismissed.

We wouldn't hear from Drake for quite a while.

41. Naked Fear

BY LATE SPRING, MRS. O'LEARY began to sweat profusely. She carried a rag and frequently mopped her brow. If she ever farted in public, which, truth be told, was rare, she bounced in her gait, covering it over by saying, "Beep, beep, beep."

As any Friday approached, we knew my parents were headed to the city. We'd be seeing O'Leary at her worst. As was typical, Lu came over after work. The gals sat down for a beer on the patio. They were looking over the *Playboy* they'd confiscated from my brother.

"Will you look at these," said O'Leary, with a tsk-tsk. "Naked as the day they were born."

"Naked as jaybirds," said Lu, adjusting her cat's-eye glasses to inspect the page. "Where is the *shame* today? If I'da ever done those kinda pictures in a magazine, before God, church and country, I'da never been able to face my dear old father again. Do they dare go to confession? I dunno, where I come from, it's a sin."

Lu let the centerfold fall open, shaking her head in disbelief. And then O'Leary disengaged her butt from the wicker chair and posed in grotesque mockery of the centerfold, her hand coyly on her arthritic hip, batting her eyes. Lu doubled up laughing.

O'Leary and Lu only expressed romantic interest in older men, in their sixties or seventies. Once Drew and I awoke to the sound of ghastly inhuman screams. We ran downstairs to knock on O'Leary's door. It was "just some cats," said Mrs. O'Leary, wistfully, "out in the garbage cans making love." I thereafter associated the term "making love" with the spine-tingling screeches of fornicating alley cats.

We were put to bed by ten. It couldn't have been an hour later when I awoke to the sound of O'Leary, calling my name. I got out of bed and went downstairs to her bedroom door, which was halfway open.

"*Jrosh*, I want to ask you something." She sounded unusually soft and wistful under her covers. She paused fitfully, gathering her thoughts. Her dentures floated in a glass of Efferdent on her night table.

"Jrosh."

"Yes, Mrs. O'Leary?"

She held a bottle of cheap sherry, a carton of which was hidden beneath her bed. ". . . Would you like to see my breasts?"

"No."

"Because you can, ya know."

"No, that's okay."

"Just thought I'd ask."

The pit of my stomach sank. I went back to bed a bit sickened that O'Leary would think anyone in the world would want to see her naked. Something resembling an arthritic, overweight chicken. The very idea was a threat, not an offer. Thankfully, that was the first and last time she ever mentioned it.

42. Catfight

CAPPING OFF OUR THIRD-GRADE school year, a fight occurred in front of the school. It was the most naked display of raw anger I'd ever seen. It was between two colored girls. They were probably in their early teens, and they'd come to pick up some younger cousins. The girls wore Keds sneakers with holes, and white, stretched-out socks fallen down around the ankles, no elasticity left. They fought with their hands, their fists, their teeth and their fingernails. I had never seen boys, or men, fight with such feral ferocity.

What triggered the fight? No one was sure. "Gimme back mah fifty cent!" one of them screamed. They dropped their schoolbooks and stared into each other's eyes. Each stare was so intimate and hateful, nothing else existed. Then they began to circle. One held a pencil.

"Don't you point that pe'cil at me, nigger!"

"Ah'll point it at your ass, fucka, and kick it, too!"

"You goan kick *mah* ass? Well, c'mon, we'll see who be doin' the kickin'. You say you can beat *mah* butt? Oh, no! We'll see whose butt get kicked!"

"Ah'll *stick* it in yo' ass, sista!" And then with a mighty roundhouse swing, she jabbed it right into the other's upturned rear-end. A piercing scream rang out. The wounded girl froze, then yanked the jagged half of a broken No. 2 pencil from her butt. She looked at it in amazement. Then she jumped onto the other girl.

"Make way, make way!" shouted some other excited teenage colored girls, scattering onlookers to give the fighters room. Shirts tore, revealing white bra straps. At first there were jeers from other colored girls rooting them on. But the crowd hushed up fast. There was no sport involved, just blind hatred. Soon there was blood on the pavement, along with fistfuls of hair like clumps of steel wool, pulled out at the roots, leaving raw sores on their heads. Both girls bit off more than they could chew—and spit out the remains. I'd never seen professional athletes expend that degree of adrenaline. They were in some altered state. No boy their age would have stood a chance. Even Cassius Clay or Frankenstein might be in over his head.

It is axiomatic that if you stand there on the street *watching* a fight, you are part of it. As in the scientific method, the very act of observing changes the nature of it. And so it went double for street fights. As I stood in awe, watching these two girls do things I'd never seen done in a fight, one of the cheering section suddenly took offense at my presence. Not of Bobo or Jeffrey, but me.

"What'chu lookin' at, white muthafucka?" My heart sank.

"He ain't no cracker," said Jeffrey.

"Who you talkin' at, little nigger?" said the teenage colored girl. "Ah'll kick yo' Black ass, too!" Even Bobo backed off.

Mr. Gaines, our school janitor, peered out from the entrance, in his overalls. The girls could have torn him to shreds. He backed away, letting the door close, and went back to his janitor's closet. Surely there was nothing in his supply closet to handle this type of mess. But a minute later he emerged holding a large fishnet.

The girls were now frozen on the ground in a mutual chokehold. One's finger seemed embedded in the other's eye, while both had death grips on each other's hair. As Mr. Gaines carefully approached, both came unglued and an unruly dance ensued, janitor vs. berserk colored girls.

Mr. Gaines maneuvered into position and tossed the net over both of them. And then the fight turned against the net. Their eyes bulged as their faces squirmed against the netting like sharks, pulling with futility at the netting. The more they pulled, the more they sealed themselves in. They had tried to blind each other, and after it was halted, it was not clear whether either had succeeded.

Mr. Gaines held the net and its bleeding contents down by standing on it. The Nassau County police arrived and maneuvered the whole mess into the back of the squad car. They hit the siren and sped off to the hospital. Once again, reality trumped any monster movie I'd ever seen.

Throughout that summer, mamas who heard about it would admonish their children: "Better behave and come on home now, befo' they th'ow that nigger net on *yo'* ass."

43. Nature Boy

ON CERTAIN DAYS, THE GOOD Mrs. O'Leary awoke and proclaimed, "What a beautiful day."

I drew back in disgust.

"Anyone can enjoy a beautiful day," she said, light-heartedly.

"Even colored kids?"

"It doesn't cost a dime."

"Who cares?"

Birds in flight across a clear blue sky, flowers in bloom, the smell of spring? That was sissy crap, for old ladies. Real beauty—though I'd never use such terminology—was found in Universal horror movies, *Famous Monsters*, Aurora models (Aurora Plastics Corp. itself was in nearby West Hempstead), plastic vomit, bicycles and the sight of George Harrison's black Gretsch Country Gentleman. Electric guitars channeled lightning from the gods, and they looked good enough to eat.

And yet . . . the rites of nature had a profound effect, even to a boy who professed to love monster stuff. So, at the risk of sounding like a sissy: During summer I would stare out in wonder at the Atlantic Ocean for hours, imagining the shores of Europe at the other end, where there were no Negroes. Gerry & the Pacemakers lived there. Autumn in Glen Cove contained all the colors of an old oil painting come to life, the air heavy with a cidery scent of apples. The suburban scent of charcoal steaks, wafting out of the twilight from unseen barbecue grills somewhere down the block or in the ether. Wild pumpkin patches. Maple, oak, ash, birch, dogwood and weeping willow trees, all with their own personalities, trees that you came to know individually, by their branches or deformities or their bark. Only Mrs. O'Leary knew their names—"over by the dogwood tree," or "under the oak tree." But I knew how to climb them, planning tree houses that never got built. Millions of red sunburst and orange-brown leaves, hills of them raked up and burned in the sidewalk gutters.

When I saw kids in Brooklyn, I couldn't imagine them growing up without earth and grass under their shoes, trees to climb or woods to run through. How did you go about the business of being a kid on pavement? No worms or crickets or fireflies or beetles or praying mantises or squirrels or serendipitous sightings of wild brown rabbits. City kids had roaches. The only thing they had over us was elevators. You could ride up and down to your heart's delight. It would have given me pause, but even I wouldn't have traded trees and grass for elevators.

I couldn't imagine how city kids made do with open fire hydrants, instead of the bay or ocean. They seemed deprived of the basic rites of childhood. My parents were from the city, that's why they were so enamored of vegetable gardens and apple trees and grassy lawns—stuff I took for granted. But secretly loved.

The downside of nature: thousands of wild apples in decaying brown piles, with apple maggots and worms boring through their cores.

44. High-Steppin' Rooster

THE LOCAL NAACP ISSUED THIS statement:

"To our great despair, on Sept. 8, 1965, Negro children will begin to suffer yet another year of inferior, segregated education at South School."

They wanted us shut down and were turning up the heat. But we didn't want to go to white schools. We didn't want to take buses into hostile territory. We liked our school. I *really* didn't want to be educated alongside the Wilshires or the Mortimers or wear Catholic School uniforms like the Applebys and go to St. Patrick's or St. Boniface Martyr School, run by hair-pulling nuns. That's where they washed your mouth out with soap. It was a Catholic thing. A practice known amongst the elder nuns as *oral soaping*. Had a bad effect on the mucous membranes. They made a kid open his mouth like a bird's beak for using a four-letter word. Even *ass* and *tit* were four-letter words. Well, *soap* was a four-letter word, too. They made kids bite the bar, chew it, and scrub it around with their tongue until bubbles came out their mouth. Sometimes the kids threw up.

I visited a white school once. Did you ever smell a class full of ripe ten-year-old white kids after an hour on the hot playground? Man, it stunk.

The first day I returned to South School, I saw a dandified fellow out on the sidewalk, surrounded by kids. The kids were oohing and aahing over something, as if he were showing them magic tricks. He had the glint of a gold tooth and a hanky on his head, protecting his pompadour. He wore the loudest, fanciest shoes I'd ever seen. It was Uncle Limpy! I joined the circle, and watched him display a gold money clip with a fat wad of bills. He was showing them his money.

Limpy flash his money all over town. Limpy grin like a piano, like a shit-eating Cheshire cat. He flash his money at Fat Emily. Emily be confused. Limpy flash his roll at the grocery store, and even flash his cash at Legertha Mae Lincoln. She tell him he might as well wipe his no-good Black ass with it, as far as she concerned, cause that money ain't come from no honest work, no decent job, no way, no how. His cash ain't nothin' but trash. That money filthy. Limpy say, "But, Baby, ahm rich. Look." He don't buy nobody nothin', don't spend his money on no one, not even Bobo. He just lick his finger and count it everywhere he go. He put it up to his nostrils and smell it in front of old ladies. He even kiss it. Yes he did, he kiss them dirty ol' dollar bills. Then he blow kisses.

There was no numbers game in the backwater of Glen Cove. But twenty minutes away, up Northern Boulevard, at the foot of the valley before Great Neck, was an older, more established Negro community called Spinney Hill. It was a Negro enclave dating back before the Civil War. That's where Uncle Limpy placed his bets. And Nigger Christmas came early. As a local hick, Limpy might get away with flaunting his wallet in Glen Cove. Had he exhibited such behavior in the city, he would have been relieved of that cash in a Harlem second. But the money was gone anyway in the next few weeks. Limpy had little left to show, except for the treasures stashed in his closet.

Bobo wasn't in my class. He'd been left back again, and despite all the extra attention from Miss Grimsby, he still couldn't read a word. There was no special education or summer school. For lack of a better alternative, until Miss Tiger figured out what to do with him, he was placed back in Grimsby's third-grade custody. Even I shuddered to think of the extra years added to his school prison sentence. Like a dunce, he sat amongst kids two years younger, including a younger brother who he smacked around. Bobo seemed oblivious to these consequences. He thought it was funny he was left back again. Mrs. O'Leary would shake her head with pity, and intone that "The only joke was on him."

We met after school. Bobo led me into Limpy's bedroom behind the collision repair shop. The man and the mechanic were inseparable. He shared his bedroom with used car parts. Littered about were spark plugs, oily transmission parts, chrome Cadillac accessories and fender spears, some scattered upon his unkempt bed. But Bobo led me to his secret closet. The boudoir of an emperor, the footwear of a king. King Limpy. I'd never seen such astounding shoes in my life, shoes to make your eyes spin. And a dozen varieties of Medalo Bops sunglasses. An Austrian alpaca sweater, the current status symbol in Harlem. ("Dat sweater cos' $56," said Bobo.) His closet reeked of Negritude.

"My uncle say a man who wear a fine Stacy get any woman he please," said Bobo. And here was his arsenal. No wonder Limpy had impregnated so many women. Twenty pairs of Stacy Adams, with the descriptive tags attached to the laces. They had fancier names than cigars.

Like the classic Orsino in urbane gray. The Cicero Burgundy Croco/Taupe Ostrich. Or the Madison Oxford Woven and Croco-Cognac Taupe. The Lorant Turquoise Ostrich Print/Croco, with a durable base for lasting confidence after a day in the cotton patch. The Demetrius Oxford in smooth/antique croco-print leather with upper leather lining and cushioned insole leather sole. The suave Matador, with buffalo and horned back croco-print leather, to express your inner nigger. The Fortino Oxford, with true snakeskin blend and printed leather for confident styling. Distinguish your Black self in The Delano, with rich buffalo leather offering a sleek silhouette for contemporary class that signals nigger-man trouble to white women. Take your look a step further with the beige Quentin Oxford with laser-cut pony hair detail. The wingtip Dayton, with extended welt non-leather sole, for the mark of Negro sophistication. The Madison with classic six-eyelet cap toe, in kidskin leather upper with contrasting stitch, genuine welt construction for durability, and winning the numbers. The Lorant, with moc toe, twin-gore instep, woven grass lamp and leather sock liner and padded footbed for tight pussy, loose comfort and a warm place to shit.

Did Uncle Limpy really consider these qualities when purchasing the shoes? And just how many buffalos and ostriches were thinned out from the plains in order to caress Uncle Limpy's feet in fake luxury? Why so many? How come I couldn't find any of these at Thom McAn, Florsheim or Nunn Bush? Where the hell can my mother take me to buy some? Never in a million years. Besides, they didn't come in little white boy sizes. I was lucky to have Beatle boots.

This was the boudoir of a real race man. What happens when a poor man gets rich. The exotic secrets of Black manhood. Like a Cadillac, each pair was a cry for recognition, social advancement. The shoes reflected aspirations and desires of a downtrodden race, a balm for egos, a peacock's declaration of sexual prowess. The hypnotic allure of nigger-man trouble for downhill white women, with all its attendant glories. The irresistible lure of depravity and ruin, drugs, beatings, prostitution and jail. What would the abolitionists have thought if they'd caught a glimpse into the next century of the infamous Hookers Ball? There may not be a Mother Goose, but there really was a Hookers Ball.

It would be impossible to sharecrop cotton in Stacys. They had a perma-gloss, impervious to shoe polish. But Stacys wore out fast. They were for poor men. A sucker's shoes, a moron's mirage. One bunion could burst a seam. You'd never catch Duke or Miles or Billy Eckstine in such a pair. Certainly not Dr. Ralph Bunche. Or even

Adam Clayton Powell. What would Frederick Douglass have made of them? Booker T. Washington? What would General Robert E. Lee have thought of Uncle Limpy's closet, had he peered a century into the future? Would he have redoubled his efforts? Abe Lincoln? Would it have weakened his resolve?

> *You put your money in*
> *You take your fat roll out*
> *You shake your moneymaker*
> *And you flash it all about*
> *You do the Uncle Limpy*
> *And you hold it up and count*
> *That's what it's all about*

Limpy executed a rich-man dance while counting his cash, shaking his high-and-mighty tail feather in the air. But a week later, he was broke again.

45. Mumsy Sinks

THOUGH BOBO APPEARED AT SCHOOL less, Mumsy had already given up. Where did Mumsy go, alone in his own world, an unsupervised fourth-grade dropout? Was the whole world his oyster? We finally found out.

Mumsy leave home alone in undershirt and mismatched Keds sneakers. The laces torn and retied in several knots. His nose running. A fishing pole over his shoulder. Mumsy skip over sidewalk, stepping on the cracks. Mumsy fly like the wind. Fly, Mumsy, fly. Mumsy stink like a stinkweed, but he happy, he alone. Mumsy laugh. Mumsy play. Mumsy cascade down hill. Uh, oh!

Mumsy can't swim. Mumsy can't breathe. Mumsy scream. Nobody hear. Mumsy daddy daid. Mumsy momma ain't around. Mumsy nostrils fill with quicksand. Mumsy go down down down in the dumps, forever one with the putrid odor of Garvies Point, with the dead cow, the huge spider, the rusted jalopies and their old runoff gasoline floating around the cow, the spouting sewage that Mr. Mortimer so enjoyed laughing at, and every other environmentally polluting substance known to man. Joined with every other smelly thing relegated to Garvies Point.

Mumsy body float up to top.

At the foot of the auditorium, Mumsy's school photo was enshrined on the wall, surrounded by a horseshoe of flowers. The memorial looked like an eerie vision of Mumsy in heaven. He had risen up from the dumps to the clouds above, surrounded by flowers. A flyer beside his photo warned children never to wander out near the dumps. There was quicksand out there somewhere. They said he went down in quicksand. The flyer also warned to stay away from train tracks where the third rail could strike you dead. Mumsy was never afraid of the third rail.

I silently wondered whether someone threw him in. Mr. Mortimer? The Wilshires? The same colored guys with the Cadillac who did in his father?

Miss Tiger gave a speech over the intercom about quicksand. Some monstrous substance that swallowed children up for breakfast. How could you tell which sand was quick? Could a playground sandbox turn into quicksand?

Mumsy be famous, the talk of the town. Mumsy get respeck. People whispered his name because he was dead, and that conferred upon him instant importance.

At home, Mrs. O'Leary shook her head with pity. "The Lord works in mysterious ways. When my time comes to go six feet under, I'll be ready. But when God takes a child. . . ." Mrs. O'Leary cried again over her own son— Drake's brother—whom she lost back in the 1940s. I was amazed she could cry over something that happened so long ago. But my mother explained you never get over losing a child. Even if it happened in the 1940s.

"Boy, you kids at South School sure have grown up fast," said Drake. I wondered how when one kid got dead, the others grew up fast.

Mumsy be dead. Pennies be on yo' eyes, Mumsy. An anonymous Black woman hurled herself upon his coffin, a woman everyone pretended not to know. In life there had been an aunt to succor Mumsy, but here was someone even closer, but she was too late. Mumsy done gone to wear dem golden slippers. That underground specialist funeralized Mumsy good.

A service was held at Lincoln House. It was my first and only time inside. Even the white teachers from South filed through its humble entrance. Miss Grimsby, her head low, and her eyeliner smeared with tears, sat amongst the kids. She was our official escort. Her hands brushed our shoulders reassuringly. Always a stray bra strap or a girdle line poking out. These protrusions bespoke of an intoxicating secret world under her clothes that I could only imagine. Dark black beauty marks and a few freckles speckled her alabaster skin. The black beauty marks stood out to make her seem like an exceedingly white person.

A crayon sign posted on the wall announced the Lincoln House credo, that this was a place for children and "a stop for weary elders." A place "to clothe our ragged." A photo from a local paper was tacked on the wall showing Mumsy's mug shot. But the newspaper ink was so blotched, his face was just a black blob of ink.

(Years later, I'd hear that venerable old racist of American letters, H.L. Mencken, had called Negro clergy "barnyard theologians," and the Negro church a "hogwaller of Christianity.")

Once at Mumsy's place, Aunt Nellie was watching silent-screen movies on Channel 13. She told us the silent movies contained dead people, who'd all died and went up to heaven. I assumed the silent screen actors were actually in heaven. Silent films were made there. And they didn't talk out loud up there.

"Where the niggers at?" asked Jeffrey. "Ain't they got niggers up in heaven?"

"Well, you see," explained Aunt Nellie, "the Lord sends us colored folks to a special heaven for colored people."

So now Mumsy must have been in that special heaven for colored people. Sort of like the song Ethel Waters sang many years ago, "Darkies Never Cry":

> *Darkies never dream*
> *They must laugh and sing all day*
> *Can't forget your troubles*

When you're thinkin' what they are
You can't find the sunshine
When you're reachin' for a star

Darkies never dream
Wouldn't help to live that way
We must walk a weary road
That never seems to turn
What good would it do to yearn?

Darkies never cry
Who would ever hear our sad lament?
Live to laugh, to die
That's the way we've learned to be content

Darkies never dream
You know what we have to pay
With a one-way passage only Gabriel will redeem
On that judgment day
When we cross that Jordan stream
That's why darkies never dream

The girls were dressed in their Sunday best. Sabrina, Fat Emily, Pamela and Torrence held bouquets of flowers and cried. Then they served Lincoln House apple pie. I had a slice. I sat with Bobo and his mother on bleacher seats around the boxing ring. Jeffrey and his mother sat beside them. Bobo was in a suit, laughing to himself at some private joke, snorting laughter through his nose. His mother was oblivious.

"Bobo Monk! Why you laughin'?" asked a crying Fat Emily.

"Because he *daid*." said Bobo, shaking his head.

There lay Mumsy's open coffin, placed in the boxing ring, the ropes of one side removed. The first dead person I ever saw, and it scared the shit out of me. He was humbly attired in a blue Sunday school jacket. Underneath he wore a new white undershirt. This one was unstained, starched clean. Two Lincoln pennies covered his eyelids. His mouth was a taut smile. His huge nostrils were flared, having been cleaned out of quicksand by the underground specialist. Small bouquets of flowers were at the head of the casket, giving off the sickly fragrance of funerals. Flowers didn't last long, and I equated them with the body—both well preserved now, but quickly destined to rot. I averted my eyes from the ring, more frightened by Mumsy's body than by any Frankenstein movie.

Our principal, Miss Tiger, walked past the coffin and shed fat tears. Miss Grimsby, who sat away from Bobo, walked past and shed tears. But then a strange woman threw herself at the coffin.

"Mah baby, Mumsy, oh mah Mumsy!"

Aunt Nellie stood by her side, holding her up. It was suspected Mumsy must have been the fruit of her womb, a woman he barely knew. Other than Nellie, the congregation pretended not to know her.

"Don't leave me, Mumsy!"

Then Aunt Nellie straightened out his eyebrows. I wondered whether she would catch dead man's fever.

"This wunta happen if his pappy around," cried Aunt Nellie, over the shoulders of condolence-bearing ladies, who patted her back reassuringly. "Ain't no way to keep on that chile every day."

Reverend Baker walked to the open casket and stood with his eyes closed. Then his nose started to twitch, as if something foul was in the air.

"Mumsy *still* stink," whispered Bobo to Jeffy.

The Reverend began a sermon.

"We of the First Baptist congregation extend a cordial welcome to all races and friends. We are here to honor the memory of a life cut short. The life of Mumsy Leech." Cries of anguish arose from the benches. "And the Lord said *Let the little children come unto me.*"

"Hallelujah!" cried Jeffrey's mother, Legertha Mae Lincoln—who'd once whipped her audience into a frenzy against me.

"The Lord almighty has called his young soul back up into the kingdom of heaven to be at his side. The Lord called him because he must have been too sweet for this worl'."

"Mercy! He was God's chile!" screamed Legertha Mae. Aunt Nellie consoled her wayward sister, who wailed aloud.

"A boy child. He never did nobody harm. He was the light of his aunt's eyes, the sunshine of her days." A wail of pain rose up from the ladies.

"Lord have mercy on this poor, poor chile!" came Legertha Mae. An altar boy approached the white teachers with a can for three-dollar donations to Lincoln House. A church choir sang "Amazing Grace" and "Leaning on the Everlasting Arms."

Mr. James DeWitt Anthony of the local NAACP was there, vowing to continue the fight for an integrated school system. South School would see its final days, he swore. Miss Tiger made a hasty retreat from the house, deeply offended once again. Anthony raised his fist, ready to head the charge against Glen Cove's wretched slum-housing conditions. In 1959, the City of Glen Cove's own housing standards appeals board had denounced the quarters as "below the minimum standards set by the Department of Agriculture for the housing of hogs." He would lead a fight to the community board over the exposed pits of hell in Garvies Point, where a lone child could wander to his death. Then he spoke of kerosene heaters that leaked fumes, overflowing and clogged cesspools, exposed electric wiring, rat- and vermin-infested quarters. It was time for a change. Mumsy's death would be a catalyst. Project housing was already being built for the poor. But little did the folks present know it would be forced project housing.

Just the day before, Anthony had led two hundred people to the steps of City Hall to protest Mumsy's death.

"We may be walkin' on dirt, but the dirt ain't walkin' on us. The city should condemn this hellhole for keeps, and dedicate it as a children's play area to this boy who has been murdered." And then, to groans of disapproval, he said, "In my day, my mother and father looked after me."

The Nassau County D.A.'s office would investigate Mumsy's death. City, county and state government agencies were alerted to join in the investigation. Rev. Baker read a statement from the mayor of Glen Cove, a bellwether of conservative Republican Nassau County politics. "On behalf of myself and the City Council, I want to express our deepest sympathy to the family of little Mumsy Leech of Glen Cove, the unfortunate victim of this tragedy." But no one was exactly sure whose family was Mumsy's.

I finally passed the open casket. Mumsy still smelled, but it was a clinical formaldehyde odor. Mumsy's face was all powdered up white in his coffin. Aunt Nellie said, "I feel like jumpin' in with him. Ain't no place he ever been where I couldn't fetch him back."

An old lady looked me squarely in the eye, paused, then asked in a kindly voice, "Why do you hate us so?"

"Momma! Momma!" screamed some little kids.

"Hey, they callin' *you*," said Nellie, who nudged a startled woman out of a trance.

"Oh," said the mother.

I sat in the back with Bobo and Jeffrey and all the kids from my class and some mothers. Bobo sniggered throughout the whole proceeding. The laughs began through his nose, choked up at the back of his throat, *then* hissed out, like a clogged steam pipe. The kids nearby all heard it, a continuous ambient noise in the background. But no one paid any mind. It was just Bobo. The mothers and colored girls wouldn't even grant such behavior the dignity of acknowledging it. Finally, Miss Grimsby's hand reached around and smacked him crisply in the head. Bobo sobered up and came to attention.

Mother Mamie White came to view the body last. She was a respected matron of Negro church affairs on Long Island. Despite Mumsy's life of poverty, she said, kids just weren't supposed to die in these parts. This was America, not a Third World country.

"Now . . ." the reverend asked on a final note. "*Who* stole the damn collards out the garden?"

Nobody answered.

"Well then. No collards, no turkey."

46. Laundry of the Night

O'LEARY WOULD MAKE NOCTURNAL trips to the kitchen. There, she prepared large slices of Velveeta or Cracker Barrel cheddar cheese, topped with whole chunks of "salty" butter on top of crackers. She always emphasized *salty* butter, never sweet, when writing grocery lists. She never ate in front of us. She didn't want to be seen struggling with her dentures, huddled over the sink in shame.

There was nothing so comforting as my parents' arrival home late at night. My mother's loving touch, waking me momentarily for a late-night kiss. The gentle reassurance that they were home, relieving O'Leary of her duties. I was safe.

But long into one Friday night I awoke into a nightmare. The door to the second-floor bedroom I shared with Drew burst open. There stood Mrs. O'Leary in her pink slippers, panting.

"Get up!"

I felt my heart pounding in my head, the same as when I was surrounded by the colored ladies. She was screaming bloody murder, but I couldn't yet fathom what about. The light clicked on. She was sweating profusely.

"Get up!" She tore the blanket from my bed. Drew sank under his own covers, feigning sleep.

"You left your warsh in the dryer. Now you can go down and get it. Now!" She kicked the side of my bed. "Move!"

I did as I was told. Mrs. O'Leary was a stickler about getting chores done, and she'd trained Drew and me well. We always cleared the table, took out the garbage and made our beds. With hospital corners. But it was now 3 a.m. The dryer was in the basement behind our spook house. I'd never gone down to the spook house at night. I'd never gone anywhere at 3 a.m. This was past the witching hour.

"Can't I get it tomorrow?"

"Oh, you'll fetch your laundry now, Professor," she said. "I'm not taking crap from you kids anymore." She seemed out of it, her blue eyes sparkling. Drew peered from underneath the covers, pretending he was asleep. Sitting Bull ran into his shoebox and emitted a staccato trill.

O'Leary marched me downstairs. Off to the gallows. I stopped at the basement door. A hard shove on the back propelled me in. I didn't want to go down there amongst the stuffed dummies with Tor Johnson masks, anonymous creeps, luminous skulls and rubber bats. Even during the day it tested my limits of fear. The basement had never been refinished for anything, it was just a basement. Dark, damp floors, the place for the boiler.

"Turn on the light!" I begged before taking another step. She switched it on. Then shoved me down several steps. O'Leary backed upstairs.

"Get your warsh out of the dryer!" The door shut. I couldn't recall leaving any clothes behind. I never left my clothes in the dryer. The good Mrs. O'Leary taught me that. But the bad Mrs. O'Leary cackled behind the door. Her voice took on a sickly, sing-song character. "You take the cake, Jrosh, you really do. Pathetic."

Halfway down the steps I closed my eyes. I smelled the furnace, the black, bubbling tar-like oil that always permeated the basement air. It wasn't an unpleasant smell. I'd have to pass our featured attraction before reaching the laundry room. The bare light bulb over the stairwell didn't offer much light. O'Leary suddenly switched it off from upstairs. I froze in the dark and was lost in my own spook house. Didn't know right from left, up from down. Scared shitless.

A string attached to a spotlight would illuminate our main dummy exhibit. I swung my arms searching for that string. At last, the string triggered the spotlight on our Frankenstein. The mask was made of green latex rubber with gray neck bolts, the Glenn Strange apparition right out of *Abbott & Costello Meet Frankenstein*. He was seated at a poker game, playing against a fake hand that reached from the rim of an old toilet bowl, holding its cards. The string also turned on a power strip that started a hi-fi, the needle of which rested at the beginning of a 78 record. It was a favorite of mine, a test recording from the days of radio, featuring the voice of radio actress Mercedes McCambridge screaming psychotically. It was turned up loud. The hi-fi was hidden in a cubbyhole, so I knew I had to sweat it out for two minutes and 31 seconds.

And so, by the light of Frankenstein, amid the radio screams of Mercedes McCambridge at 3 a.m., I ventured to the laundry room for my clothes. There were none in the dryer. There were none in the washing machine. I hunkered down for the night with the dummies, trembling. This would be my bed till the crack of dawn, when Drake O'Leary came in from a night on the town. He often slept in the basement.

For God's sake, Josh, what are you doing sleeping in the basement? he asked, and escorted me up to my bedroom.

47. A Week With the Janitor

BOBO BECAME ABSENT FROM school more and more. I guess I felt a need to carry on his tradition of being disruptive. Many times over my four years at South, my parents received the familiar call from the principal, alerting them to my behavior. This time, for saying a word so subversive it couldn't be repeated over the phone, and required my mother's presence in the office.

Miss Tiger appeared particularly agitated this day. The NAACP was always breathing down her neck, and was picketing regularly to close our school.

"So," my mother asked, bracing herself in a chair before the principal's desk. "What did he say this time?"

"Now, Mrs. Friedman, I don't want to alarm you. We've dealt with more serious disruptions, and clearly, there are worse language violations in terms of hallway etiquette. But I feel it's better to nip this in the bud before it gets out of hand. He *said* . . ." Miss Tiger gripped the armrests on her chair and leaned forward. "He said: *cockamamie doo-doo.*"

"I beg your pardon?"

"That's exactly what he said."

"He said *what?*"

Miss Tiger summoned the strength once more to utter the unspeakable, spying the door so that no one else was within earshot. Slowly, with emphasis on the vowels, she mouthed, "*Cock-a-maim-ee doo-doo.*" Then sat back and folded her arms, waiting for a response.

"I see," said my mother. "Well . . . what does it mean?"

"That's just it!" shot Miss Tiger. "We don't know. I was hoping you could tell us."

The phrase was vaguely Yiddish sounding, had a scatological ring to it, and may have even denoted, as far as Miss Tiger was concerned, something subversive or communist or *Jewish* in nature. It clearly made her insane. But my mother, always cooperative with school procedure, well inured to corporal punishment in hard-to-handle cases like mine, began to doubt Miss Tiger's judgment for the first time. Was the principal cracking under the strain?

"Well," came my mother, uncomfortably, "I don't think he *meant* anything by it. I don't think it means anything really, just, you know, a make-believe word."

Whatever the meaning, which I didn't know myself, I had shouted it like a morning rooster in the crowded hallway. "Cockamamie doo-doo!" And then, from out of the blue, I felt something clasp over my ear. Like a hooked fish yanked out of the water, I looked up to the incensed face of Miss Tiger. She provided my ear a one-way ticket to the principal's office, pulling the rest of me with it. I had to sit facing the wall for an hour. And now, the next day, my mother was summoned.

"There are limits to what is appropriate language in school, and what is not, which we must abide by. Of course, there is a time for loud play outdoors. But we can't have a child in the hall crowing potty language like a nut, and keep order. I'm sure you can understand."

"My husband and I will have a talk with Josh. We'll make sure he doesn't say it in school again."

Miss Tiger was grateful, and sure it wouldn't be repeated.

Pretty soon, all the colored kids were joyously crowing "Cockamamie doo-doo! Cockamamie doo-doo!" through the halls. It was mutiny. Strangely enough, the phrase incensed grown-ups, Black or white. One colored kid told me he got an ass-kickin'.

(One parent to another:)
What'd he say?
He say, 'Cockamamie doo-doo.'
Howdy Doody?
No. Cockamamie doo-doo.
What?! Don't 'chu be talking that shit in this *house. Beat his ass.*

The teachers were none too happy, and the blame circled around my way again. Like Mrs. O'Leary, it never occurred to those in charge of children to just *lighten up*. Tiger went into crisis mode.

All teachers were put on alert, should I utter the offending phrase again. When finally I did, I was taken out of class and assigned to the custodian. I was to accompany him on his chores, and not leave his sight. Miss Tiger referred to Mr. Gaines as the custodian, a modern honorific, never the janitor. You heard about special kids who got to be honorary mayor for a day; well, I got to be honorary janitor. This privilege had never been bestowed upon anyone, not in the decades Mr. Gaines toiled at South. A refreshing alternative to the monotony of the classroom.

Mr. Gaines was a quiet older man in a green uniform. An Uncle Remus sort of fellow, but perhaps without the wisdom. He was not one to laugh at doo-doo, considering he had to confront such matters in reality. He kept a low profile and attended to chores without any direct involvement in school activities. Until I was thrust upon him. I soon learned he single-handedly kept South School in ship shape. So, in fact, he was heroic.

Mr. Gaines locked the doors at closing time, and was somehow there to open them in the morning. When it snowed, he shoveled the pathway and salted the pavement. He attended to the boiler room, which kept the old school warm in winter, and kept the "lavatories" up to health code.

He did floor waxing at night, a solitary task. He didn't listen to music or get in anyone's way with his mop and pail. I don't think most kids were even aware he was there.

Jeffy saw me as the kids single-filed down the hallway. "There go Jock! There go Jock!" I smiled proudly, mop in hand, like a mongoloid idiot. I was someone special and got to do important grown-up things with the janitor. And the kids laughed, "Hey, Jock, hey, Jock!"

Mr. Gaines had his own janitorial closet, the polar opposite of a race man's private domain like Uncle Limpy's. Aligning the shelves were canisters of Janitor in a Drum, ammonia, industrial rolls of one-ply toilet paper, hand towels. Acme Bleach, Armor All, rubber plungers, squeegees, brooms, a yarn mop. Smelleze. Zorb-It-All. OdorXit. OdoBan. Odorcide. Central to the large closet was a rusty basin with running water. There he filled his metal bucket, with a water press for the mop. A yawning stain colored the back of the basin where the water emerged in uncivilized streams. I saw the Negro net he had used to neutralize the girl fight. There was even a little space to lie down for a snooze.

Never fully satisfied, Mr. Gaines continually tested new products on the market against older ones. Most appetizing was a jug of something called Janitor's Dream, with a smiling mop man. The man depicted on the jug was a Negro—but the package designer apparently lightened him up a bit, so it would be vague as to whether he was an octoroon, quadroon or high yella.

It reminded me of when Mrs. Appleby, across the street, bought her live-in maid, Laverne, a new mop for Christmas. *"It'll make her so happy,"* said Mrs. Appleby, delighted with the choice. When Laverne went back to South Carolina for the summer, the Applebys burned her mattress in a gutter bonfire with the leaves. They said it stank beyond repair. It was one of the young Appleby daughters who saw a group of little colored girls for the first time and shouted, "Look! Baby maids!"

"Do the mop in figure eights, like in the Navy," said Mr. Gaines, teaching me the ropes. "A clean sweep, like this."

His duties: sweep, vacuum, remove coffee stains from office carpets, vanquish dust, clean and supply restrooms, collect and throw out trash, replace light bulbs. Empty ashtrays in the teachers' lounge. Set up tables and chairs in auditorium or meeting rooms. There were other custodial chores done at night when the building was closed, like mopping and waxing floors. It was too slippery to do it during school hours. The custodial job required a man who was able to work alone. He was exposed to irritating cleaning detergents. Dusting and sweeping required a lot of bending, stooping and stretching. He tended to the furnace and boiler in the basement catacombs of South School, where no kid but me had ever roamed. He was picking up after white people, all right. But they were white teachers whose careers were in service to Black children.

While we debriefed in Mr. Gaines' office, which was the closet, a vomit call came in by intercom from the principal. Except she referred to it as "vomitus" on the floor, in Mrs. Phillips' class. Mr. Gaines, the first responder, would now demonstrate the most heroic of his janitorial duties. He pulled from his arsenal a bottle that reminded me of the climax of Dr. Seuss' *The Cat in the Hat Comes Back*. The Cat doffs his hat to present Little Cat A, and A presents B, on down through the alphabet to Little Cat Z. And Little Cat Z, who's nearly invisible, lifts *his* hat to present Voom. Why, Voom cleans up anything, clean as can be!

> *Now don't ask me what Voom is*
> *It's different than Comet*
> *But boy! Let me tell you*
> *It sure cleans up vomit!*

Except this stuff was orange, and it was in a bottle with

no name. It looked like orange kitty litter and was not sold in stores to civilians. You had to be a certified school janitor. Mr. Gaines and I carried a broom, dustpan and pail up to Mrs. Phillips' class. He opened the bottle and sprinkled liberally, like fairy dust, over the harsh chunky mess on the floor. All the kids in Mrs. Phillips' second-grade class stood back in a semicircle of wonder. Right before our eyes, the Orange Voom worked its janitorial alchemy and absorbed the mess to a solid. Better livin' through modern chemistry. We swept up five minutes later. Mrs. Phillips gave Mr. Gaines a relieved look of sincere thanks, and me a pat on the head. We left the room as heroes.

Another day, some boys came running out of the boys' room, afraid to use it. God knows what lay ahead. The call came in to Mr. Gaines.

When we entered the boys' room, I saw Mr. Gaines' face grow grim. "Somebody doin' they bidness in the wrong place," he said, shaking his head, tsk tsking. There were no urinal screens or mothball deodorizer blocks in boys' rooms. Somebody shat in the urinal, and it couldn't have been Mumsy. If there was one thing Mr. Gaines seemed thankful for, it was that the Lord made toilets flush. Because when they didn't, he had to deal with it head on.

But I was curious. Since when were bathroom habits (as well as someone's private parts) part of the business world?

"Why do you call it business?"

"Well, son, what would you call it?"

And then I had an epiphany. "I know, Mr. Gaines. It's cockamamie doo-doo."

"*Cockamamie doo-doo?*" repeated the custodian, scratching his chin. "Yeah, son, I believe you right. That *is* some cockamamie doo-doo."

Miss Tiger had him report to her office about what happened in the urinal.

"Well, Mr. Gaines, just what *did* you find in there?"

"Why, Miz Tiger," said the custodian, in the oratorical tones of the Kingfish. "I believe we found us here a case of *cockamamie doo-doo.*"

48. Mother Tumbles

THE PRIMARY O'LEARY GRAND-
children were undersized and undernourished, though not
quite as unhealthy looking as the Wilshires. They were the
offspring of Drake's tiny oldest brother, Timothy. Oh, the
grief she endured from them all. Hushed phone calls late at
night from county jails, even to bail out Timothy.

Mrs. O'Leary called me and Drew "spoiled rotten"
whenever she returned from a visit with her own. We had
plentiful toys, her grandchildren didn't. Once a year, her
four grandkids came to visit their "Mimi" at our house.
They sniffed around our bedrooms like an army inspection.
"Spoilt," they nodded to each other, confirming their worst
suspicions. Their haunted, intimidated faces spoke volumes
from the moment they arrived. Ours was the family of rich
Jews, they figured, that employed their old grandma, their
"Mimi," the matriarch and anchor of their brood. God knows
the stories they'd heard about us.

"Drew-the-Jew, Drew-the-Jew, how do you do?" asked
the oldest kid, shaking hands with my brother. Drew was
clueless as to why his religion, which he knew nothing
about, was foremost on their minds.

After they left, Mrs. O'Leary would remind us of how much
better behaved they were than us. *They* minded their elders.
But then, she would qualify that by tearfully admitting that
she felt much closer to "you boys" than her own, and actually

loved us more. And through the years she was with us—the second decade being better than the first—that could not be denied. Mrs. O'Leary changed dramatically, warming with old age. She would eventually come to laugh at doo-doo jokes, and even try smoking pot—but that turnabout would not take place until the early '70s.

Drew and I surrounded our parents as liberators when they returned from the city, breathlessly telling of O'Leary's latest torture. We begged not to be left alone with her again.

"Who, Mrs. O'Leary?" they said, incredulously. She *couldn't* be all that bad. And then O'Leary came out in tears, doing her act. She would make grand statements of moronic wisdom, in the voice of Oliver Hardy, with British overtones when she tried to sound smart or self-assured.

"Boss, I tried to tell those boys not to climb on the roof, I nearly had a heart attack. My God, if anything ever happened to them! I merely said, 'Boys, please, get down before you get hurt.' You know I love these boys like my own, Boss, I would *never.* . . ."

Our parents consoled her, patted her back as she cried, feigning disbelief that we would accuse her of any abuse. She was, after all, the envy of all our parents' friends, an Irish charmer. Oh, how lucky my folks were to have Mrs. O'Leary. All their friends wished they could find such a lady to join their family. And with a brogue, yet, even though she was three generations removed from the Potato Famine.

My cries for help, along with Drew's, were but a silent scream for years.

But if it weren't for my mom and dad's presence, with only Mrs. O'Leary in charge, we'd have gone insane. Whenever I begged her to move out, she became apoplectic, leaving the room sadly. She had nowhere to go.

When Mrs. O'Leary drove, she grunted and groaned with each turn of the wheel, like steering an old ship. Power steering was a luxury option, something she didn't have. She often cussed at other drivers on the road. If they made one perceived wrong move, they were automatically branded an idiot. If Gandhi drove by, he'd be reduced to a goddamned moron, five Nobel Peace Prize nominations and all.

Once when Drew, Kipp and I were in the back seat, her Buick station wagon's brakes completely gave out. We coasted for blocks. She hit a tree in the driveway to stop the car, then plunged her head down toward the wheel, in praise to God.

"You boys could've been killed! How would I face your parents then?"

Drew, Kipp and I thought it was cool. We enjoyed the brakeless joyride immensely—as much as Willie Wilshire enjoyed coasting down hills with his brakeless bike. "Do it again, do it again!" we cheered.

One Mother's Day, Drake came over with a bouquet of flowers for his dear old mom. She kept a hidden crate of cheap sherry underneath her bed, which no one in the world was supposed to know about. But you could smell the sickly sweet aroma of the sherry outside her door. She was hung over from her secretive drinking the night before.

So on Mother's Day, she fell down the stairs. I heard her weight tumble and crash. She'd fallen down the stairs before, but I could tell this fall was bad. I heard Drake from my bedroom.

"Mother? Mother?"

"I'm hurt, Drake," cried O'Leary, motionless on the floor.

"Oh, Mother, just get up," Drake demanded, with annoyance.

"I can't."

"Oh, Mother, please!" insisted Drake, becoming angry. He hovered over her, shaking his head in disgust. He offered her his hand to help her up, but when she couldn't move her own arm, he drew it back.

"Get up, Mother!"

"I can't."

"Mother, you're pathetic."

"Help me, Drake."

"Oh, hell, just forget it!" he yelled, then stormed out the door into his car. He sped off.

I was not at all intimidated by Drake. But I was mortified by the sight of O'Leary lying there in a pile of arthritic helplessness. I approached with my hand. She couldn't move. I was able to call for an ambulance, whose attendants rolled her onto a stretcher and left our driveway with the siren on. That evening, my mother drove her home from the hospital. She had dislocated her shoulder and would remain in a huge cast for many months.

"My own son left me for dead," Mrs. O'Leary announced to my mom. "He left me lying helpless on the floor. Thank *God* Josh was there to get me to a hospital. He's a good boy."

The dislocated shoulder was another injury to add to her crippled body. One more source of agony as she moaned through the night each time she turned in bed. Yet she was resigned to her crippled figure, refusing to do anything about it. When asked if she'd consider seeing a doctor, she turned her head in stoic refusal.

She told Lu that I was her hero. Her son was nothing but a bum. I was revolted by the idea of being Mrs. O'Leary's hero. Why couldn't I be Miss Grimsby's hero? Drake had raced out the driveway that morning, in what his mother referred to, during past altercations, as a "mood." It was not a good day for the O'Learys.

Drake disappeared for a long while.

49. Chased

At THE AGE OF TWO OR THREE, IN the late 1950s, I played alone in my front yard. Horse-drawn wagons still passed my house, the last vestiges of old Glen Cove, before the suburbs completely displaced such things. There was still a farm somewhere. I would wave to the farmer, he would wave back.

Three strange colored dudes came boppin' down Robinson Avenue. Teenagers perhaps, but they might as well have been giants. One in the middle stood taller than the other two. He wore a handkerchief do-rag over his conk. He bounced up and down with each step. I waved at the edge of my lawn, the same way I'd wave at a choo-choo train. And suddenly, without a word, one of them smacked me to the ground. They traded a few kicks, then they bounded back in formation, not a word amongst them, as if having swatted a fly in the way. I lay there too shocked to cry. One of my earliest rude awakenings to the outside world of big people who tyrannized someone smaller.

Young colored women loitering outside the A&P, chewing gum, smoking. Their hair was in curlers and white handkerchiefs, and they wore capri-style slacks. I heard them hissing as my mom held my hand, wheeling a grocery cart. Then they began cursing aloud, and the only word I understood was something about being white. My mom hurried, pulling me along. They sidestepped along, hissing insults that my two-year-old self could not comprehend. But the voices were thick with hatred. I sensed panic in my mother, as she wheeled the shopping cart faster, pulling my hand along. Oranges fell from a grocery bag, rolling down in the gutter. She did not stop. We were at a trot, the fastest my mother could go, the ladies hissing racial threats at our heels, like sideways-running Halloween cats. My mother, breathing heavily, kept going. She didn't let go of my hand, or drop the shopping bag till we reached the car. Cars remained unlocked in those days. She hoisted me and the grocery bag onto the front seat and drove off. She never mentioned a word about it again.

The world had essentially been a fairy tale, never far from a parent's loving touch. Saintly mother singing songs from *My Fair Lady* as she did the dishes. You played with stuffed animals, crawled, swatted mobiles that hung over your crib. Every need attended to, there was no need to cry. The world was essentially a place of song and laughter and Gerber's vanilla custard. Like floating through some pristine Garden of Eden.

And then, like an innocent child in a village that has never known anything but tranquility, the sudden invasion of Mongols on horseback, beheading, burning and slaughtering everything in sight. Your antenna felt the electrical surge of hatred transpire like lightning. Larger humans would tyrannize smaller ones simply because they could. These incidents were a harbinger that all was not right out there. Something dark and sinister could lash out and violate you without warning.

50. Arm Size

SOMETIMES MY ENTIRE WORTH rested on whether or not I could fight. When you lost, you were worthless. "May the better man win" took on a literal meaning. The winner felt victorious in every regard, as if you were only as good as whom you could lick, like cavemen. This was reinforced by adult women, like our principal, and certainly some of the colored mothers. Glen Cove was a medieval society amongst children. Predators stalked the earth in search of beating you up.

I figured my dad could kick anybody's ass, and this gave me a small degree of comfort. He worked out every day at Vic Tanny's Gym on Madison Avenue in New York during lunch breaks. As for his novels, he considered writing to be like heavy lifting. You "rolled up your sleeves" and went at it. He never behaved like an *artiste*, he always spoke about it like it was blue-collar labor. But he was fit as a lumberjack, unlike other working men in the neighborhood. He took me to Vic Tanny's in Manhasset on weekends. While my dad exercised, I ran up and down the sit-up boards. I bent down and tried to pick up the heaviest dumbbell I could. I figured that was how you worked out. The only kid present, I was an annoyance to the serious weightlifters.

Arm size was religion to them. The bigger the arms, the stronger the man, I supposed, with all the wisdom of a Popeye cartoon. With big arms, you could take care of yourself in all aspects of life. "Gotta pump up," men told each other at the curling irons, "got a date tonight." Weightlifters were convinced the only things women noticed were their arms. What more did you need to impress girls? I prayed for big arms when I grew up. Mine were skinny, a matter of shame, and there was nothing I could do about it. No amount of weights could bulk up my pre-adolescent biceps. What confused me, however, was that the Beatles and the Rolling Stones didn't have big arms, yet millions of girls fainted over them. Didn't they notice how skinny Mick Jagger's arms were?

As was custom, my dad bought us two V8s from the vending machine at the end of our Saturday workout. The V stood for Vegetable, and the 8 was how many vegetables were used for the drink. It came in a little can, and should have been called V9—the ninth flavor being the metallic taste of the can. Some bodybuilder, employed as a greeter by the club, would flex his arms, making a muscle for customers on the way out. His bicep was the size of a grapefruit. I was awed. When I asked how I might bulk up like that, he merely advised, "Eat a lot of rye bread, sonny."

As we walked to the parking lot, I begged my dad's assurance as to whether he could take this guy. He dismissed the subject, but I didn't let up. He had his own threshold of patience when humoring me about these matters. "I'm a lover, not a fighter," he said. But I didn't want my dad to be a lover. I needed to know that he could lick all the bullies that tyrannized my existence. Even though he didn't.

"Yeah, I could take him," he finally assured me.

"But, Daddy, he's got even bigger arms." This bothered me.

"Yeah, but I know some tricks," my father winked.

I breathed a sigh of relief. Knowing some tricks could defeat huge arms. I wished I could learn these tricks, but he didn't let on.

51. The Chinaman

"REMEMBER THE CHINAMAN?"

Mrs. O'Leary elbowed Lu as they prepared supper in our kitchen. They used to perform a sickly singsong when they were young girls. There was a Chinese man come to live in old Oyster Bay, opened a laundry or something.

"Remember that poor old man?" Both old gals remembered in unison. He walked down the street in traditional garb, like Fu Manchu. Mrs. O'Leary, Lu and their kid gang serenaded him in singsong:

> Chink, chinky China-man
> Chink, chinky China-man
> Yellow-belly, squinty eyed
> We—hate—you!

Maybe there was something cute about it then, but today they were like six-hundred pounds of drunken girlish lard. They'd since softened their stance about other races. I remembered a day after school when my friends were over.

"Ah smoke thigarettes," said Mumsy, indicating he'd like one of Lu's.

"Not around here you don't!" came O'Leary.

"Now that takes the cake," said Lu. "A kid. How old are you, sonny?"

"Nine," said Mumsy.

"And your mother lets you smoke?"

"Ain't got no momma," said Mumsy.

"Who minds you?"

"Just Aunt Nellie."

"Poor kid."

"We ain't poor," said Mumsy.

Bobo asked for a beer. "Boy, are you barkin' up the wrong tree," said O'Leary.

"Imagine that," came Lu.

"Would you like some milk and cookies?"

"Yeah!"

After they left, Mrs. O'Leary became sympathetic toward the colored kids. Her voice turned pitiful. "Those colored children can't afford proper clothes. Only rags not fit for school. You should feel *sorry* for the colored, Josh."

"I don't feel sorry for them."

"Well, that's because you're spoiled."

I was offended by Mrs. O'Leary's—and my mother's—feelings of pity toward the colored kids. I didn't feel sorry for any of them. Except Mumsy, because he had been alone, smelled bad, and was now dead.

52. Bobo Goes on *Wonderama*

"**B**OBO GOIN' ON *WONDERAMA!*"

"Hecha Momma?"

"No, *Wonderama.*"

"Wondermomma?"

"*Wonderama.*"

"Bobo goin' on Wonder*momma*? Win some toys?"

"Yeah, Jeffy, he goin'. And it's *Wonderama.*"

"Wow!"

A million kids watched *Wonderama* on Sunday mornings. The prizes! The glory! Jeffrey was gabbing a mile a minute with the colored girls. You could clean up on *Wonderama,* when Sonny Fox read the list of loot a kid could return home with. The Sunday morning kiddie show gave out all the latest toys, for good little girls and boys. Some lucky kid's winnings sometimes piled all the way to the ceiling.

"Ain't never see no niggers on that show, that right Jock?"

Bobo would probably be the first Negro child ever on the show, a development whispered by some liberal pal of my dad's, who provided the tickets. He'd be the Jackie Robinson of morning kiddie TV. But unlike Robinson, Bobo would also be the last Negro child to appear for some time. He would single-handedly set back the participation of Negro children in the morning TV arena for months, if not years.

The kids in school gave us a heroes' send-off. Our class was abuzz the week before. "Bobo and Jock goin' on TV!"

Even Miss Grimsby herself came forth, proud that two of her last semester's pupils had made good. She smiled upon us. The idea of a colored boy receiving an open-armed pile of prizes—especially a kid who didn't have any toys to begin with—was awesome. Bobo and Jock goin' on TV!

Bobo showed up bright and early to my house that morning. My parents drove us into the city. All parents bid farewell to their kids at the studio, then were required to leave for four hours. Once we filed in past the entrance at the WNEW Metromedia studio, at 205 East 67th Street, the gate shut closed, like a jail. They could have been leading us into a gas chamber, for all anybody knew.

Wonderama looked like a three-ring circus on TV. Our group of fifty kids was taken aback by how cramped and claustrophobic the studio actually was. WNEW occupied the building of the extinct DuMont Television Network, the earliest of all TV networks. They transmitted from the top of the Empire State Building. Off-camera personnel herded the kids according to strict bandstand-seating procedures, in order of height. Right away, I suspected something was amiss. The personnel didn't smile. They hardly talked to us, other than to issue orders. None of the adults seemed happy to be there on a Sunday morning. The lights were hot and in your eyes.

Most of the boys wore little suits and ties. I wore my Lord Fauntleroy suit with new Beatle boots. Bobo wore his purple Continental sharkskin suit. He was all smiles, polite, a perfect gentleman. Some executive came out to shake Bobo's hand and pose him with the host for a photo op. Some other host was substituting this morning for the normally acerbic Sonny Fox. Before the broadcast, a *Kommandant* came out to warn all the kids, now sitting in bleachers. She'd be watching monitors for any sign of misbehavior. "And don't think you can get away with it. You can't." If they saw a kid give the finger or even do donkey ears during the opening wave of hands, that kid would be pulled from the bleachers

and sent to a "detention room." Zero tolerance, no second
chances. "So don't try any funny stuff," she warned. "Now,
let's have fun."

"Attention kids—scream when the red light glows. Now
quiet, please!"

"Don't move! Quiet on the set. Cheer when the red light
glows."

The host and star looked like a used-car salesman, in black
suit and tie, with cuff links and a cleft in his chin, slicked-
back hair. Cleft in chin, devil within, Mrs. O'Leary would say.
This was a liberal show, which just had Robert Kennedy on,
discoursing on improving Negro education. The host sang a
song called "Kids Are People, Too." He looked at Bobo, as if
to add, *and so are Negroes.*

Then he went into:

> *Does anybody here have an aardvark?*
> *Does anybody here have an aardvark?*
> *There's an elephant here*
> *And a kangaroo there*
> *But does anybody here have an aardvark?*

I was disappointed that acid-tongued Sonny Fox was off
this week. Even through his sarcasm, you could tell he was a
generous, warm-hearted individual. I wished the sub would
have been Soupy Sales or Paul Winchell or Chuck McCann—
any of whom would have been great. But this substitute guy
seemed fake-happy, put-on friendly.

First up was the classic "snake cans." Contestants
opened cans, mostly filled with spring-loaded "snakes."
Whoever found the can containing an artificial bouquet of
flowers was asked a trivia question—*What fruit grows on
cherry trees?*—and then won a prize.

The kids were constantly instructed to wave cross-
armed as the show led in and out of commercial breaks.

Bobo lip-farted the whole time. In the opening barn dance, Bobo danced up a storm and the camera followed him, a standout amongst the white kids. He danced the boogaloo like James Brown. The host approached Bobo with the microphone to make opening patter.

"Well . . . What's your name?"

"Albert Francis Monk. But everyone call me Bobo."

"And where are you from, Bobo?"

"Glen Cove, Long Island."

"You're quite the dancer—where'd you learn those steps?"

"Arthur Murray."

The host looked bemused, as if hosting a show called *Negroes Say the Darndest Things*.

"And now a word from Arnold Brick Oven Cookies."

The kiddie showman, all smiles and charm on camera, went limp every time the camera's red light went off. He had a sour expression as the makeup girl patted him down. He became brusque in a way that implied he knew her more intimately than just as makeup staff. Between scenes, whenever a Three Stooges short played, he drank his coffee black. A cigarette dangled from his lip. He referred several times to the makeup girl's "gobbler," as if references to children's songs had infiltrated other parts of his life.

The beginning of our downfall occurred during the second dance segment, while "Little Egypt" by The Coasters played. The show featured sly rock 'n' roll songs, playlets that could be enacted by puppets, which they intercut with kids on the dance floor. *Wonderama* was topical, broadcasting live for several hours. There was no instant replay, and video keepsakes or kinescopes of the shows were not made. But some boy named Smitty fell to the floor writhing in agony holding his groin. The *Kommandant* didn't catch what happened. Poor Smitty was helped off the set.

Bobo worked his way through the dance floor, doing the boogaloo, then spotted a second victim. He inched up to the kid and executed a perfectly evil knee to the balls. Down went the kid, buckled over in shock. This time they saw it. Those with a keen eye watching live TV also noticed the attack in the middle of the screen during the mournful New Orleans whine, "Mother-in-Law." The director cut to a commercial, while Bobo was grabbed by the scruff of the neck by *Wonderama* MPs and hauled off the floor, protesting his innocence.

"He done it, he done it!" yelled Bobo, pointing a finger at me. Since we were together, they figured I was in on it.

They marched Bobo and me down a long hallway. The *bad-cop* lady led us to detention. *Wonderama*'s fabled lock-up was a dark secret. It was for badly behaved boys who'd blown it. There'd be no pile of presents for us.

The show had barely been on an hour when we were removed. This meant another three hours in detention. Something we were familiar with at school. The kiddie cops who brought us there were adhering to some protocol they had obviously performed before. Our gifts were confiscated. No candy for us. We were told we were banned from *Wonderama* forever—a curse we'd always have to live with. At the moment, it seemed like doomsday. When the *Kommandant* turned on her heels and left, the lock clicked on the door. Then the lights went out. And we stood there in darkness.

"Hey, Bobo, what you have to do that for?"

"I ain't done nothin'."

"Yeah, you did, everybody saw. Now we get no toys."

"Fuck them toys."

After a half-hour in the pitch dark, we had to piss. And we were thirsty. The door remained locked.

"Hey, Bobo, you think they forgot us?"

I wondered whether they'd even remember us in here and return us to our parents. Or would we be prisoners of this *Wonderama* gulag till God knows when? Did they punish kids beyond the duration of the show? Could they get away with kidnapping, did they have some official juvenile incarceration powers? And what about this lifetime ban from *Wonderama*. Did it curtail your freedom in the world at large? A black mark that followed you through life, like a bad report card? Their arrogance seemed assured, as if they held truant-officer powers to punish kids who violated the sanctity of live television. And Bobo had really fucked up big time.

I was scared and felt like crying. I wanted my mom and dad. But Bobo still didn't give a shit. I heard a loud stream of piss from Bobo's direction. He started to laugh. Then we heard a key or something fumbling with the lock. The door opened. An old Black janitor in a green uniform stood squinting at the door.

"Who dat?"

"It's us."

"Who?"

"They put us here."

"You from dat *Bamarama* show?"

"Yeah."

"Ooooh, y'all musta be bad. Dis where dey take misbehaviors."

"We ain't done nothin' bad, mister," said Bobo. "They just don't wanna give us no toys."

"Well, you musta done somepin'."

"Hey, Mister, let us go. We just wanna find our mommas and go back home."

"Hmmm," said the old man, considering. "Okay, well, y'all follow me."

We followed him down a hall that led through the Metromedia newsroom. We were AWOL. But there was an adult with us, so we couldn't get blamed. It was a slow news day, Sunday morning, and nobody was in the studio. Just muffled Teletype machines, where wire stories came tapping in. The old man stopped to dump some trash pails into a bigger one with wheels.

"Now y'all wait here a minute and be quiet."

Far up on a wall a silent TV monitor broadcast a shocking personage, looming out at us.

"It's Mrs. O'Leary!" I panicked.

Bobo looked at the image and went bug-eyed. "How she know where we at?"

"I don't know! But she found us!"

By some miracle, I thought, she had tracked us down to this escape and was letting us know her old eagle eye was watching, as usual. I was absolutely shocked. But on closer inspection, I saw the image was of a man—a bulldog-faced old guy who looked like Mrs. O'Leary's twin brother. The Teletype machines suddenly took off in a muffled staccato flurry. I read a roll of paper the keys were beating against. It announced the death of someone important, a Prime Minister. Probably the fat, old guy, who looked like Mrs. O'Leary. But his name was not O'Leary.

I quickly flicked the off switch on the Teletype machine. "Turn 'em off, turn 'em off," I ordered Bobo. "They'll hear 'em and find us here!" Bobo jumped to flick another off switch, and we repeated the procedure on all the other machines. We did this behind the janitor's back. The Teletype activity came to a halt. The room was once again silent. We followed the janitor out back to the studio where we were finally ushered out by my parents. The *Kommandant* cast a cross, suspicious eye on me and Bobo. But she couldn't prove anything.

And that was how Channel 5 Metromedia News remained oblivious to Winston Churchill's passing through the entire cycle of that Sunday's news. Every other station led off with it. WHERE'S WINSTON? NOT ON CHANNEL 5 read one tabloid newspaper story.

53. Mr. Anthony Returns

BOBO DIDN'T SHOW UP BACK IN school that Monday. But I was nearly greeted as a conquering hero. It was big deal enough that Bobo was singled out while dancing. He answered three questions on the air. That was more than he ever answered in class. After that, kids wondered what the hell happened. Where did we go? I didn't tell.

A year had gone by since the first NAACP meeting in our auditorium. Our school still hadn't integrated. The NAACP now wanted South School closed. Pickets grew more aggressive by 1965. An event called Freedom Week began at First Baptist Church, 7 Continental Drive, and marched to City Hall. One-hundred-fifty residents from Back Road Hill, including clergy, mothers and children, marched two-by-two, just like in Mississippi. They held placards:

A DESEGREGATED SOUTH SCHOOL IS A HUMAN AND MORAL RIGHT

SCHOOL SEGREGATION BREEDS DROPOUTS

HOW MANY MORE GENERATIONS OF NEGRO CHILDREN WILL RECEIVE INFERIOR EDUCATION IN GLEN COVE?

Flyers said, "Equal education is the basis for good citizenship. Join the protest against racism in our nation, by contributing to the fight for freedom. Make out checks to the Glen Cove Freedom Fund."

Mr. Anthony returned to school with a small delegation. He took offense when someone mistook him for the custodian. "I am Phi Beta Kappa . . ." he asserted, reeling off credentials and launching into a tirade. Then Superintendent Dr. O'Kane showed up, but was somehow mistaken for a TV repairman—a detail disclosed in the *Glen Cove Record.*

I was called out of class again, back to the auditorium. Clueless as to what was going on. Anthony took the podium:

"Miss Tiger, we know the School Board will not arrange busing for the pupils of South, to end racial segregation. And we see that South *still* has not been able to enroll any more white children. But what confuses us are reports of this white boy—the one pointed out last year. The sole white child among our less fortunate Negro children, the one supposed to set an example. *And a little child shall lead them.* We hear tell that this white child is seen about the school pushing a *mop and pail*? And popping a *shoeshine rag* in class? The tools of ignorance! Miss Tiger, we don't follow your logic. Just what message does *this* send?"

I wished Mr. Gaines could have been there to explain that a mop wasn't an ignorant tool. It was pretty smart to have around when someone vomited. Tiger was once again flabbergasted by Anthony and the NAACP's odd logic. They actually held the belief that white children should be models for Negro children. If that were so, I might have led many a Negro child to ruin. No, Tiger didn't see me as a role model for anything. She didn't even like me, and that was putting it kindly. If anything, she wanted me out of class for being disruptive. And the "Disruptive Child Clause" had just come into being. It seemed custom-designed for Bobo, who would soon drop out before such a clause could claim him.

The NAACP argued that the Disruptive Child Clause symbolized white misunderstanding and disparagement of the values of the lower-class Black community. The concept itself of a "disruptive child" was indicative of white cultural bias against Negro children. So it was a tricky proposition.

Yet, for political reasons, Miss Tiger still needed me as an example, her one ace in the hole. To show that South School was integrated. Which it wasn't. No other white family in Glen Cove would send their children there.

> *You cannot place little white and Negro children together in classrooms and not have integration. They will sing together, dance together, eat together, and play together. They will grow up together and the sensitivity of the white children will be dulled . . . This is the way it has worked out in the North. This is the way the NAACP wants it to work out in the South, and this is what Russia wants.*
> — (Mississippi Circuit Court Judge) Tom P. Brady[1]

The *Brown v. Board* Supreme Court decision of May 17, 1954 declared that racial segregation in education was a denial of equal protection under the law and therefore unconstitutional. Most assumed the ruling was directed at the Southern states. An editorial in the *Jackson Daily News* reflected the state's response: "Mississippi will not obey the decision. If an effort is made to send Negroes to school with white children, there will be bloodshed. The stains of that bloodshed will be on the Supreme Court steps."

One of those stains involved the brutal killing of 14-year-old Emmett Louis "Bobo" Till in 1955. He allegedly whistled at and accosted a married young white lady in Mississippi. Emmett and his cousin, visiting from Chicago, amazed their country cousins that summer with stories of life up North. They could sit anywhere on buses or at integrated movie theaters. He bragged of having white girlfriends, the forbidden fruit. One of the local boys remembered that

---

1   Tom P. Brady. *Black Monday: Segregation or Amalgamation . . . America Has Its Choice* (Winona, MS: Association of Citizens' Councils, 1955)

Emmett and his friend "relished their ability to dazzle us with their lack of fear of white people. It never occurred to us at the time that they always made these boasts when there were no white folks around to challenge them."

The sharecropper children believed the snapshots of white women in Emmett's wallet were real. They had been cut from magazines. A crowd of local kids dared him to enter Bryant's Market. "You talkin' mighty big, Bo. There's a pretty little white woman in there in the sto'. Since you Chicago cats know so much about white girls, let's see you go in there and get a date with her."[2] Emmett became a visiting local celebrity at the start of his Southern holiday. By the end, he'd be a national one. A little streetwise education in the Chicago school system might have hipped him to what he was in for.

It turned out Emmett's father, Louis Till, had been convicted of raping two women and killing a third during World War II in Italy. The army executed him by hanging in 1945. Not even the Till family knew this at the time of Emmett's death. They just knew he died in World War II. Southern segregationist senator, James Eastland, dug up that bit of information weeks before the killers' trial. Presumably to sway public support from his mother, Mamie Till, in the weeks before the trial.

But what seemed remarkable about Emmett, if the testimony of one of his killers was to be believed, was his unrepentance in the face of imminent death. Emmett's great-uncle, the sharecropper Mose Wright, bravely stood up in court and identified the two men who kidnapped Emmett at night. "Dar he," he famously said. The white crackers claimed that their intention was to scare Till into line with a pistol-whipping and threaten to throw him off a cliff. Till underestimated the hatred of the South, of which his momma had warned. He was supposedly defiant, insolent, unrepentant concerning whatever his actions were toward

2   Chris Crowe. *Getting Away with Murder: The True Story of the Emmett Till Case* (New York: Dial, 2003) 51.

the white lady behind the grocery counter. She was 21, a local beauty-pageant winner, now the wife of grocery owner Roy Bryant, with two kids.

> *The loveliest and the purest of God's creatures, the nearest thing to an angelic being that treads this terrestrial ball is a well-bred, cultured Southern white woman, or her blue-eyed, golden-haired little girl. . . . The social, political, economic and religious preferences of the Negro remain close to the caterpillar and the cockroach . . . proper food for a chimpanzee.*
> — (Mississippi Circuit Court Judge) Tom P.
>
> Brady[3]

After they were acquitted and couldn't be tried for murder again, Emmett's two killers sold their confession to *Look* magazine. "We never were able to scare him," said J.M. Milam, Bryant's half-brother. "They [Northern rabble-rousers] had just filled him so full of that poison that he was hopeless. . . . When a nigger even gets close to mentioning sex with a white woman, he's tired o' livin'. I'm likely to kill him. . . . 'Chicago boy,' I said, 'I'm tired of 'em sending your kind down here to stir up trouble. Goddamn you, I'm going to make an example of you—just so everybody can know how me and my folks stand.'"

According to Milam's story, he challenged the boy at gunpoint. "You still as good as I am?"

Milam claimed Emmett's response was "Yeah."

"You've still 'had' white women?"

"Yeah," came Emmett. Milam fired his .45 point-blank into Till's skull.[4]

---

3   "Judges: The Education of Tom Brady," *Time* 22 October 1965, 11 January 2010 http://www.time.com/time/magazine/article/0,9171,941426,00.html?iid=chix-sphere
4   William Bradford Huie. "The Shocking Story of Approved Killing in Mississippi," *Look* 24 January 1956

In photos, Milam and Bryant sure looked like the nigger-hatin'-est peckerwood brothers you ever saw. But looks don't tell. So did the prune-faced 19th century abolitionist John Brown, and he martyred himself to end slavery. So deeply ingrained was Till's killers' belief in white supremacy and upholding the old ways of the South, they didn't see what they did as evil. Acquitted by an all-white jury, they too were unrepentant for the rest of their sorry lives.

What happened to Till was ten years gone. None of the little kids at South knew the name of Emmett Till. Except, oddly enough, Bobo. He was born the same year Till was killed, and thus received Till's own nickname—Bobo. Maybe Bobo was reincarnated from Till.

When rural white crackers in Mississippi hanged someone, they didn't fuck around. They knew their noose, which branch to hang it from and how to make it snap. The Black university, Tuskegee Institute, compiled a statistic of some 3,500 *reported* mob lynchings of Blacks since 1882. Most were accused of homicide, assault or rape. An additional 1,300 lynchings were of whites. Strange fruit hanging from trees. Aside from the 1863 Draft Riots, only two lynchings occurred in New York State, one white, one Black. Both in the 19th century.

The Tuskegee definition of a lynching, from 1940: "There must be legal evidence that a person has been killed, and that he met his death illegally at the hands of a group acting under the pretext of service to justice, race, or tradition," with a group defined as "three" or more persons.[5]

Contrary to popular myth, The Tuskegee accounting attributed only 19.2 percent of lynchings to rape. Trivial offenses accounted for 11.5 percent: "disputing a white man," "asking a white woman in marriage," or "peeping in a window." "Eyeball rape" was not specifically pointed out, but must have figured into that category. The Tuskegee statistics were so exacting, they figured "1.8 percent for insult to white persons."[6]

The type of Northern Black militants that would emerge in the late '60s would have popped Milam and Bryant's thermometer. Their worst nightmares couldn't have anticipated the likes of Eldridge Cleaver or Stokely Carmichael or Bobby Seale. Or even hearing Cassius Clay's mouth, or his cornerman/*provocateur* Bundini Brown's scrunched-up Black face on TV, pronouncing how much he just *loves* all those white women. If they thought Emmett Till was out of line, what might Till's killers have made of Bobo and Miss Grimsby? Because they went *a little too far*—having gouged out one of Till's eyes and thrown his body into the Tallahatchie River with a heavy metal fan barbed-wired around his neck—they disgraced white Mississippi in the eyes of the world. They done spoiled it for all the crackers of the South, becoming the first white men ever indicted for killing a Negro in Mississippi.

The Till case spawned the American Civil Rights movement. Though the legalese of the Supreme Court Justices left loopholes, the *Brown v. Board of Education* decision, in theory, became doctrine throughout the South. But years later, the NAACP identified 24 schools outside the South that were still segregated. Above the Mason-Dixon line. (Or as Black folks sometime referred to it, the Smith & Wesson line.) Now the NAACP went to war, and unbeknownst to us, our school was on the front line.

Manhasset's Valley School capitulated and changed to "equitable-districting of Negro students in the public schools." Port Washington's Sands Point Public School gave in and desegregated. Great Neck's Spinney Hill desegregated. But Glen Cove would not. South was still the last segregated school

---

6   Robert A. Gibson. "The Negro Holocaust: Lynching and Race Riots in the United States, 1880-1950," 2010, Yale-New Haven Teachers Institute, 11 January 2010 http://www.yale.edu/ynhti/curriculum/units/1979/2/79.02.04.x.html

on Long Island.

I could tell by the scornful look from Anthony that he didn't like me. He never addressed me directly, just gave a fleeting look of contempt. The only adults who took a shine to me, it seemed, the ones who could trade a doo-doo joke or two, were those with a low station in life. The "bad examples," as Mr. Anthony might say. Mr. Gaines, Mr. Shuggs, Drake O'Leary. Ones looked down upon by anyone who thought they were a little further up the ladder.

"All I can do is reflect the feelings of parents to whom I speak," Mr. Anthony continued, in his auditorium speech. "If they run me out of town and tar and feather me, but desegregate the schools tomorrow, I'll wash off the tar and feathers and be satisfied. . . ."

Another NAACP member stood up and announced she had graduated from a segregated school in North Carolina and that she "swore before God that my children wouldn't have to go through the same thing I did—but South School is almost as bad. Segregation is an evil."

"Mr. Anthony has never even been in our school," interjected Tiger, from the audience. "It might help the whole cause if he would come and visit us. No one mentioned all the good things that happen here."

"The good things?" came Anthony. "Textbooks depicting Negroes and whites in reasonable situations are not available."

The President of the Teacher's Association issued this statement:

> *We, the teachers, deplore the evils of segregation, whether by accident or design. Collectively and individually, we support the aims of those whose goal it is to make all Americans equal in fact as well as law.*

We find it equally reprehensible that an attempt should be made to further the cause of equality in Glen Cove by resorting to distortion and fabrication . . . we cannot stand silent when the integrity of members of the Glen Cove teaching staff is impugned either through malicious falsehood or ignorance of the facts. . . .

Every school system has established machinery for remedying just complaints and for investigating and clarifying unjust ones. Had the NAACP spokesman taken the trouble to avail himself of this machinery he would have found that these charges had no basis in fact: that no child was ever in fact demoted at South School for being tardy; that the children at South School do not in fact sit with arms folded after lunch while children in other schools are permitted to play; that the children at South School are as well prepared for the curriculum of the Middle School as any children in Glen Cove.

We are sure that the majority of the parents of children at South School who know first hand the depth of the devotion of Miss Tiger and her staff to the welfare of the students in the school will join with us in deploring such an unjust tactic to further a just cause. We call on the NAACP to stick to the facts and we will support its fight for equality. . . .

What was going on in New York City at the time? Well, in 1965, according to Black psychologist Dr. Kenneth B. Clark:

Negroes seldom move up the ladder of promotion in urban school systems. There are only six Negroes out of more than 1,200 top-level administrators in New York City, and three Negroes out of 800 are full principals. Practically all of the Negroes are

*to be found quite far down in the organizational
hierarchy—a fact discouraging in the extreme to
Negro teachers and indirectly damaging to the self-
image of Negro children who rarely see Negroes in
posts of authority.*[7]

Bobo began showing up for school less and less. Then he
just dropped out. They say one disruptive child can bring
down a whole classroom for an entire year. In fourth grade,
I began to like school. Some of us seemed to grow up a little.
Our fourth-grade teacher was a humorless old lady, and
thankfully didn't lick gold stars and affix them to homework.
I fantasized that Grimsby would provide me one more gold
star for old time's sake, lick it, and put it on my forehead.
There you go, Josephine.

Although the teachers never mentioned it, the
NAACP's efforts were reaching critical mass, and action
was underway to close the school. White teachers who'd
dedicated their lives to teaching Negro kids at this school
would lose jobs. Miss Tiger knew she was losing her school.
And Mr. James DeWitt Anthony was jubilant.

7   Kenneth B. Clark. *Dark Ghetto: Dilemmas of Social Power* (New
York: Harper & Row, 1965) 137.

54. Bubba From Down South

THE LAST TIME I EVER WENT HOME TO
Bobo's, he took me to a gathering at some porch on Back Road
Hill. Someone's Uncle Bubba was visiting from the South.
Jeffy's momma, Legertha Mae Lincoln, wore an apron and
was busy preparing things for the gathering. Though it was
only two years, it seemed like long ago when I was lynched.
Nobody even remembered. Uncle Bubba sat on the stoop
with a guitar.

"Who dat Dirty Water y'all listen at?" asked
Aunt Nellie.

"Muddy Waters."

"Yeah. What he sound like?"

"Well, that boy play the newer style up in Chicago. I don'
go for that stuff," said Bubba.

The mere sight of a guitar was cause for excitement.
You didn't see them in person very often, and whenever
someone had one, it drew a crowd. I got my first guitar at
the beginning of fourth grade, a cheap Harmony acoustic.
I still had no idea how people got fantastic sounds out of
them, or what their hands were doing. George Harrison's
black Gretsch Country Gentleman was the coolest looking
object on earth. Even more so than my Schwinn Phantom
bike. The black knobs and silver switches on an electric
guitar were a total mystery.

But Uncle Bubba's guitar seemed to be made of weather-beaten metal, with a resonator device in the sound hole. He placed his left hand topside over the neck, thumbing open bass strings, tuned down low. This guy from the South had the biggest thumbs I'd ever seen. Strange rhythms reverberated. It wasn't how John or George played guitar.

Mr. James DeWitt Anthony of the NAACP was on the porch visiting, adding to the special occasion. He checked in with *the people* periodically. He beamed at the old man like the old man was someone special. Anthony was casual tonight, his sleeves rolled up for the weekend, his tie loosened over an open collar. He was sitting on the porch with a drink in a rare display of leisure. This was not his *milieu*, but the music seemed to trigger some ancestral emotions from his past, and he seemed pleased to be present.

"Brian Jone, he int'oduce Wolf on teenage TV," Uncle Bubba told Anthony. Mr. Anthony acknowledged the name of Wolf, and even I knew whom they were talking about. I recently saw *Shindig* with Howlin' Wolf introduced by The Rolling Stones. His music was utterly mysterious.

Anthony poured from a bottle of cognac. The label said Armagnac. "I like the delicate aroma in the glass," he announced, swirling the purple liquid in a snifter. As he inhaled the aroma, he began talking French, what seemed like total gibberish. "A mélange of spices, fruits and candies. But the alchemy stems from a blending of Gascony grapes— *Folle Blanche*, *Ugni Blanche*, *Colombard* and *Baco 22A*. Their distillation and aging are a patented technique, which stems from the Moors. Have some?"

"Naw," said Uncle Bubba, "I likes my 'shine." He gulped a swig from his own jelly jar, swiping a shirtsleeve across his lips. Then he went into some serious blues. Anthony's face became beatific.

> *Blues before mornin'*
> *Tears are fallin' down my cheek*

The most miserable time
Of every day, of every week

"Play some of those *big leg, big leg* blues," requested Anthony, growing more interested by the moment. "I sure do like them big legs." Anthony glanced down at his oxfords. "My, these shoes are rather tight," he said, loosening the laces. The bluesman obliged.

A kettle on Legertha Mae's porch was ablaze with firewood underneath. Legertha laid out brown globs of something on a large greased pan. It was obviously her special pan. It wasn't long before they started to splatter in the sizzling lard. I'd never encountered such a strong food smell, which permeated the air. The Seder never smelled like this. A smell that resembled pure excrement, except ten times stronger, as if spiked by ammonia. Apparently chitlins were supposed to be washed out first, but she never did. If ever there was a moment of culture shock in my childhood Black Cracker days, this was it.

Big laig, big laig
Kickin' 'round inside my head
Tall tail, tall tail
Make me leave my family bed

"Got some fresh chitlins cookin' for ya here, Mr. Anthony. And mustard greens. For special times, since y'all come to hear Uncle Bubba," said Legertha Mae, grunting over the kettle. Mr. Anthony rubbed his belly, making hungry sounds of anticipation.

"Gimme dat hooch," said Anthony, grabbing the bluesman's moonshine, and discarding his own bottle of Armagnac. After a few swigs, Anthony rose. He began undulating to the rhythm of *big legs, big legs*, as if in a trance. This was Aunt Nellie's cue to slowly sway on over toward him. She put down the box of cornstarch she continually licked from. They both undulated together, Anthony's sinewy hind end suddenly upturned and gyrating. He still wore his black-rimmed glasses, and his tie had completely loosened up around his open-collared neck, now wet with perspiration. Eyes shut, he held tightly to the bluesman's jelly jar in his hand as he slithered. When he opened them, he noticed me.

"Why, it's the little white boy. How you doin', white boy?"

"Mister, he ain't white," came Jeffrey, to my defense.

"Chitlins am ready!" said Legertha Mae.

A gang rushed to the kettle, folks pushing ahead in line. But the honored guests were served first, being Uncle Bubba and Mr. Anthony. I was served last.

"A delicacy," said Anthony, scarfing chitlin to mouth and washing it down with hooch. Except some excrement remained smeared on his hands and face. "Good times. Indubitably so," nodded Anthony, swirling the liquid in his jar. "Boy, these shoes are mighty tight," he said, loosening the laces yet some more. Taking his place on the stoop, Anthony's pants legs rode high above his ankles, revealing black socks. His knees appeared bony, his legs skinny, which somehow made him appear even more erudite. Aunt Nellie sat with her own big bare legs crossed, on the opposite stoop. As usual, she kept licking her finger in a box of cornstarch.

Suddenly, in mid-step, Anthony lifted a pants leg. He shook his leg and urine streamed out from under the cuff. "Oh, Lawd!"

"Well bless his heart," murmured Aunt Nellie, with sympathetic concern. I'd heard old ladies say this whenever somebody vomited or shit their pants.

"No matter," came Anthony, patting his wet trouser leg. He was now in his stocking feet. "All part of the good times." The NAACP official took stock of himself, shrugged, and got back into the rhythm. "Let the good times roll. *Laissez les bons temps rouler!*"

"Want some souse?" asked Aunt Nellie, holding out a plate of something fearsome. Everyone was in a generous spirit. She chewed and gnawed at something that refused to give. It looked like a pig snout. I begged off.

"These are some fine fixins, I do declare," said Anthony, finishing the last drop off his plate with a swipe of his tongue. "*Compliments au chef!*" Legertha glanced up askew, too busy running the show to consider his odd praises.

"But listen here." Mr. Anthony inched up on Legertha, in confidence, with a more somber furrow over his brow. "Uncle Bubba wouldn't happen to have any of that fine, sour, old-time *gumbo dirt*? You know, from down home in Ol' Miss. Oh, how I sometimes pine for the sloping red-clay banks of Leflore County, along Highway 49."

"What? You crazy? I ain't seen hearda dat since my mammy's mammy done keeled over in a donkey ditch."

"My own mother sent me a shoebox when I was at Sorbonne," confided Anthony. "Baked, seasoned with vinegar and salt. Addictive."

"My last boyfren say it make yo' mouf taste like mud. That's why I do this here starch," said Aunt Nellie. "Want thome?"

From the back of the dimly lit porch, the embers began to die under the kettle. It was a bountiful evening, and any kids from my school who were there were happy and well fed. Then came a loud thwack. The unmistakable pitch of a firm hand slapped upside a waxed bald head. Mr. Anthony held his face, as Aunt Nellie warned, "Doncha be puttin' yo' goddamn hands near *mah* nakedness. *Mah* nature is true, and not for you, egghaid."

By the time I left, Anthony was stretched out on the porch, unconscious, satiated, glasses akimbo, his white shirt smeared in intestinal hog grease, with chitlin manure caked on his face. But he still had a beatific smile. Little kids ran wild on and off the porch, and paid him no mind. But Legertha Mae came out to shoo them off the porch.

"Mr. Anthony done disgraced hisself," she said, shaking her head at the sorry figure on the ground. "Can't take dat nigger out no place, no how."

55. Better Dead Than Black?

JOHN DAVID WILSHIRE MEASURED my pocketknife cross-angle against his fingers. It was a fake stiletto ordered from a Bazooka Bubble Gum wrapper, and I was proud of it. It was against the law if the blade was over four fingers long.

"That's how long it's gotta be to kill someone," he said. "That ain't four inches. You can't kill nobody with that."

John was the most laid-back of the Wilshire kids. We used our knives to whittle on tree branches and play mumbly peg. Nobody did any killing yet. But if you were under sixteen and caught carrying a knife in public, one with a blade over four inches, you were a juvenile delinquent. Fifteen inches long was a felony. Big Willie Wilshire was officially adjudged a juvenile delinquent. So was Bobo. Both were candidates to be removed from school under the new Disruptive Child Clause. They were a menace to the welfare, peace and safety of the children of Glen Cove.

"What do they teach at the nigger school?"

"I dunno, just regular stuff."

John David Wilshire spread his fingers on the ground, then flicked the knife in-between each one. As the game of mumbly peg progressed, you upped the ante. You had to do it faster. Then you had to do it with your eyes closed. Then you positioned your knife on the top of your head, and let it flip to the ground, where it would stick upright in the earth. If it didn't stick, it was the next guy's turn. The first to complete the cycle won. It was John Wilshire's favorite game. Sometimes the conversation turned philosophical.

"I'd rather be dead than Black," said John Wilshire. "Wouldn't you?"

I'd heard other whites make this odd declaration.

"I dunno. Maybe not."

"You wouldn't?"

"Well, maybe so then, I'd rather be dead, too."

First, it didn't seem like a proper juxtaposition, being dead or Black. Like, would you rather be tall or old. The apples and oranges didn't mix. Someday you'd be dead anyway. So weren't you saying you'd rather not have been born at all? And if you never existed, how would you even qualify such a distinction as being dead or Black?

Years later, I read a Civil War-era quote from a Mississippi white man, who said, "I'd rather be dead than be a nigger on one of these big plantations." But that didn't apply today—unless they meant they'd rather be dead than live in the slums. Nobody thought it through, but I wondered whether those white crackers would reconsider, once they stood on the gallows with a noose around their neck.

DEAD

- Six feet under
- Food for worms
- Possibility of soul being saved or damned, if the Applebys were right
- Future unknown or nonexistent

BLACK

- Pride and power of finally being among the Black race, even though my home might stink
- Less parental supervision
- Learn to box at Lincoln House
- Wear Lorant Turquoise Ostrich Print/ Croco Stacys, like Uncle Limpy
- Get to dance to lots of James Brown records

Yeah, there was no doubt about it. I'd rather be Black than dead.

56. Get My Kid Out of That Shvartza School!

AROUND THIS TIME, DREW GOT beaten up for the first time by colored kids. He was in second grade. My mother went ballistic. He was delivered home black and blue, by a policeman. He'd been attacked outside on the long walk home. He didn't cry, just shrugged it off, all in a day's work. As he'd once said about kindergarten, "It's hard work, ya know."

"Enough is enough!" she yelled to my father. "Get my kids out of that *shvartza* school!" *Shvartzas* was what my grandmother called Negroes. It was Yiddish, or *Yinglish*, a more or less neutral term, referring more specifically to cleaning ladies. I'd never heard my mother say it before. And certainly not the more pejorative, *shvoogie*.

I tugged at her for her attention. "Hey, it's no big deal, I got beat up a hundred times." But she didn't hear. This was little Drew, momma's boy. He never strayed from home. He was not tough or athletic like me or Kipp. He did play baseball in Little League with a noble effort, but he was an artist.

She and Mrs. O'Leary kept watch over him every ten minutes, after he was delivered home. But Drew was oblivious, just laid there watching cartoons with his black eye. Stoic as an Indian. More consigned to his fate than me. He had no fear going back to school. The only thing that scared him was a chimpanzee show called *Chatter*. He ran from the room in a panic when the shrill opening theme—

Chatter, what's the matter with you!—came on TV.

My father still considered it unethical to remove his sons from South just because it was a Negro school. The boys would stay put. But things had gone too far, as far as my mother was concerned, and Drew didn't belong in the school. A racial time bomb was ticking.

Never much of a big brother to Drew or Kipp, I usually recoiled when told to watch over them. Whenever we were instructed to hug each other for photographs, it felt forced and unnatural. We just never displayed affection. If you asked us if we loved each other, well, we couldn't honestly answer that question. Besides, an admission of such would be too embarrassing. Our loss.

Did the Wilshire brothers love each other? Would they have been embarrassed to say so? The O'Leary brothers, Drake and Timothy? My guess would be they'd have shrugged indifference, said they didn't love each other.

Unlike ethnic hatred in Europe or Africa or Asia, Americans, when the chips were down, didn't *really* mean it. Even Drake O'Leary or Mr. Wilshire would give an honest Negro a break. Or come to a Negro's defense if they knew he was in the right. Americans would temper their prejudice and be fair in the long run. That's why they were Americans. That's what made them different from all other civilizations. There was never an Inquisition, Crusades or Holocaust on these shores.

But then there's Emmett Till.

57. The Last Halloween

WHAT ARE YOU GOING TO BE ON
Halloween?
Ahmma be Smokey Bear. He blow the flyer out!
The Wo'f Man.
Superman!
Hey, Emily, what you gonna be, Hecha Momma?
No, ahmma be a beauty queen. My momma bought me a
beauty wig at Woolworf.
Hey, Bobo . . . what you gonna be for Halloween?
A nigger.

Like Big Willie Wilshire, Bobo didn't play games like everyone else. He didn't wear costumes on Halloween. He'd become scary enough without one.

Emily's beauty wig blew away, across the street, amongst the leaves, in a gust of autumn wind. She waddled after it but couldn't catch up. She broke down crying on the curb, taking off her dewdrop glasses. Sabrina tried to offer solace, but Emily sobbed big, fat-girl tears. In an act of chivalry that I nearly felt ashamed of, I retrieved it. This didn't mean I had any special feelings for Fat Emily—only that I could outrun a wig in the wind, and she couldn't.

"Here go your beauty wig."

"Oh, thank you," she said, wiping her tears, with kindness in her voice. *Fat girls have feelings, too.* She pulled the wig over her head and preened.

"Now you Hecha Momma mammy," Bobo taunted.

I bought the *Do-It-Yourself Monster Make-Up Handbook* by Dick Smith, put out through *Famous Monsters*. It required professional makeup. My mother bought me an assortment from Paramount Theatrical Supplies in New York: assorted greasepaint sticks (regular and water-soluble), sable makeup brush, non-flexible collodion (for scars), Factor nose putty. I'd never heard of any of this stuff. Four ounces of Stein stage blood cost 75 cents, as did Stein Black Tooth Enamel, for blocking out teeth. You could get something called "crepe hair," made from wool, by the yard. You attached it to your face with Stein spirit gum. Naturo Plasto mortician's wax was a soft, flesh-colored paste that came by the tin. Undertakers used it to restore injured faces. They used it on dead bodies, which made it far too scary to actually use on yourself. A black pencil was used to enlarge the nostrils. You used something called collodion and acetone to make gelatin scars. They were extremely flammable. The idea was to turn smooth, youthful skin ugly.

To remove all this crap you were supposed to use Stein Alpine cold cream or Paramount cold cream, from Paramount Theatrical Supplies. But my mother made me use her regular cold cream, she insisted it was the same. Stein's spirit gum remover was needed to remove the spirit gum. You were never supposed to use non-cosmetic material, like shoe polish, which was dangerous for the skin.

Yet, with all this professional makeup, I still couldn't figure how the hell to make myself look like Frankenstein, Dracula or the Wolf Man. I couldn't even create an authentic-looking scar. Or even turn myself into a Negro. But I always had the sense that real monsters roamed the earth, and the ones in monster movies were just loners like me. I gave up with the makeup and opted for a mask.

Halloween was the only night you could legally wear a mask in public, according to New York State law. A policeman told me this when I went out wearing a Don Post Phantom of the Opera mask one night. It was the only night you could take candy from a stranger. Halloween was like sex, a night of adrenaline rushes. You lost yourself in another persona. All bets were off. That kid throwing eggs or smashing pumpkins—that wasn't you, that was someone behind a mask.

At some point in the '60s, the evening reverted from an innocent candy-gathering excursion to an eve of destruction. You suddenly began to hear news reports about poison candy or razor blades in apples. It seemed hard to slip a razor blade into an apple without upsetting the surface. Someone would have to be a psycho. New Jersey actually passed a law by 1968 mandating prison for anyone caught boobytrapping apples. Were there such homicidal maniacs in the lazy suburb of Glen Cove?

Well, there was a 1964 news story about a deranged New York housewife who parceled out steel wool, dog biscuits and ant poison (marked with skull and crossbones). She dropped it in the bags of kids she considered too old to be trick-or-treating. Nobody was hurt. She was arrested and pled guilty to endangering children. But practically all other such stories were myths or hoaxes, often started by children. The Halloween sadist became urban folklore. It gave rise to the sense that children were no longer safe in America. A mistrust of others, a deep-rooted fear of strangers.

A yearly costume parade took place in front of our school, before trick-or-treating began. A lot of big colored kids showed up, older brothers and sisters, who all returned to South School for the event. They were required to use their wits because their parents didn't spring for the predictable, store-bought pablum like the Lone Ranger, Tonto, Bozo or Casper the Friendly Ghost masks, the hard plastic ones with rubber bands that white kids wore.

Po' cullid kids used homemade ingenuity to spook

themselves up. Much better than anything I attempted with my expensive makeup, and more startling than any mere mask. Over the years, I recall:

A porkchop
Bacon and eggs
A Fu Manchu Cheegro (Chinese Negro)
A black cat in Medalo Bops sunglasses
A silver tinfoil mummy
A medicine cabinet
Black Bride of Frankenstein
Black Abraham Lincoln

The kids from South trick-or-treated on their own turf. They had projects now, and could go from apartment to apartment. They never ventured up to our neighborhood. But the Halloween of 1965 was different.

"Hey, Jock. Let's go trick-or-treatin' up there by yo' house. Eat some candy from the white peoples."

"Okay."

"They got marshmallow pumpkin candies up there? Ah love them marshmallows."

"Yeah, they got everything."

White kids never trick-or-treated on Back Road Hill, and I never saw colored kids up our way. Drake said the colored "preferred to trick or treat from their own." But I knew my mother would be extra pleased to see colored kids if they came knocking.

Bobo, Jeffrey and James had high hopes for sweet bounty. I loaned Bobo a mask. My mother put extra amounts of candy in their bags. At the onset of darkness, we set out. Packs of small kids trick-or-treated with parents strolling along. I'd been allowed out on my own, unsupervised, since second grade.

And so we trick-or-treated. House by house. Our bags

filled slowly. Seemingly neutral, white people tossed in the goods. The Applebys, with a look of surprise, parceled out Brach's Witches candy. Mrs. Mortimer pruned her face. Maybe if there had been one Negro amongst us, it would have passed unnoticed. But here three sets of colored hands held open their bags. She coughed up some candy, but I imagined she gave less to the colored kids.

The tension built for me as we rounded the corner to Lindbergh Avenue, where the Wilshires lived.

"This a scary-lookin' house," said Jeffrey. "It haunted?"

"Sorta haunted, yeah," I said.

"Dey real ghos' inside? White ghos'?

"Yeah, they're white."

"Do a ghos' wipe they butt?"

"Probably not these ones."

We walked the dirt path to the front porch. A bunch of Wilshires leaned by the door, others pitched their legs up on porch beams. A jack-o'-lantern glowed. Mr. Wilshire had actually sprung for candy—though it was the cheapest in the neighborhood. They dispensed single candy corns from a paper bag with their filthy fingers—the only unsanitary issue of the night.

Even on the front porch with the door open, the elusive stink of the Wilshire's living room hit me in the face. Stale urine? A million cracker family farts that left their olfactory imprint in the worn fabric of their furnishings? The human stink of poverty, regardless of race, creed or religion? Something gone rancid that emanated through the pores of nigger-hating crackers that stunk a bit more? Was this what the homes of poor Confederates smelled like during the Civil War?

I wore a cheap Frankenstein mask, and figured they wouldn't know it was me. Big Willie's sister dropped a candy corn in my bag, and then the next . . . and then Big Willie reached out his hand to stop her.

"Wait a minute." He noticed a colored boy's hand holding an open trick-or-treat bag.

"Hey, Friedman. Is that you? Is one a you Friedman?"

"No," I said from behind my mask, like an idiot.

"You bringin' niggers up here? To take our candy?"

He yanked off my mask, breaking the rubber string. "I knew it, goddammit you! Bagel boy. Bringin' niggers 'round here."

"What's up, you outta candy corns?" came an older voice from inside the Wilshire house. I knew it wasn't the voice of Whitey Wilshire. He'd been shipped off to Vietnam in the early years of the war, later to return in a body bag. *Apocalypse Whitey*.

"It's Josh Friedman, from down the street. He brought the niggers up here."

"The what?"

"Niggers!"

Someone came charging from round back, through the hubcaps and used tires with the hound on a chain, barking like a bat outta hell. Eggs pelted our backs as we turned and fled.

"Git out! Eat your own nigger candy!"

"Egg da niggers! Egg da niggers!"

And then bigger kids and friends from inside the house spilled forth, grabbing ammo from egg cartons. A fusillade of Bohack Grade A's flew at us as they gave chase. The Wilshires went through enough eggs on Halloween to stock their kitchen for a month, but they'd rather use them to pelt people. You'd think they'd be out collecting free candy to fill their bellies, but I knew they preferred to steal it from other kids.

"Ah'll go back 'n' kick his ass," said Bobo, when we got back to my porch. We got paper towels to wipe off the eggs. Big Willie and Bobo had never encountered each other before. It was hate at first sight. Both preferred to wear no mask or costume for Halloween. They made no pretense toward the spirit of the holiday. They only wanted to wreak havoc, and had enough monster in them already. Bobo wanted to recruit some big colored kids from the Hill and come back. But such events would come on another day. By the time race riots broke out at Glen Cove High, I was long gone.

58. Bobo Attacks

BOBO DROPPED OUT ENTIRELY AFTER a couple of months in fourth grade. How he got away with it, I couldn't figure. He'd be seen occasionally wandering alone on the Hill, but no longer played with kids from South School. He was clearly a goner.

Wherever he went, a little white mutt followed at his heels. The poor dog was completely cowed, as Bobo reprimanded and scolded him.

"Hey, Bobo, why you hit that dog?" asked Jeffrey.

"He call me a nigger. Now he take his whuppin'."

He wasn't funny anymore. Just angry. He hated white crackers. He hated everything.

Mrs. O'Leary had taught me to never point a knife at anyone. I couldn't master a fork, preferring to this day to hold it like a caveman. But it was drummed into me that your steak and bread knives should always point away from others at the table. It was a concept that her own son, Drake, would never heed.

I didn't see Bobo for months until one day in the woods, not far from school. I was alone and so was he. He approached smiling, then pulled a knife. And then he pointed it and came at me. I raised my arms to block, instinctively, and the blade slashed me along the forearm. That seemed to satisfy him and he walked off, laughing.

I walked home stunned, holding my left arm. All I knew was to head home. There was a gash about six inches along the soft side of my forearm. The blood dripped down slowly as I walked home. Bobo's face had taken on a fearsome resemblance to King Kong's. The angry Kong, eyes glaring, the face of the devil. Devoid of humor or charm or the desire to play. Ruined, a mutant, infected with ghetto pathology.

I came in the back door and presented my arm to Mrs. O'Leary.

"Bobo stabbed me."

Mrs. O'Leary looked at it, expressionless.

"Don't you care?!"

She didn't answer. She didn't say a word. Just matter-of-factly got up and said to follow her. In a dream state, I followed her out to the car. She had me get in the front seat. As she drove I saw her hands shaking on the wheel. She kept a sturdy bulldog face, the same as Winston Churchill, and didn't speak a word.

"Why don't you care?!" I asked. Still no answer. She pulled into the emergency entrance of North Shore Hospital, a place she seemed to know. And led me in. I was in a state of shock. Nurses laid me on a gurney and wheeled me through a door that crashed open. The same way doors crashed open at Coney Island spook houses. It felt like I was going into an aluminum spook house. Then everything was white. White uniforms, hushed voices, white nurses with white hats. I gave them my arm. Everyone seemed assured, acting out some protocol, like they knew what they were doing.

Then I was wheeled in somewhere else. A man dressed in white with a facemask came in and took charge. He spoke with an exceedingly calm voice, grandfatherly, relaxed, totally confident. Everyone obeyed his instructions as he called for odd-sounding instruments, the names of which I'd never heard. My arm was laid out on another table, a screen in front, where this man, Dr. Bang, sat on a stool. He was so easygoing, I wondered whether he even cared, like Mrs. O'Leary. I smelled alcohol, felt cotton swabs, heard nurses answering Dr. Bang, but didn't know what they were talking about. They knew exactly what to do, which was great, because I didn't. Like a feral animal remaining still, I sensed I was in the right place and these people would take care of me. The pain was offset by the calmness of these caretakers. The whole procedure seemed to take place outside of time; I couldn't tell five minutes from one hour.

They told me I was getting stitches, a bunch of them. Yes, I thought, give me stitches. I never wanted stitches, but yes, I thought, give me stitches, whatever it takes to fix it. I'm glad for the stitches. Bobo attacked, cut me, then went off laughing. No different to him than doing the boogaloo. An outrageous violation, the worst I'd ever experienced. That was out in the woods, over near school. And now I'm over here, these people are here to fix it, a safe haven.

Mrs. O'Leary drove me home a few hours later. She was unemotional, barely audible, still frozen. I accused her of not caring. She later explained she was in a state of shock the whole time. It was in such a dangerous spot, it had just missed a main artery, where I would have bled to death. And now she returned the favor of getting me to the hospital, as I had for her after she fell down the stairs.

There had been white kids who were barred from playing with me. But I had never been barred from playing with anyone, until now. Bobo was *Negro non grata*, both at school and my house. I don't know why he wasn't arrested. I wanted him killed. But he just seemed to disappear. I only saw him one more time.

It was toward the end of my fourth grade year, when a battle took place on a cliff between white and colored kids. They'd all be forced into the same schools next year. Most kids my age were oblivious of this, but some of the older kids were up in arms. Bobo had already achieved the distinction of being the youngest dropout in Glen Cove. But during this prelude to race-riot fever, Bobo was on the front line.

The Wilshires rigged a trap at the bottom of the cliff, as they'd seen in war movies. A hole was covered over with twigs and leaves, for colored kids to fall into. They brought metal garbage can covers for shields. They set barricades and stashed rock supplies. Bobby Mortimer had a slingshot.

The colored kids never considered such luxurious armaments; fists and rocks would suffice. But none of them told me where to meet up before the battle.

And so I arrived alone after school, in a crossfire of rocks and apples. I felt like a boy without a country, unsure of my status, claimed by neither army. I watched the Wilshires egg-bombing colored kids from the top of the cliff. They rolled a tire and chucked all kinds of crap from their backyard down the hill. Burned-out light bulbs, hubcaps. Big Willie lit off packs of firecrackers, tossing them down from a tree. He was in his happy place.

I came to the edge of the cliff with the whites and chucked a few rocks down at the colored kids. I purposely threw with bad aim, but after a few rocks flew back and nearly missed my head, I started throwing for real. I scored a few direct hits with worm-eaten crab apples.

Some big colored kids swarmed over the top of our barricades, swinging sticks. The next thing I knew I was running with a bunch of white kids as fast as I could. We ran into the Wilshires' garage and dropped to our knees, out of breath. Bobby Mortimer shook my hand, and Big Willie clapped me on the back. I felt a new kinship to the white kids around me, like I was one of them, among my own. The feeling was odd, but it felt good. I had made the club.

I was finally a white cracker.

James DeWitt Anthony's final statement about the closing of South School, which occurred at the end of the 1966 school year:

> "It's a good thing we won't see another generation of Negro children subjected to the atrocities of segregated education . . . It is sad and tragic, however, that over the period of recalcitrance and obstinacy one full generation of Negro children which was in school at the time of our plea has now completed primary school and has been damaged by segregated education. It is our hope the damage can be rectified as they continue through the upper grades."

Writer-guitarist JOSH ALAN FRIEDMAN done learn to read and write at South School in Glen Cove. Evidence of this be the non-fiction books *Tales of Times Square*, *Tell the Truth Until They Bleed* and *I, Goldstein* (with Al Goldstein). He done wrote some comix, too, featuring the art of his brother Drew, collected in the anthologies *Warts and All* and *Any Similarity to Persons Living or Dead Is Purely Coincidental*. And he co-edit *Now Dig This: The Unspeakable Writings of Terry Southern*, with Terry son, Nile. Yes he did. *Black Cracker* be his first novel.

"TELL THE TRUTH

JOSH ALAN FRIEDMAN

UNTIL THEY BLEED"

PAPERBACK, EBOOK, AND LIMITED EDITION HARDCOVER

Praise for
Tales of Times Square
by Josh Alan Friedman

"Reminiscent of *New Yorker* writing at its best, but with much more humor. . . Unforgettable, and good enough to turn Jimmy Breslin or Studs Terkel pale mauve with envy."
—*FT. LAUDERDALE SUN-SENTINEL*

"Amazing stories!"
—*SAN FRANCISCO EXAMINER*

"Friedman manages to paint a devastating portrait of a culture of vice."
—*WASHINGTON TIMES*

"...bustles with brilliantly colorful accounts of peep shows and porn kings, one or two of which might actually make you sorry they all got the boot."
—JOHN DEFORE
SAN ANTONIO CURRENT

"A fascinating study of life in New York City's entertainment hub."
—*VARIETY*

"If you miss the old Times Square but don't feel like sitting through *Taxi Driver* again, check out the expanded edition of *Tales of Times Square*."
—DAVID KELLY
NEW YORK TIMES

"The most essential anthropological study produced by the 20th century. Upon its arrival, the book was electrifying. A no-holes-barred blast of the sin business's smoldering hell-holes, with momentary explosions of pure paradise. Two decades later, Tales is an historical document of an era that quite simply does not seem like it could have ever possibly existed.
But, oh, did it ever."
—SELWYN HARRIS
MR. SKIN

FERAL HOUSE

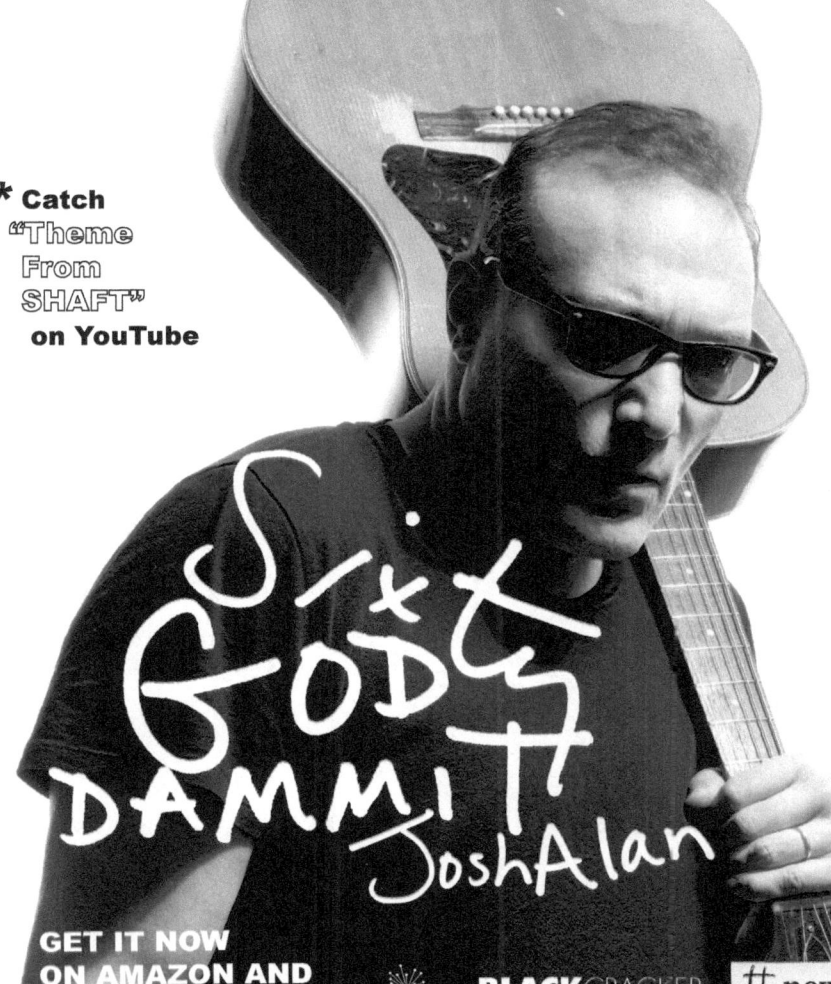

Listen to this Guitar →

Six GODt DAMMIT JoshAlan

BLACK CRACKER   # new texture

IS IT WELL WITH YOUR SOUL?

Jacket photography by Todd Burke © 2013

REV. RAYMOND BRANCH

"I'VE GOT HEAVEN ON MY MIND"

recorded live at the Heavenly Rainbow Baptist Church, South Los Angeles

Recorded and mixed by Todd Burke
Produced by Wyatt Doyle and Mike McGonigal

LIMITED EDITION **LP** AND **CD** AVAILABLE NOW

VISIT REVBRANCH.COM # new texture  yeti

Art: Samson Pollen
Books worth fighting over.
WEASELS RIPPED MY FLESH!
TWO-FISTED STORIES FROM MEN'S ADVENTURE MAGAZINES OF THE 1950s, '60s & '70s
featuring
LAWRENCE BLOCK
JANE DOLINGER
ROBERT F. DORR
HARLAN ELLISON
BRUCE JAY FRIEDMAN
WALTER KAYLIN
KEN KRIPPENE
MARIO PUZO
ROBERT SILVERBERG
WALTER WAGER
Man's Life
edited by Robert Deis with Josh Alan Friedman & Wyatt Doyle
HE-MEN, BAG MEN & NYMPHOS
COLOR EDITION
classic men's adventure magazine stories by
WALTER KAYLIN
edited by Robert Deis and Wyatt Doyle
CRYPTOZOOLOGY ANTHOLOGY
strange and mysterious creatures in men's adventure magazines
EDITED BY ROBERT DEIS, DAVID COLEMAN & WYATT DOYLE
A HANDFUL OF HELL
CLASSIC WAR AND ADVENTURE STORIES BY
ROBERT F. DORR
EDITED BY ROBERT DEIS AND WYATT DOYLE
THE MEN'S ADVENTURE LIBRARY
BARBARIANS ON BIKES
A high-octane visual archive from vintage men's pulp adventure magazines
BIKERS & MOTORCYCLE GANGS
EDITED BY Robert Deis & Wyatt Doyle
AFTERWORD BY Paul Bishop
THE MEN'S ADVENTURE LIBRARY JOURNAL
I WATCHED THEM Eat Me Alive
Killer Creatures in Men's Adventure Magazines
EDITED BY ROBERT DEIS & WYATT DOYLE
THE MEN'S ADVENTURE LIBRARY JOURNAL
CUBA
SUGAR, SEX, AND SLAUGHTER
Cuba and Castro in Men's Adventure Magazines
EDITED BY ROBERT DEIS & WYATT DOYLE
The Library is open.
THE MEN'S ADVENTURE LIBRARY
MOST TITLES AVAILABLE IN PAPERBACK, EBOOK, AND DELUXE HARDCOVER W/ADDITIONAL CONTENT
MENSPULPMAGS.com
new texture

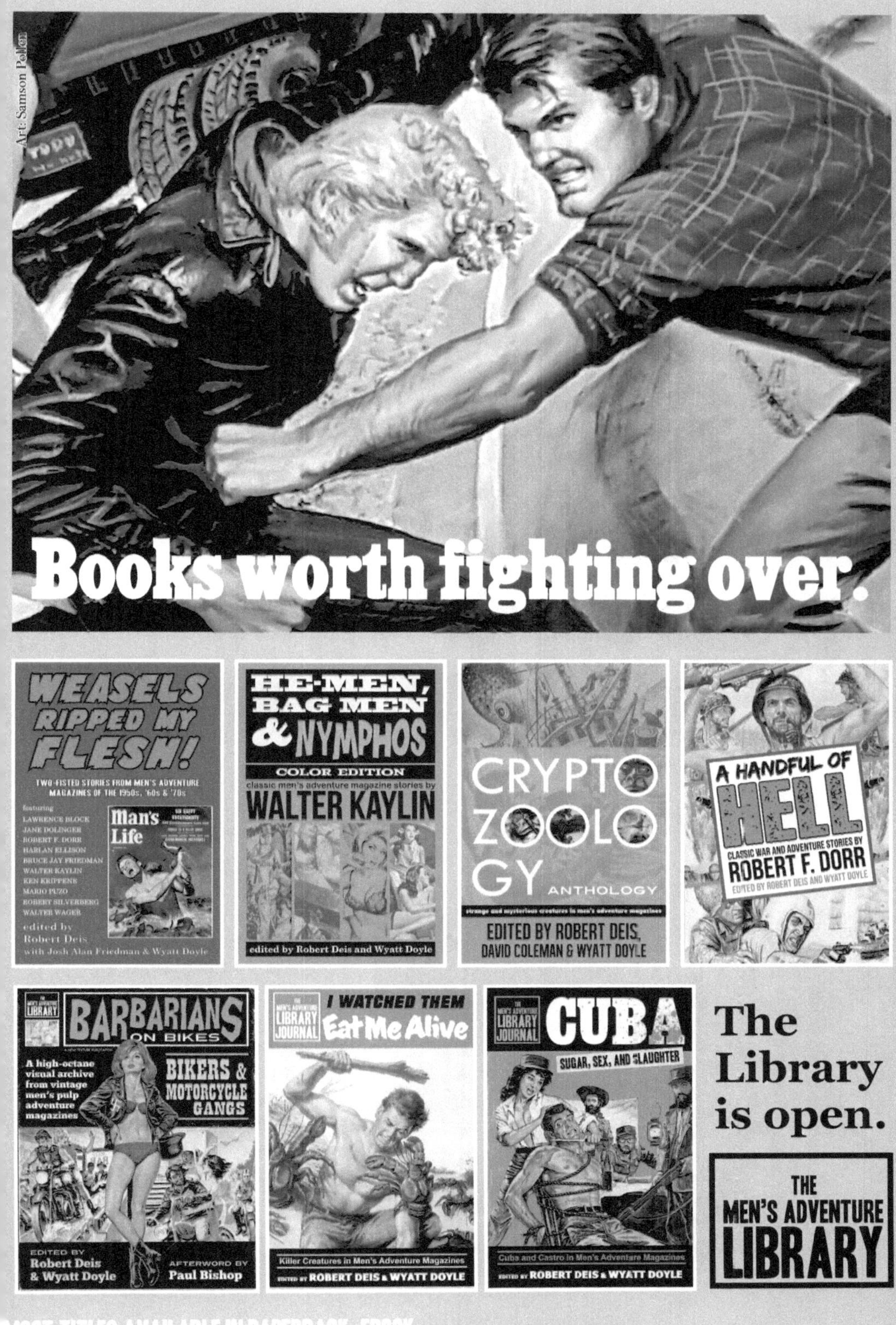

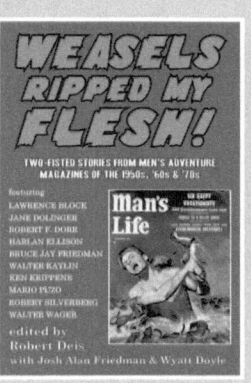

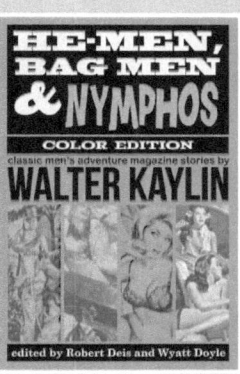

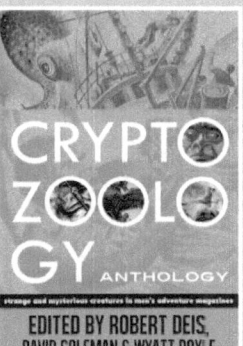

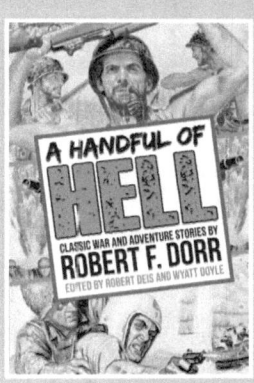

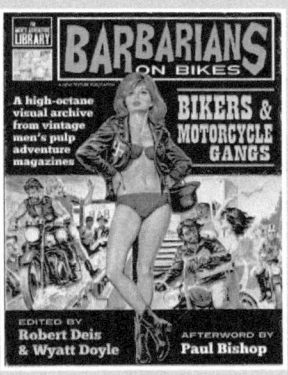

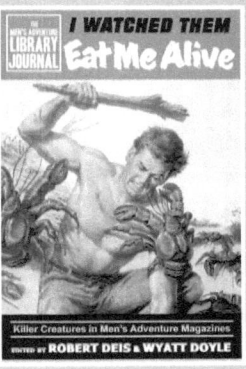

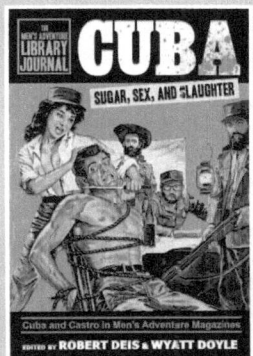

WYATT DOYLE

"**[Doyle]** has the elliptical, post-modern zen understatement of a Richard Brautigan, with a poet's gift for the carefully-chosen detail and a playwright's gift for dialogue.

"I admire his eye for the unexpected juxtapositions of detail among the seemingly mundane, juxtapositions of detail that provide a window of insight into life, into society, into truth. This quality is as strong in his fiction as it is in his photography."

—Bill Shute,
Kendra Steiner Editions

PHOTOS BY WYATT DOYLE

STOP REQUESTED *stories*
illustrated by Stanley J. Zappa
softcover and deluxe hardcover

DOLLAR HALLOWEEN *photographs*
hardcover

I NEED REAL TUXEDO AND A TOP HAT!
photographs/stories
88-pg softcover
104-pg deluxe hardcover

PHOTOS BY WYATT DOYLE

BUTY-WAVE IS NOW CLOSED FOREVER
photographs
88-pg softcover
104-pg deluxe hardcover

JORGE AMAYA DOESN'T LIVE HERE ANYMORE *photographs*
88-pg softcover
104-pg deluxe hardcover

new texture

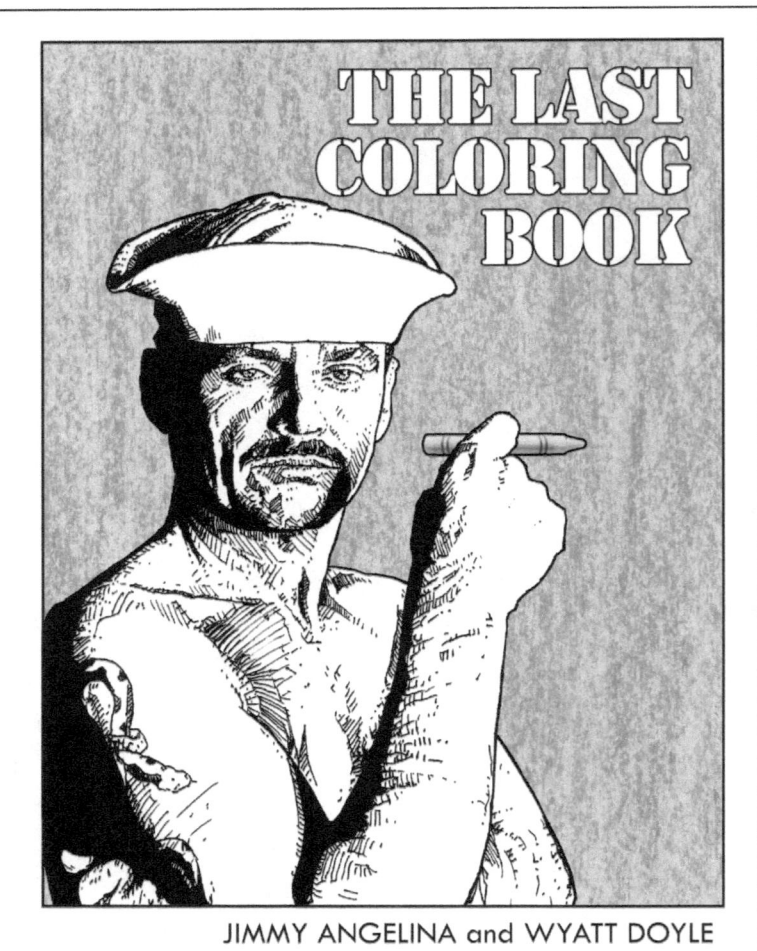

THE LAST COLORING BOOK

JIMMY ANGELINA and WYATT DOYLE

Ceci n'est pas un coloring book

lastcoloringbook.com

Ceci n'est pas un coloring book non plus[1]

new texture

The Revolution will be on the Moon.

n u l u n a

Andrew Biscontini

photo © 2010 Wyatt Doyle

new texture